RUIN THE FRIENDSHIP

K.SINKO

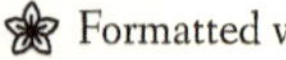 Formatted with Vellum

For anyone looking for a Nicolas Giuliano-sized present underneath the tree this year, this is for you. ;)

Hey loves!

Thank you so much for picking up a copy of *Ruin the Friendship*. It means the absolute world to me that you're supporting my art.

This book is categorized as an adult romance with use of language, innuendos, and intimate scenes on page. If you prefer a closed-door modification, feel free to skip chapters 19 and 23.

Happy holidays, xx.

Prologue

THE CRICKETS WERE CHIRPING, the fireflies were glowing, and Sam's head was buzzing. She shifted branches of the juniper shrub in her parents' backyard and maneuvered into the tiny alcove, holding the branches steady as they rustled back into place to keep quiet. She sat, then laid out on the dry grass, the soil beneath her still warm after another stifling ninety-degree day in Willow. She blinked up at the stars, enjoying the feel of the Hudson's cool breeze as it climbed up the river bank. She took a deep breath and closed her eyes, her edges fuzzy from the two hard seltzers she drank earlier, right before her brother declared they all play a game of sardines.

Branches swished to her left. She sucked in a breath, keeping as quiet as possible.

Large hands circled her wrists and tugged. "Get up, you can't be that drunk."

Sam frowned at the sound of Nico's voice as he pulled her into a sitting position. "Be quiet, people will hear you."

"I'll be quiet once you sit up properly."

She ripped her wrists from his grip. "I'm not drunk. Just a little buzzed."

Nico frowned back at her as he took a seat, angling his Knicks hat backward on his head.

She rolled her eyes. "How did you find me so quickly?"

He perched his elbows on his knees and leaned back, his fingers loosely threaded together. "This has always been your spot, Sammy girl. You used to hide here and read your books."

She glared at him, a smirk on her face. "Maybe because it was the only place I could get peace and quiet from you and Jeff being utterly obnoxious."

He grinned. "But being utterly obnoxious is so *fun*."

She rolled her eyes again. They sat there in silence, listening for the others to find them. But after a few minutes of waiting, she wondered if they would be stuck hiding next to the juniper bush for a while.

He tilted his head toward her. "How was the rest of senior year?"

"It was...*fine*. I'm glad it's over."

"Jeff told me Dylan broke up with you."

"Jeff needs to mind his own business."

Nico shook his head. "I don't think your brother knows how to mind his own business."

She let out a snort. "Isn't that the truth."

He hung his head between his legs and chuckled, keeping the sound of his voice soft so no one would hear.

Sam crossed her legs. "Did Jeff tell you why?"

"Why Dylan broke up with you?"

She nodded her head.

Nico's brow furrowed. "Do I need to beat him up?"

Sam pulled at the uneven threading at the edge of her

denim shorts, not looking him in the eye. "He told me I was a bad kisser."

She could see Nico's hands tighten into fists in her periphery. "Excuse me?"

"I mean, that's not the only reason," she defended. "He said he felt like we needed space to do our own thing in college, or whatever. Then he went on about how I don't have enough experience or something stupid, all because I wouldn't sleep with him. I stopped listening after that."

Nico blew out a breath. "What a fucking idiot."

"Don't say that."

He swung his gaze to hers, the chestnut color in his eyes darker. "Don't call him an idiot?"

"No, don't swear. It's unoriginal."

Confusion spread across his features. "What?"

"It's a filler word. People only use it because they don't have any other words to say. They're unoriginal, and quite frankly, dirty and gross."

His eyes widened, and he coughed out a laugh. "Since when do you have such high and mighty opinions about swearing?"

Sam placed her hands in her lap. "I always have. I just feel brave enough to share them now."

His eyes narrowed. "Then were you at least brave enough to tell your ex he's an idiot?"

"I told him he didn't know what he would be missing before I walked away from him." She shifted, feeling uncomfortable that she was sharing all of this with *Nico.* Her brother's best friend, and probably the number two most annoying person in the whole world—right behind Jeff. Nico had been coming around for almost sixteen years now, the perfect partner in crime for her brother to pull off the most elaborate schemes to annoy her. Like learning how to pick locks on YouTube so she never had privacy. Or the time they lined the mattress of her bed with whoopee cushions. It was easier to place him in the category of *Jeff's annoying best friend*, and not in...whatever he was right now. It was making her stomach do weird things, and she wasn't sure how she felt about it.

Sam puckered her lips, like she was tasting something sour. She turned away from Nico's gaze. "Although who knows, maybe I do suck at kissing."

"I *highly* doubt that."

Her eyes dropped into slits as she turned back toward him. "What are you doing right now?"

"Um, hiding?" he said, gesturing to the space between them.

"No, I mean, to me. You need to stop...whatever this is. It's unnerving."

"You mean stop being nice to you?" His smile blew wide, the corners of his mouth tucked behind that dumb dimple that girls at Willow High used to whisper about. They used to come to Sam and ask for an introduction—all because her brother was *best friends* with Nicolas Giuliano. Sam was thankful the day they graduated so she could have three peaceful Jeff and Nico–less high school years.

"Yes," she deadpanned.

"Oh, come on." Nico clicked his tongue. "I'm always nice to you, Sammy girl."

"The nicest thing you've done to me is move to California so you could go to Berkeley and get out of my hair."

Nico ducked his head again, the sound of his laugh like an exasperated wheeze. She wasn't surprised—he'd always found annoying her amusing.

She crossed her arms and looked away. *Where is everyone?* Jeff surely had to think of her hiding spot soon—Nico wasn't wrong, she used to hide from the two of them all the time in this very spot. Or maybe Jeff was too distracted by someone else. She saw the way Veronica Lawson had been looking at him.

"Sam."

She turned to face him. Nico had been calling her *Sammy girl* for years now. She wasn't even sure where the nickname originated from. He never just...said her name like that.

She picked at the chipping red nail polish on her thumb. "Yeah?"

"I really don't think you suck at kissing."

She let out a huff. "Not like you'll ever know."

"Why not?"

Her back went ramrod straight, and she pressed her lips together tight.

Nico smirked at her reaction. "Come on. You haven't ever thought about it?"

She blew out a breath. "Thought about *kissing you?* No, literally never."

His grin widened. "*Literally* never?"

She fixed her eyes on a blinking firefly close by. "No, that's gross. You're the most annoying person ever."

"Fine then. If you hate me so much, then kissing me will mean nothing. And I can tell you if Dylan was right or wrong."

"I don't hate you." She swallowed. "And I'm not kissing you."

Nico shifted, moving his body so he sat criss-cross next to her, angling his chest in her direction. "Come on, Sammy girl. Just one kiss. It's not like it will ruin everything."

She blinked, dropping her gaze to his loose cotton gray T-shirt and his dark-washed jeans, the way they molded to his lean thighs perfectly. She hesitated, then turned to mirror his sitting position, their knees bumping together.

The stupid smirk on his face sunk deeper into the dimple on his right cheek. "Are we being brave?"

"Shut up."

He snickered, tilting his head up. "Prove Dylan wrong."

She felt hot, from the ground below her to the rising heat in her cheeks and the radiating warmth coming from the body opposite her. Maybe it was the heat, or the slight buzz that reverberated in her head, or the fact that she was simply bored because no one had yet to find them. Whatever it was seemed to cloud Sam's judgement as she slipped her hands to Nico's knees.

Nico chuckled. "Okay then." He didn't hesitate, moving his hands to her legs, his palms and long fingers covering the width of her thighs.

"This is so dumb," she grumbled, her eyes on his hands, the way the tips of his fingers dug into her skin.

"No, it's not."

"Promise it won't ruin everything?"

"It won't. We're doing it for science."

She squeezed his thighs. His muscles were still lean and tight from all those years on the basketball team. "For science."

"Exactly."

She blinked up at him. They stared at one another in the dark. His expression made it seem like this was more of a challenge rather than a moment where they were about to kiss.

"Prove Dylan wrong," she repeated.

Nico grinned, leaning in. "Atta girl. Prove him wrong."

The two of them drew close, their noses about to brush, their eyes locking.

Then they both laughed.

Sam stifled the sound by covering her mouth, then reaching up to cover Nico's. It didn't do much for the noise, his breath warm on her palm, his lips soft. He gripped her wrist, like he needed her to hold on so he could finish laughing.

She shook her head, a smile still painted across her face. "I'm glad the idea of kissing me *amuses* you."

He shook his head, shaking off the rest of his laughter with it, his palm still around her wrist. "Come on, we're adults, we can do this."

"You make it sound like we're about to get a colonoscopy."

"Oh, I think we're about to have a lot more fun than that."

"If that's your bar for having fun, then sure. On a scale of colonoscopy to fun, I would say kissing you would be right above getting teeth pulled and right below stubbing your toe."

He pressed her hand to his chest. "You wound me."

"I speak the truth."

He grinned as he leaned in again, gripping her thighs. She copied him, bracing her hands on his. *Am I really about to do this?*

The sound of crickets filled the silence.

Nico's legs shifted underneath her grip. He released a hand, then seconds later, a finger traced up her neck and under her chin. Goosebumps flecked across her arms. He tipped her face up, and before she could properly look at him, Nico brushed his lips against hers, then pressed in.

His kiss felt like electricity. Static energy that finally burst free, a zip of...*something* climbing high up her spine while simultaneously dipping low in her belly. She could feel the cadence of her heart pick up speed, the tempo thrumming in her ears as the person she thought she hated kissed her gently. Carefully. Politely.

Sam angled her face, opening her mouth against his. Nico followed her lead, gliding his hand from her chin to around her nape, pulling her closer by her neck, his fingers digging into her hair. She slipped a tongue in his mouth, her thighs going numb at the sound of the small hum in the back of his throat. She moved her hands to his hips and gripped them tight, thumbs digging into the divots above his hipbones.

She felt like her whole body was on fire. *Nico. Nico. Nico.* How could this be happening? How could she have been so wrong about him? Was this...Was kissing supposed to be like this? Had this been how she felt about him the whole time? Was that weird feeling in her stomach a...a *crush*? Did she have a crush on Nicolas Giuliano?

The thought of crushing on Nico, of how she might actually be *feeling*, had Sam detaching her lips from his and pulling away from his grasp.

They stared in silence at one another, breathing ragged, eyes locked.

She brushed her fingers across her lips. "Nico," she whispered.

He nodded, eyes wild. "Yeah."

"Yeah?"

"Yes."

"Are you feeling how I'm—"

"Yes. Get over here."

Sam rocked forward, reaching for his shirt at the same time he hooked his fingers through the belt loops of her shorts, tugging her to his lap. She fisted the cotton as she dipped down to kiss him, his hands greedy as they slipped under her tank top and explored the bare skin on her back. He dragged his fingernails down her spine, sucking on her bottom lip as she arched into him.

"Oh, Sammy girl," he rasped, his pinkies dipping into the back of her shorts. "Where have you been this whole time?"

Heat crawled up her spine at the feel of Nico's *hands* on her, the rough sound of his voice on her skin.

He dragged his teeth up her neck, biting her gently. "He's an idiot, Sam. An idiot."

Her thighs squeezed around his hips. He groaned, grabbing her chin and fastening their lips together again. He tasted like firewood and bad decisions. She wanted to lick the skin along his neck and learn what that tasted like too.

Lick...Nico's neck? What was going on with her?

She wrapped her arms around his shoulders. Nico dipped down, kissing along her arm. "I'm so stupid, I'm so stupid," he whispered.

She flushed. "Why are you stupid?"

"For wasting all this time," he muttered. "For not having you like this sooner."

"I was with Dylan," she whispered as he nuzzled into her neck, sucking on the soft spot above her clavicle. She could feel herself bruising. Feel Nico leaving his mark.

"Never again," he growled, dropping kisses along her jawline. "He will never get to touch you ever again."

Then he distracted her with a mind-numbing kiss, the kind that had her like soft putty in his hands. She was pliable and willing in Nico's arms. She let herself go. Let him take control with his hands and his teeth and his tongue.

"What the hell is going on here?!"

They broke apart and scrambled away from one

another, standing up to face a red-faced, violently angry Jeff Carter.

"I-it's nothing," Sam speedily defended, dusting off her legs. There was no dust or dirt. Only the memory of sitting in Nico's lap. She needed something to do with her hands.

"I wouldn't say it's *nothing*," Nico added with a mumble, leaning toward her.

"Get away from her," Jeff spat. "Six feet. Far away."

Nico took a step forward. "Jeff—"

"How long has this been going on?" her brother asked, his eyes darting between the two of them. "Have you been sneaking around behind my back?"

"*No*," Sam replied. "It hasn't been going on. It only just happened. It was only a kiss. A-a stupid joke."

Nico stiffened next to her, then shifted back and forth on his feet.

Jeff pointed at her. "Is this your way of getting back at Dylan or something?"

Sam flicked her gaze to Nico. His eyes were already on her, his expression guarded. At first, the kiss *was* a way to get back at him. *Prove him wrong.* It was meant to be an experiment. For science. Nothing more than a simple exchange between friends. Maybe a lesson or two on how to improve her technique.

But Sam couldn't lie. That kiss quickly shifted into something far more than she expected, and she felt off-balance. Like she was living in the Upside Down. A reality she didn't even know existed...but could never look away from again.

Her hesitation didn't help in calming her brother down. Jeff was shaking with anger. "No," he said, whipping his head back and forth. "Absolutely not. This will not be happening. The two of you. Just...*no*."

Sam sucked in a breath, but didn't get the chance to reply.

"I don't think that's your call to make," Nico interrupted.

"You're my best friend, and she's my sister. *No.* No, no, *no.*"

"Jeff..." Sam whispered.

He pointed a finger at her again, his hand still trembling. "Stay the fuck away from him."

"*Jeff,*" Nico growled.

Jeff ignored him. "You will go to NYU and you'll have your pick of anyone you want, Sam. But not him. This will not happen."

"Why *not?*" Nico bit back.

But Jeff wouldn't respond to his best friend. Wouldn't even look him in the eye. He bolted from the alcove and ran for the house.

A solid, warm hand covered her forearm. "Sam—"

"I'm sorry, Nico."

"*Sam,* wait—"

She wrenched from his grasp and took off after her brother. She didn't look back.

She found him in her room, ripping apart the blankets and pillows on her bed.

"What are you doing?" she asked, snatching his discards off the floor.

"Looking for evidence." He huffed.

Sam paused, watching her brother rifle through her desk and dismantle her room, examining his face. His cheeks and neck were cherry-red, his eyes wide as he searched. He didn't look angry. He looked...*embarrassed.*

She reached for his arm. "Jeff."

He shrugged her off.

She scoffed, then grabbed his bicep and yanked him away from her things. He stumbled backward, his eyes scanning the corkboard above, covered in pictures and old choir concert programs and friendship bracelets from summer camp. She squeezed his arm, trying to get his attention. "What's going on with you?"

"You can't have him," he muttered.

"Okay, but—"

"*No*, not him." Jeff swiveled around and faced her. "Anyone but him."

Sam took a deep breath, scanning the face she knew so well. The freckles on his nose, the small scar on his left cheek from the time he fell off his bike racing Nico down the bank, his mahogany-colored hair flat on his head, not combed and styled neatly in the way he'd worn it more and more during his two years at Cornell. And his eyes, full of hurt and embarrassment and, if she wasn't mistaken, shame.

The truth hit her like a ton of bricks. "Are you—"

"Don't tell anyone," he whispered. "I-I haven't told anyone at home."

"But have you told people at Cornell?"

"They know. I...I haven't hidden that part of myself from anyone there."

"But you hide yourself here," she concluded. She dropped her grip from his arm and hugged her stomach. "You hid that part of yourself from us. From Mom and Dad. From me."

He shook his head, face still red. "You don't get it."

"Then explain it to me." She took a step closer. "Jeff, Nico has *two moms*. If anything, our families would always be accepting. You know you're in a safe space with us..." She hesitated, her words strained. "You know that, right?"

"I know it's a safe space, but I..." Jeff sighed, then leaned in. "What was I supposed to say, huh? That I'm pretty sure I like guys and that I have been in love with my best friend since I met him?"

"*Yes!* If I had known, I would have...I would have—"

"Not kissed him?" Jeff huffed. "I'm not stupid, Sam. He likes girls. I don't. It's simple."

"But I-I—" The sentence died in her throat. *Wouldn't have kissed him?* Maybe it would have been easier to not have. To not know what Nico's hum would sound like with their tongues tied and his hands on her back, or to feel her stomach dip when he made all of his declarations.

I'm so stupid.

For not having you like this sooner.

She touched her lips, the memory of his on hers, like a ghost.

"I know I'm safe with you, with our family but...I didn't want to come out and still have this big secret to hide." Jeff's face softened. "Don't do it," he pleaded. "Don't be with him. You can have anyone else. But please, not him."

Sam blinked up at her brother. "He'll be with someone eventually, Jeff." The thought of Nico being with *someone else* made her throat go dry. She wiped it from her mind, trying her best to focus on her brother and not on the fact that everything she felt for Nico had to stop before it could even start. She could do it. Lock Nico back up into the compartment she always put him in. *Jeff's annoying, gross best friend. Jeff's annoyingly hot, good-with-his-hands best friend.*

"If it's someone else, then I won't have to watch it all the time. It's...more manageable this way."

She hugged her stomach tighter. "And you? What will you do?"

He shrugged. "Hope that I fall for someone else."

They remained there for a beat, his confession lingering between them.

He cleared his throat, his hands pulling at the edges of his Cornell College of Agriculture T-shirt. "Promise me, Sam."

"Promise what?"

"Promise me you won't be with him. I won't ever get in the way of your love life again, I promise you that. But...*please*. Promise me this."

It was one kiss. It wasn't supposed to ruin everything.

But it did. And it was all Sam's fault.

"Okay," she breathed, telling herself *I can get over this. It was only a kiss.* "Okay. I promise."

Jeff hugged her, then left without a word, closing her door with a muffled click.

Sam tiptoed to her window, looking out to the backyard and the alcove behind the juniper bush.

He was still there, pacing in the dewy grass. His hat fisted in one hand, the other running through his hair.

Sam closed her eyes, tears trickling down her cheeks as she backed away from the window and switched off her light.

Four Years Later

Chapter 1

"I really should have put on a bra."

The sliding doors at Willow Food Basket swooshed open as Sam stepped around a line of pumpkins and hay bales. She pulled her jean jacket tighter as she breezed past the bags of cranberries and baskets of butternut squash, heading for the prepared foods aisle as she adjusted her earbuds.

"Girl, I feel like that could work *in your favor*," Yumi joked on the other end of the line.

Sam heard rustling. "Yu, why did you call? This should literally only take me five minutes and I'll be back at the house."

"Your mom wanted me to tell you she needs celery as well." She could *feel* her best friend's smirk through the phone. "But now I want to know if anyone notices you're not wearing a bra."

Sam turned on her heel and retreated back to the produce section. "Again, it's a small town. People talk."

"Which means everyone will be gossiping about how Sam Carter was in the Food Basket, bra-less and buying celery and boxed stuffing?" Yumi cackled. "*Scandalous!* A harlot! Alert the press!"

"You don't get it," she grumbled, making her way to the open fridge and the pile of bagged celery stalks. "Why does Mom need celery?"

"I don't know, something about chopping it up and throwing it in with the stuffing to make it healthier." Yumi dropped her voice low. "I didn't think it was possible to be so stressed over burnt stuffing, but your mother defied all odds."

She sighed, grabbing a bag and tucking it underneath her arm.

"Actually, I take that back. Nothing compares to Omma at Seollal when she overcooked the rice cakes and couldn't serve Tteokguk." Jingling came through the other line, likely from Yumi's stack of charm bracelets Sam knew she fiddled with when she was nervous—or overthinking something. "Frightening."

"Thanksgiving happens once a year," Sam added. "It's *one day*. Why can't she not worry about being healthy for one day?"

"Because she wasn't taught to, girly pop. The world taught her that eating is bad and being skinny is good and you have to always watch what you put in your pie hole. Then walk ten-thousand steps and drink lemon water after to 'quiet your cravings.'"

Sam crossed the deli counter, recognizing Harley Guthrie on the other side, carefully folding thin slices of bacon into brown paper sheets. She grabbed the brim of her NYU cap and dipped it low as she scurried into the prepared food aisle. "Funny. It sounds horrible, and at the same time, eerily similar to the stuff we're writing."

Yumi sighed, and Sam felt it in her bones. They were on

the same page about this, ever since they started as editorial interns at *Nourished* the previous summer. They did a lot of the grunt work, as expected of interns. Coffee runs, stock image research, email management, being the butt-end of the joke on numerous social media posts and videos that went wrong. Sam didn't mind it at first; she just wanted to move past the intern phase and get a job in editorial so she could write about nutrition and actually make a difference. When she was promoted to a staff writing position right alongside Yumi, she *finally* felt like she had her break. Until Garrison, the nutrition editor, handed her and Yumi a spreadsheet of search terms and told them to write "service pieces" so *Nourished* could be the top searchable nutrition magazine on Google. Terms such as *fat-burning foods* and *detox juice cleanse* and *how to get a Miley Cyrus body*.

She'd thought her writing would make a difference, but found herself doing exactly what she hated most: writing dumb articles for the internet that would cause readers to develop seriously scary, unhealthy habits. But if she wanted to work her way up in that world, she had to bite her tongue.

At least she and her roommate were on the same page about it all. Yumi and Sam moved in together after that summer, splitting a studio apartment in the Upper East Side in Manhattan, where they transformed the living room into a second bedroom with a partition that they did *not* tell their landlord about. The rent for a studio had been too good to ignore, and Sam and Yumi committed to doing it for a year. But at the rate they were going, with their pitiful annual salaries, they concluded it'd be more than a year before they could upgrade into a two-bedroom. Maybe in Long Island City. Or Bushwick, though it'd probably be too trendy for them to afford by then.

"We'll work our way up and out of these positions,"

Yumi reassured her, pulling Sam from her borderline existential crisis in the middle of Willow Food Basket the day before Thanksgiving. "Now, before you get all moody on me, tell me how many people you've recognized so far."

"Four," Sam grumbled, slowing down in front of the boxed stuffing mixes. There were barely any left. "Actually, five. I saw someone at the deli counter."

Yumi cackled again, the pure delight in her best friend's voice making it hard for Sam not to smile. "*Five*. God, small towns are so interesting. People just like, *know* you."

Sam scanned the limited selection, either cheap store-brand or "heart healthy" options that looked like they probably tasted like chalk. She frowned. She wanted the good stuff. "Don't you sometimes get that when you're back in Washington Heights?"

"Not even close to the same. I know some of the shop owners, but anyone I grew up with is long gone by now. They all left the city, like my parents."

"Any word from them yet?" Sam asked, picking up a box that said *Stuffing, Without The Bread!* and then throwing it back on the shelf.

Her friend sighed. "Nah, not yet. They're too busy with Halmeoni. I know they were planning on taking her to Namsam to see the flowers. There probably aren't many left in bloom, but Halmeoni has no concept of what season it is. Plus, it's like, ten at night in Seoul."

Sam's heart dipped for Yumi. Her parents were across the globe taking care of her grandmother, whose brain had slowly started deteriorating from dementia. It was why she was here with Sam and her family on Thanksgiving. She hadn't asked yet, but Sam was already planning on bringing her home for Christmas as well. "Do you want to try and call them again?"

"And not be on the phone with you while you parade around your small town without a bra on? Fat chance. This is *far* more entertaining."

She picked up a store brand box that looked a little more promising. "To give you even more context, people don't just know you in a small town. They know *everything*. The color bands you wore on your braces and what grade you got in sophomore biology and who you kissed underneath the bleachers at the homecoming football game."

"You were kissing people underneath the *bleachers*?"

"I was being hypothetical," she grumbled. She snatched two boxes of mix.

A sneaker squeaked against the linoleum floor a few feet to her left. Without thinking about how her mission was to *hide* from whoever walked in the store, Sam followed the noise, her eyes on a pair of white Nike Air Force 1's. Her heart skipped as she blinked up. Then her stomach dropped.

There was so much about him that had changed. His bushy brown hair seemed a little more tame, trimmed smartly so the waves sat evenly at his crown. The youthful softness in his face was gone, now hardened into the jaw line of a young man, smooth and clean-shaven. He wore dark gray joggers and a navy-blue sweater, the sleeves pushed up to his elbows. He clutched a bag of corn muffin mix in his hands, his corded forearms flexing, an expensive-looking silver watch on his left wrist.

But those chestnut-colored eyes...she would know them from anywhere. Know them from days playing by the river. The late-night video game marathons she was occasionally allowed to crash. And the night four summers ago when he guided her onto his lap and murmured confessions into her skin, leaving his mark with his tongue and his teeth.

He blinked at her, the color in his cheeks deepening with each excruciating moment that passed.

"Oh, a car pulled up," Yumi chided on the other line. "I think your brother just arrived—"

Nico's not supposed to be here. Last she knew, he was living in San Francisco. He graduated from Berkeley and never returned to Willow, accepting a job at Nubo and working there as a software engineer. He seemed settled there, enough for his moms to travel for an extended stay during the holiday season every year, all so they could be closer to him.

This was information Sam had learned online, through the very social network that Nico worked for. She couldn't help her curiosity. She didn't care for social media much, but she was curious about what Nico was working on. Sam would click through the different features of the app and imagine Nico behind a computer, coding complicated languages to bring those user experiences to life. It was the closest she'd gotten to him in the years since everything went down between them.

But he should be out there, not *here*. In the Willow Food Basket. On Thanksgiving weekend.

"Nico," Sam whispered.

Yumi killed her rant. She heard shuffling, then the soft closing of a door. "I'm sorry, did you just say Nico? As in...*your Nico?* Oh my fucking god!"

Nico's eyes widened. He inhaled loudly through his nose, like he was trying to calm himself down, his eyes scanning her greasy hair tucked underneath her hat, her ratty old Willow High Choir T-shirt and worn denim jacket, and a pair of old sweatpants that pinched her hips. The festive *Gobble Up!* turkey socks Yumi gifted her were embarrassingly visible thanks to the sandals she'd slipped on, hoping she would be in and out of the store quickly. She didn't think she would run into too many people. She didn't think she would run into *him*.

"What's going on? Are you guys just like, staring at each other? Is he still super hot? Oh god, like, swallow his face. Make out in aisle four. And keep me on the phone while you do it."

"Nico," Sam whispered again, ignoring the way Yumi was rattling off requests on the other line. "What are you—"

Nico dropped the bag of corn muffin mix in his hand, the plastic splitting open as the dry mix careened across the floor. He clenched his fists and turned, then walked down the aisle and right through the swooshing front doors, past the pumpkins and the hay bales and the line of cars. Sam didn't move an inch as she watched Nico climb into a black Bronco toward the back of the lot.

"He's gone," she whispered.

"He *left*?!" Yumi cackled with delight again. "Dear lord, what a thrill! I *love* small towns!"

Nico slammed the front door of the house. A soft ping followed as the harvest wreath dangling from the hook inside fell to the ground.

Mama jumped from the kitchen, wooden spoon in her hand stained from the cranberry sauce she'd been mixing. Her curly brown hair was piled high in a bun at the top of her head. "*Nicolas*! What are you, twelve? Why are you slamming the door?"

He closed his eyes and pressed his temples hard, hoping the pressure would stave off the headache he felt coming on. "Sorry, Mama."

"Everything all right?"

Nico dropped his hands and glanced at Mom, glasses perched on the bridge of her nose, her short blonde hair neatly straight, not a strand out of place.

She frowned. "Never thought I would have to say this again, but—"

He sighed and reached for the wallet in his back pocket. He flipped it open, snatched a dollar bill, and placed it in her open palm.

She stuffed it in the pocket of the cardigan she'd changed into, buttoned neatly to the top. "Need I remind you how much money you lost that summer when we had to make this rule?"

He rubbed his neck. "Yeah, yeah, I get it."

Mama crossed her arms, her loose floral dress brushing her bare ankles with the motion. "No corn muffin mix?"

He clenched his teeth, his jaw locked. He could have easily gone to another store in town, but he'd been distracted. His mind raced faster than the unnecessary speed he pushed his Bronco getting back to the house.

She furrowed her brow. Mom cocked her head.

Nico cleared his throat. "No. Completely out." Then he kicked off his shoes, mumbled that he had some work to do, and climbed the stairs two at a time. He carefully closed his bedroom door, leaning against it as he slid down to the carpeted floor.

Nico had expected to see Sam. It was a holiday and Willow was the smallest of small towns in New York and, to top it all off, Jeff had been begging him for *months* to meet him at Gilroy's for a drink later. When his ex–best friend emailed him last year with a long-winded apology for derailing their friendship, they fell into a cordial email relationship. He hated the formality of it—he desperately wanted to send Jeff stupid *SpongeBob* references or *Futurama* memes he saw online—but getting to that point felt like an upward battle, espccially when Nico still had so much he needed to say. He didn't want to convey it all in an email, and he certainly didn't want to follow up with how he was feeling after Jeff bravely came out to Nico and told him about his new boyfriend.

His name is Daniel, he'd written. *I'm in love. And I want you to meet him. Gilroy's, the night before Thanksgiving?*

Nico had already told Jeff the news. Nubo was rapidly growing, the photo-sharing app now number two in the App Store, and the company was bringing on swaths of new employees. OmniCorp, the company that acquired Nubo, was impressed by his work as lead engineer and thought he had the "tenacity to lead." He was promoted to the east coast director of engineering, and they wanted him to transfer to the OmniCorp offices in New York City. It meant he could be back on the east coast and his moms could spend the holidays in their house in Willow. It meant he could maybe fix his broken relationship with his best friend.

It also meant he would probably see *her*.

So, yes. He expected to see Sam.

What he didn't expect was how seeing her would fundamentally tilt his world on its axis.

He had spent the past four years trying to get over what had happened between them, moving through the stages of grief at a painstakingly slow pace. Denial that he could never have Sam in the way he desperately wanted. Anger at Jeff for making it impossible for them, for the way Sam completely blocked him out after that night. Bargaining through all of the ways they could make it work, how the three of them could fix things. The cavernous pit of sadness of losing both Carter siblings in one fell swoop.

But all of that work disintegrated instantly with one look at her. One look at her, and all of his favorite memories with Sam came rushing back, like scooter races through the neighborhood or the way she schemed when they played Monopoly. Yet, even if she wore the same old sweatpants and T-shirt from high school he remembered well, he could see all the ways her body filled them out, the curves that'd transformed Sam from the girl he used to know to the woman he never got the chance to. His mind replayed the way that body felt wrapped around him that night. He wanted to run his hands through her silky black hair again. Sink his teeth into her bottom lip, blush-pink and soft and full.

But the sound of his name coming from those lips startled him into reality, causing him to act like a complete imbecile as he dropped the box of muffin mix to the floor and walked away from her.

So much for getting over it. After seeing Sam, Nico was pretty sure "getting over it" would never actually be an option for him.

Chapter 2

Sam slinked into the kitchen from the side door connected to the garage. A bellowing, cackle of a laugh came from the living room, followed by a number of loud voices talking over one another in excitement.

Jeff's home.

Sam placed the bag of groceries on the counter and made her way to the living room where he was holding court.

Her brother was *beaming*. Flushed cheeks and a toothy grin, his hair still bleach-blond despite Sam's insistence that blond was *not* his color. She watched from the doorframe as her brother blinked up at his boyfriend, his shoulders tucked under Daniel's long, lanky arm. Jeff looked at him like he was his world, and Sam could easily tell why. Daniel was *hot*. Dark hair, a little scruff, round tortoiseshell glasses, a button-down tucked inside slim slacks and a tweed blazer over top. He was like a nerdy, academic Johnathan Bailey. Daniel had molded into his new professor role at Cornell easily, moving from a teacher's assistant to assistant professor in the agriculture department. It was why Jeff never left Ithaca. Jeff told his parents it was because of a job, working as an agriculture manager for one of the firms that assisted smaller wineries in grape production. But he told Sam the truth—he'd fallen in love with the TA and wasn't ready to leave.

"It's a bit scandalous," Jeff had murmured on the phone two years ago. "A scandal I would have gone through with, don't get me wrong, but Daniel is too proper. He wants to wait until after graduation to get together."

"I like him already," Sam said with a smile, tucked inside her too-tiny twin bed in her student apartment at NYU, horns blaring outside, music pouring through her window from the bar downstairs that unfortunately *always* had live music until two in the morning.

She could *feel* his eye-roll on the other line. "Ugh, you're no fun."

"When are you going to tell them?" she whispered, like she needed to make sure her words wouldn't travel across the island, up the Hudson River, and through her parents' bedroom window.

"Soon," he replied. She could sense he was smiling. "I promise."

He kept to his promise. They traveled to Ithaca for Jeff's graduation, watching him walk across the aisle, his newly dyed blond hair peeking out from under his cap. That night at dinner, in the same sentence that Jeff shared the news about his new job, he also shared the news about his sexuality.

Now, two years later, Jeff had the courage to bring Daniel home for the holidays. The "story" they were going with was that they recently met through mutual friends in their industry, and this was their first holiday together. But Sam knew the real one—the story that involved clandestine meetings at night and promises in the dark. She liked that one better. She liked seeing her brother's love story unfold.

"Sam!"

Jeff jumped out of Daniel's arms and threw himself at her.

It'd taken time for them to work on their relationship. After that fateful night that'd started with an innocent game of sardines, Jeff had been attentive to her. Kind in a way she hadn't experienced in a long time. Instead of being her usual annoying older brother, he asked her thoughtful questions. He listened to her frustrations when she was in school, when the classwork felt too hard and New York City felt like too much. He never made fun of her for those late-night calls. Their relationship evolved into a friendship, with shared memes and jokes through text, video calls over coffee or wine, weekend visits to the city so Sam could take Jeff to all of her favorite spots—the Strand and Black Fox Coffee and the boathouse at Central Park.

Sam liked having her brother in this way, a sibling who also felt like her closest friend. She'd pretended like everything that happened was no big deal, that kissing Nico meant nothing to her. She'd kept her sadness hidden, locked away in a small box and placed on the shelf of her closet. She only let herself play around with the feeling when she was at her lowest, when she felt lonely and wondered *what if.*

Nico was Jeff's best friend, and despite how *she* felt, that relationship far outweighed those new, unfamiliar feelings. She'd wanted them to heal. Wanted them to fix what she had so clearly destroyed that night. So she'd kept her distance—and she had no idea if Jeff and Nico were even talking anymore. She never brought up the subject. It felt like poking a sleeping bear. Or pointing out the elephant in the room that became a little more translucent with each passing year.

Jeff squeezed his arms around Sam. She smiled and returned the hug, smelling his usual cologne and a hint of the french fries she knew he loved to snack on when he made the road trip back to this side of the state.

Her chest ached. *Nico's home.* She wanted to bring up who she saw in the store, *wondered* if Jeff had any idea that his former best friend was back in town. But Sam wasn't sure if she could talk about it in any coherent way. So she bit her tongue and squeezed her brother again before he pulled her over to the circle to meet the love of his life.

Her brother slipped a hand around his boyfriend's waist. "Sam, this is Daniel."

Daniel's smile was coy, an eyebrow raised in her direction. Technically, she had already met Daniel—on a video call with Jeff one morning when he popped onto the screen after a morning run. She'd sat there and listened as the two of them bantered over Jeff's lack of exercise, and when Sam confirmed that no, Jeff would *never* be the kind of person to "go for a morning run," that got a cackle out of her brother and a fake scowl from Daniel. Her chest had felt warm when she hung up minutes later.

Sam tilted her head, trying to mimic the same kind of smile as she held out a hand. "Daniel, so lovely to finally meet you."

Daniel rolled his eyes, then stepped closer to give Sam a hug. "Good to see you again," he whispered in her ear.

She blushed, watching the way Daniel casually rejoined Jeff, the two linked at the hip.

"*Blech*, show-offs," Yumi interrupted with a pout. She crossed her arms, her charm bracelets dangling with the motion. "Daniel, do you have any hot single brothers?"

Daniel's face fell, his cheeks flushing red. "No siblings."

Mom breezed in, a plate of bacon-wrapped dates on a plate and a bottle of Crozes-Hermitage in the other. Her frizzy brown hair was loose at her shoulders, wisps of gray visible along her forehead. Dad, dressed neatly in navy slacks and a white polo, his jet-black hair slicked back neatly in place, silently opened the cabinet behind them and pulled out six wineglasses.

Despite Daniel looking clearly uncomfortable by the situation, Yumi persisted. "Cousins? Uncles?"

Jeff moved his hand to Daniel's nape, massaging small circles into his neck. "We don't talk about Daniel's family. They are dead to us."

Mom froze, platter of dates still in her hand. "What?"

Daniel's face melted into a smile, shifting quickly into an expression that seemed a lot more easy-going than Sam was willing to believe. "A story for another time," he reassured her. "These look delicious, Mrs. Carter."

Mom sucked in a breath, then smiled back at him as she held the platter out, offering Daniel the first date. "Well, you can call me Mom, if you ever feel comfortable."

He thanked her, then popped the date in his mouth. Yumi and Jeff quickly followed, each grabbing two before she'd even set the platter down on the coffee table.

Sam held out a glass as Dad poured her wine, content to remain quiet as Jeff and Daniel shared their love story. Or at least the revised version—that they met after Jeff graduated and had been dating for less than a year, making sure to exclude any mentions that they'd been cohabitating for almost *two* years now.

Mom clapped her hands, not noticing Dad as he handed her a glass of red wine. Some of it sloshed to the wood floor. She continued beaming at Jeff and Daniel, unaware of

Dad's accident. Sam silently laughed into her hand as she watched him wipe up the wine with his sock, then wink at her.

Her mother finally accepted it, still oblivious to the spill, and raised it high. "To finding love."

Jeff's face lit up as Daniel tucked him closer, holding his glass in midair. "May we always be in pursuit of it."

A resounding cheer came from the group. A twinge of sorrow swept through Sam as they clinked glasses, wondering what it meant to always be in pursuit of love. Was she even trying to be in pursuit of it? She'd done what was expected of every young undergrad: put herself out there at parties and on-campus events and even in her classes. But there'd never been that *spark*. The feeling that always brought her back to Nico, the low growl when he'd kissed her, his hands exploring her skin at her back. Jeff had been able to move past his feelings for Nico and find someone new. Would she ever be able to do the same? Or was she irrevocably ruined by Nicolas Giuliano?

Jeff lifted a finger and pointed at Yumi. "Don't worry, sister number two. We can find you someone tonight."

Sam frowned. "Tonight?"

He moved his pointer finger to Sam. "Tonight. We're going to Gilroy's."

She groaned, tilting her head back. "Everyone goes to Gilroy's the night before Thanksgiving."

"*Exactly.*"

Yumi cheered, lifting her glass in the air. "*Yes!* Small town night at the local bar! I am *so* in."

"Would you like to come, Mrs. and Mr. Carter?" Daniel asked politely.

Dad's face grew serious. "I have work to do."

Mom placed her hands on her hips. "Jackson, come on. It's a holiday."

He shrugged. "Technically it isn't. The firm won't run itself." Then he looked at Sam and winked again, like she understood hard work and getting things done. He had no reason *not* to believe that of Sam. When trying to do the "normal" college thing didn't work out, Sam dived deep into her studies—and had graduated Summa Cum Laude that spring.

Jeff rolled his eyes. "Mom, it's okay. It's mostly just a gathering of sloppy high school grads. You won't have fun."

Dad frowned. "Who's driving?"

"Me," Daniel volunteered, cocking a brow at my brother. "I don't have any desire to get 'sloppy.'"

Yumi and Jeff covered their mouths in an attempt to stifle their laughter, then the two of them fought over the last bacon-covered date.

Daniel flushed and looked at Sam.

"You kind of handed them that one," Sam teased.

He huffed. "I'm going to get a run for my money, aren't I?"

"You haven't already learned this about Jeff?"

Daniel chuckled. "Touché. I guess that's what makes him so interesting."

Sam watched as her best friend and brother squabbled over who deserved the date, while Mom tried to mitigate the argument and Dad stoically sipped on his wine.

"*Interesting* is certainly a way to put it," Sam replied.

Yumi snatched the date and stuffed it in her mouth, then ran for the stairs. "Sam, follow!" she yelled with a full mouth. "We have to get ready!"

"*You suck!*" Jeff yelled as Yumi disappeared to the second floor.

Sam poured more wine, then lifted her glass to Daniel. "Welcome to the family."

Daniel smiled and clinked her glass, his green eyes sparkling behind his specs. "I'm happy to be here."

When Sam entered her room, Yumi jumped out from behind the door and slammed it shut.

She cupped her glass, making sure not to spill her wine. "Jesus, Yu."

Her best friend pranced onto the bed, still unmade after Mom woke her up from a glorious late-afternoon nap to *go to the store now, it's an emergency*. "I want every juicy detail about what just happened."

Sam pointed to the door. "You already know the story. They've secretly been dating for—"

She rolled her eyes. "Not *them*. The store. The man-who-must-not-be-named."

Her chest deflated. She placed her glass on her desk. "Oh."

Yumi clapped, like she was summoning the information she demanded. "Details, Carter. Spill. Now."

She groaned as she turned around, falling backward on the bed with a soft *plunk*. "So I saw Nico."

"And you totally eye-fucked, didn't you."

She shoved her. "Stop."

Yumi cackled, her laugh reverberating off the walls.

Sam squeezed her forearm. "Quiet down or I'm going to stuff Mister McStuffin in your face."

Her friend laughed again, grabbing the stuffed white bunny and holding out of Sam's reach.

She launched herself at Yumi, reaching for the stuffed

animal she's had since she was five when she won it at the Willow Summer Solstice Fair. She beat Nico and Jeff at the ring toss, and proudly called him Mister McStuffin. They made fun of her for it, but she didn't care. Mister McStuffin had taken up a permanent spot next to her bedroom pillow ever since.

Sam snatched it from Yumi's grasp and hugged the bunny close for protection as she lay back down on the bed. "Be nice. He's been through a lot."

Yumi twirled the bunny's soft ear. "I bet if Mister McStuffin could talk, he would tell you how *desperate* he was for you to get some action."

She scowled. "Nothing has worked out yet, you know that."

"Has nothing *really* worked out, or is someone not allowing it to work out because of a certain hot makeout that ruined her love life forever?"

Sam covered her eyes with the stuffed animal. "Stop," she grumbled.

Yumi wrenched the animal from her grasp, then gently dropped a kiss on the bunny's nose and tucked him next to Sam's head. "Did he even say anything to you?"

"No. He dropped the bag he was holding and walked out of the store."

She sighed, sprawling out on the bed next to Sam, the two of them staring up at the discolored plastic stars still stuck to the ceiling. "That's romantic."

Sam held up her hands. "*How* is that romantic? He looked at me like I was a ghost."

"Probably because he saw how hot you got and was all flustered and couldn't think straight."

"Oh, yeah right." She lifted her feet in the air, her

Gobble Up! socks still on. "I'm sure I looked irresistible with these things on."

"Hey, don't bash the socks I got you. They're cute."

Sam hooked their arms together. "They are cute, Yu."

The two of them lay there in silence for a beat, looking up at the stars, the glow of the setting sun peeping through the trees outside of her window.

Yumi careened herself into a seating position before jumping to the floor. "Come on," she said, pulling on Sam's ankles. "We gotta get ready."

Sam groaned again. "Please, go without me. I don't think I can handle high school tonight."

"But what if *he's* there?"

She blinked, then propped herself up on her elbows. "I highly doubt Nico Giuliano is planning on going to the *dive bar* the night before Thanksgiving."

"But didn't you tell me he was like, mister popular or something? Wouldn't he want to go back to the bar and *live his glory days?*"

She shivered. "Nico wasn't like that. He was..." She hesitated, trying to find the right words.

Yumi's smirk was telling. "Are you going to tell me he was *different?* Misunderstood? Popular in a 'I'm too nice to know the power I actually hold over you' kind of way?"

She frowned. "He was popular because he's hot. Jeff was popular because he was funny. Put the two of them together and it was a recipe for high school disaster."

"I love your use of *present tense* in that sentence?"

Sam glared. "Excuse me?"

"You said *he's hot.* Present tense. Because you still think he's hot."

"Don't make me throw Mister McStuffin at you. He just got comfortable."

Yumi grinned, then tugged on Sam's ankles again. "Come *onnnn*."

She hesitated. "Yu?"

Her best friend cocked her head to the side, a strand of hair falling out of her left space bun. "Yeah?"

"What if he is there?"

Yumi's expression softened. "There's only one way to find out, my girl. Now get up and get out of those socks. We gotta make you hot."

Chapter 3

Two steps into Gilroy's and Nico's shoes were already stuck to the floor. He tugged on them with force as he made his way past the packed entrance as far too many people he recognized flashed their IDs at the door. He did the same, scanning the bar, his hair masking some of his face in hopes he wouldn't get stuck talking to someone before he could find Jeff.

A peel of laughter came from a booth at the back of the bar. He saw a familiar-shaped head, his hair bleached blond and his arm slung around the shoulders of a taller man in a tweed jacket. Sitting across from him was a Korean woman he did not recognize, and next to her was the woman he would know anywhere.

Sam sat with her legs crossed, wearing a silky-looking black skirt and a black tank top, her bare arms perched on the table as she covered her mouth in laughter. Her hair shaped her round face and fell loose at her shoulders, trailing down her back.

I can't do this. He thought about how easy it would be to leave. He could turn around and hop back in his Bronco, drive the eight minutes back home, then text Jeff to tell him he came down with something. He'd sit at the table with his moms tomorrow, fully embracing his new title as *the world's biggest coward*. It didn't sound so bad. He could live with that.

"Nico!"

Too late.

Hilary Barton jumped in front of him, the hot-pink top she wore dipping dangerously low on her chest before disappearing into high-waisted jeans. The last time he saw Hilary was his senior year prom, when she cried to him that she wished he cared more about her than he did his best friend. Nico thought the idea was ludicrous. Why would he back away from a decade-long friendship for a girl he'd only been dating a couple of weeks? Two days later he told her their priorities weren't aligned, and let her down as gently as he could. She threw a lunch tray at his face in response.

"I can't believe it, it's actually *you*." Hilary jumped and threw her arms around his shoulders. "God, it's been forever."

He tensed, then lifted a hand and patted her back, finding only bare skin. Her tank top was backless. Nico blinked back up at the table, noticing a set of honey-green eyes trained in his direction.

He dropped his hand.

Hilary grabbed his shoulders and pushed him back, scanning his appearance. "Well, don't you look nice with your Ralph Lauren and your Rolex," she cooed. "Aren't you supposed to be in California or something? What the hell are you doing here?"

He swallowed. "I moved back. I live in Manhattan."

Her eyes blew wide. "Manhattan? Oh my god, I'm in Hoboken now! We should *totally* hang out."

"Nicolas!"

Nico grinned at the interruption from the person heading in their direction. He cupped Hilary's hands and unlatched them from his shirt. "That would be the siren call."

She huffed, eyeing Jeff, who now stood beside him. "You guys are still friends."

Jeff grinned. "Never stopped."

Hilary rolled her eyes and stepped away.

Nico felt his heart pounding in his chest as he faced his best friend. Technically they *did* stop. He knew their friendship was on the line at that moment. Would things feel different, or would they continue on like nothing ever happened?

The two of them stood there for a beat, years of unspoken words floating between them. Words he wanted to let free...but he didn't know how.

Jeff cleared his throat, then pointed at Nico's clothes. "Who did it? Who taught you how to dress properly?"

Nico snorted. "I taught myself."

"No more Knicks apparel then?"

He smirked. "It makes an appearance from time to time."

Jeff sighed. "I guess some things never change."

Nico's gaze lingered on the booth in the back, watching as Sam shifted her weight and crossed her legs.

Jeff poked his shoulder. "Thanks for coming."

"Of course." Nico gave Jeff his full attention. "I want to meet the love of your life."

Jeff beamed. "And you will." He shoved his hands in his pockets. "I just had something I needed to say first."

Nico sucked in a breath, ignoring the way his chest burned as he nodded.

"I'm sorry, for the last four years. For ignoring you and our friendship. For letting that moment get between us."

"You already apologized for that," he answered tightly. "In your initial email."

"I know, I know." Jeff exhaled. "But I needed to say it to you in person. I was a shit, and I'm sorry."

But why? Nico asked himself that question over and over the last four years. Why Jeff reacted the way he did, and why his best friend refused even the idea of him and Sam being together. The burning in his chest didn't subside, but he nodded anyway. He wanted to get past this part. He wanted to get to the table, and to at least say *hello* to Sam after his incompetence to do so in the grocery store.

Nico clenched his jaw and nodded.

Jeff beamed again, then grabbed Nico's arm and pulled him to the booth. When they arrived, Jeff dropped his death grip and held out his hands for the man Nico presumed to be Daniel. "Babe! This is Nico. You may not recognize him from my photos because apparently my best friend has discovered designer clothing."

Nico snatched his phone from the pocket of his dark-washed jeans and held it between them. "Old photos, huh? If you're going to act that way, then I think it's time for Daniel to see your *pop punk phase.*"

Jeff sucked in a breath, then narrowed his eyes. "Asshole. You're playing dirty."

He shrugged. "Keeping you humble, that's all."

"I would actually love to see your pop punk phase," Daniel chimed in, standing up to shake Nico's hand.

"Babe, for the love of *god*, please don't."

Nico winked at Daniel. "I'll show you later."

He grinned. "Looking forward to it."

The three of them stood there in silence for a beat, the

thumping beats through the speaker soothing into something acoustic and soft.

A throat cleared behind Jeff, followed by a high-pitched *ahem.*

"You wanna share with the crowd?" said the woman he didn't know.

Jeff rolled his eyes, then turned. "Yumi, keep it in your pants."

She shot him a devilish smile in return. "Can't if I'm wearing a skirt."

"You disgust me."

The two of them bantered back and forth, giving Nico enough time to fix his gaze on Sam, uninterrupted.

She blinked up at him from the booth, where an empty glass with a bare toothpick sat in front of her. He watched as she leaned back into the leather, her hands clasped loosely in her lap.

"Sam," Nico said with a nod.

The slightest smirk curled up her mouth. "So you *do* remember my name?" she teased.

He bit his bottom lip and widened his eyes. She responded with a silent chuckle, her shoulders bobbing lightly in amusement.

Jeff grabbed Nico's arm. "Come, sit. Lots to catch up on."

Nico blinked down at Sam's empty glass, then eyed the rest of the group's drinks—a mix of half-finished pints and glasses with melted cubes of ice.

He shrugged off his coat. "Let me buy the next round first." He hooked it on the wood panel at the side of the booth, the wool coat ruffling Sam's hair. A whiff of coconut and vanilla trickled up to him, unusual in a place that smelled like stale beer and even staler memories.

He swallowed. "What does everyone want?"

Yumi shot up a hand. "Tequila soda, two limes."

"I'm good, keeping to one tonight so I can drive," Daniel said, pointing to his pint.

Jeff dipped his head in Nico's direction, an evil grin spreading across his face.

Nico pointed at him. "No, absolutely not."

Jeff clapped. "Absolutely *yes*."

"There is no *way* you will convince me to do a Jägerbomb right now."

"Jägerbomb! Jägerbomb!"

Someone from the bar cheered. "Did someone say Jägerbomb?"

Nico turned, finding the bartender eagerly waving a bottle of Jäger, ready to go. "He'll take one," he yelled over the music, pointing to Jeff. "I'll have the IPA."

The bartender's shoulders fell as he placed the bottle back on the shelf and pulled the tap.

Nico squared his shoulders to the booth seat right beside him. He dropped his voice. "What are you drinking?"

Sam tapped a finger on the stem of her empty glass. "Martini, please."

He nodded and turned on his heel, squeezing his way through the crowd to put in the rest of their orders.

She orders a martini at a dive bar?

His mind wandered as he watched the bartender pour drinks. Beside the fact that Sam recently graduated from NYU, Nico knew nothing else about her life. He'd tried to find her online over the years. She didn't have any kind of social media—he checked Nubo for her name at a frequency that could be considered borderline stalkerish. Jeff was tight-lipped about her in his emails, only sharing the small update that he went to her graduation in May. He wondered if she still lived in the city. He wondered what bars she frequented and when she became the kind of person who ordered a martini when she was out. He wondered if she ordered martinis alone...or if she was with someone else.

His gut tightened at the thought as glasses were placed in front of him. He threw down more than enough cash to pay for the drinks plus tip. He reached for the martini and tequila soda first, but was stopped by a wet, pale hand.

"Hey, man, before you do that—"

Nico blinked in surprise at the bartender. "What?"

He dropped his grip. "Want to put in a good word for me with Sam over there?"

"Sam?" He turned to the table, watching her nod along to whatever story Jeff was sharing as he dominated their attention.

He shifted back, eyeing the guy's soaked-through Metallica T-shirt and the receding hairline he was poorly trying to hide with his backward flat-brim. "Who are you?" Nico asked.

The bartender perked up. "Dylan."

His chest flared again. "No," he said firmly, tucking glasses in the crook of his arm so he didn't have to make another trip and look at Dylan's extremely punchable face.

"*Dude*, come on," Dylan pleaded. "We used to date. Help me out, man."

He clenched his jaw then leaned forward, eyes narrowed. "You were wrong, by the way."

"Come again?" Dylan replied, brow furrowed.

Nico couldn't help the devious edge to his smile. "You were wrong. She's an *excellent* kisser."

Dylan's face went white as Nico straightened, then,

feeling infuriated, snatched the leftover tip money. Back at the table, he gingerly set down the glasses, his mind racing at Dylan's insistence on wanting a "good word" and Nico's immediate reaction to protect her from him. Like she was his...even though she was far from it.

Jeff cheered as Nico placed them on the table, then scanned his side of the booth with a frown. "Don't think we have enough room for you over here."

Yumi shimmied closer to the wall, making more room. "Here, we'll scootch in."

Sam's head whipped in Yumi's direction. He watched in rapt attention as the two of them had some kind of silent exchange before Sam conceded. The color rose in her cheeks as she made enough room for him to take a seat. The booth was too small for personal space, their thighs pressed together, ankles knocking into one another. He could feel her body warmth radiating through the silk of her skirt, smell the lingering coconut and vanilla as she brushed a strand of her hair behind her shoulder before pinching the stem of her martini glass and taking a sip.

He took a long swallow of his beer. Then another.

Jeff clapped his hands. "*So.* Nico just moved back."

"No *way*," Yumi replied, dragging out the last syllable a little *too* long.

Jeff sat up straight. "Yes! He's been in Manhattan for a couple of months now."

Sam stilled, the tip of her glass brushing her lips. "A couple of months?"

"Yeah! Isn't that wild? The gang is back together!"

Nico dipped a shoulder to Sam's level. "I got promoted. The company relocated me."

"What company?" Daniel asked.

"OmniCorp."

Groans escalated across the table. Except for Sam, who remained silent as she fiddled with the toothpick in her glass, poking at the lemon peel that fell in.

"They are evil," Yumi groaned. "The number of hours of my life I have wasted scrolling on Nubo."

He grinned with his teeth. "Glad to hear it."

Jeff pointed at him. "She's right. *Evil.*"

Daniel shrugged. "Sounds like he's good at his job if you're all addicted to it."

More groans from Jeff and Yumi.

"Not Sam," Yumi quipped. "She's too much of an adult to have a social media addiction."

"I have a Nubo," she chimed in, the softness of her voice a contrast to the loud bar.

His stomach flipped. "You do?"

She nodded. "It's set on private."

"And she never posts." Yumi rolled her eyes. "Or scrolls. I have to tell her to open the app and like my stuff, otherwise she would be oblivious."

"Not a fan of it?" Nico asked in Sam's direction.

She shrugged. "It kind of makes me sad."

"Boooooo!" Jeff shouted. Yumi joined in with him.

Nico cocked his head at Jeff's glass. "You going to do your Jägerbomb or you going to whine like a little kid."

Jeff's eye twitched as he lifted the shot glass.

"Dear god, I'm nervous," Daniel joked.

Nico leaned in with a wicked smile. "Come on, Jeff."

"Yeahhhhh, Jeff, don't be a pussy!" Yumi cheered.

He noticed the way Sam flinched at Yumi's use of the crude word.

Jeff dropped the shot glass into the energy drink, then tipped it back and swallowed it all in a few gulps.

Daniel shook his head, eyeing Nico. "If I have to take him to a hospital tonight, I blame you."

Nico grinned into his glass. "Feel free to send me the bill."

A finger tapped on his leg underneath the booth. Nico flinched, the beer in his glass sloshing and almost tipping over the side.

"Excuse me," Sam said. "I need the bathroom."

"Oh, right, yes." Nico hopped out, hypersensitive of the small spot on his upper thigh where she poked him. Sam slipped out from the leather seat and didn't look him in the eye as she stepped around his frame, then made her way to the restrooms on the opposite side of the bar.

Yumi requested small-town gossip and Jeff barreled right in with all of the juiciest drama he could come up with, pointing out different people who were in their vicinity. Nico picked up his beer, eyes still on the spot where the swarms of people swallowed Sam out of sight, then finished off his drink in a single gulp. When he placed the glass down on the table, he noticed Daniel watching him closely.

He tapped his empty glass. "I'm off to get another."

Jeff and Yumi were oblivious to his statement, but Daniel nodded. His gaze was a little too knowing, like somehow Jeff's boyfriend knew something he didn't.

Maybe Daniel did, because as soon as Nico reached the line at the bar, hordes of familiar faces closing in, his feet led him in the direction of the bathrooms. He tucked himself in a shadowed corner near the women's, and as soon as the door swung open and a curvy silhouette in black appeared, he grabbed her wrist and pulled her into the dark.

Chapter 4

The firm hand at her wrist pulled her to the old phone booth in the corner, unlit and lingering with the faint smell of used cigarette butts that filled the ashtray in the corner.

Nico twisted her around, the expanse of his back covering the entrance to the booth, his chest pressed into hers and his hand gripping her wrist wedged between them.

Her eyes flicked down to his hand. He loosened his grip, but didn't let go.

"Sam," he breathed.

She huffed. "Two months, Nico?"

She couldn't see his full face, just shadows and dark eyes that flitted across her features. "I know. I'm sorry."

"Are you and Jeff friends again?"

"He emailed me a year ago, and we've been catching up. He told me to come tonight. I didn't...I wasn't sure if you would also be here."

She frowned. "Where else would I be?"

He lifted his shoulder in a sorry attempt at a casual shrug. "With a boyfriend or something."

Her chest twisted, like a damp cloth that was being wrung dry. "No something. No boyfriend."

Nico brushed a thumb across her pulse. It all felt like too much. His proximity. His touch. Those eyes.

She wiggled her wrist free from his grasp and leaned against the wood behind her, attempting to make some space.

Nico's body instinctively followed, but then he caught himself and pressed himself upright. He crossed his arms. "He didn't tell you."

She shook her head, even though it was a statement rather than a question. "It's...odd. I feel like—" She paused, rubbing her clavicle, like she could smear off the hurt that her brother painted there. "I feel like he would have told me something like that. He and I...we're *friends* now. We talk all the time."

Sam watched as Nico's lips curved into a sad smile. "I'm glad to hear that."

She glared. "Yeah, well, maybe if someone didn't take up *all of his time* growing up, I would have been closer with my brother earlier."

He snorted. "Fat chance. He hated your guts then."

She crossed her arms, mimicking his stance, a smile curling up her lips. "And I hated his guts too. And yours."

"Still hate my guts?"

She turned her head, fixing her gaze on the Halloween costume contest poster from a couple years ago, a large rip in the bottom left corner.

"Jeff and I...We got really close, after that night." She took a deep breath. "It kind of changed everything between us."

Nico leaned against the side of the booth, making sure to be in her line of sight. If he wasn't so infuriatingly tall, then she might have been able to avoid him. But his frame crowded the space and she had no other option but to look into the deep chestnut color of his eyes. So much of Nico had seemed to change—his wardrobe, his haircut, the width of his arms. But those eyes looked exactly as she remembered. The same eyes that frequented the dark corners of her deepest dreams.

"I was going to apologize for that night," Nico started. "But it sounds like you should be thanking me."

She rolled her eyes. "No. If anything, I should apologize. I didn't say anything to you. I didn't—"

"Sammy girl."

She sucked in a breath. Hearing those two words, her nickname dripping from his tongue like honey, had her poor attempt at an apology slipping from her grasp.

"We were young and you were sad." He cleared his throat. "And the only thing I could think about that night was proving your stupid ex wrong and kissing you so you could forget about him."

She exhaled. "Well, you were successful, I guess."

The corner of his mouth curled upward. "Glad to be of service."

Sam gaped at him. "You're unbelievable."

Nico pointed a thumb behind him. "He's looking for a second chance, by the way. Asked if I would hook you guys up."

Dread pooled in her belly. She'd seen Dylan working the bar, and had done her best to avoid the longing glances he sent her way. She'd even asked Jeff and Daniel to grab the first round so she and Yumi could claim the empty booth in the far corner. Away from Dylan's prying eyes. "And what did you say?"

"I told him you're an excellent kisser, then took back my tip."

She covered her face with her hands. "*Nico.* You didn't."

"Come *on*, Sammy girl," Nico whined. "Don't ruin my fun."

Warm hands grasped her wrists. Nico pulled her hands from her face, then held them close to his chest again, like he was locking her in place.

Her gaze was on their joined hands. "So, you guys are friends again," she whispered.

His throat bobbed. "And sounds like you guys are too."

They remained there in silence, the booming music shifting into a song Sam couldn't recognize. Something softer and sweeter.

"I missed you," she admitted. "I thought you were so annoying most of my life. But I missed you."

"I missed you too." He swallowed. "You both," he corrected. "I missed you both."

Sam blinked up at him, unable to avoid the elephant that'd wedged itself into their hiding spot. Unavoidable and no longer translucent. "Do you think we can fix what we ruined?" she asked him.

"I hope so," Nico replied in a whisper. "I really do."

Another silent beat passed between them. His hands still held her wrists.

He must have noticed at the same moment, as he squeezed and then dropped her hands. "Should we go back?"

"I should go first."

"I'm supposed to be at the bar. I was going to hit the bartender on this corner in case Dylan ended up spitting in my drink." He shoved his hands in his pockets. "Want another?"

Sam nodded. She shifted her weight, squeezing between the small space Nico made for her to exit the booth. When she turned to properly look at him, the glow of the orange light in the hallway dangling above them, his expression was more obvious. A little curious. A little wistful that any of this could actually be happening after all of this time.

They would go their separate ways tonight, then head back to the city and live their separate lives. There were two million residents in Manhattan, and eight million people flooding the streets during the working week. The chances of running into him were slim.

So it didn't seem like much of a big deal when she gave him a rueful smile and said "Oh, and Nico?"

His left brow quirked up. "Yeah?"

"Get gin in my martini this time. I hate vodka."

He smiled, leaning against the frame. "Shaken or stirred?"

"Stirred," she replied. "And dirty."

He huffed and hung his head.

She didn't wait to see his expression as she slipped into the crowd and headed back for their group, unable to fix the smile across her red-painted lips.

"You forgot to mention that he's *hot*."

Sam sat across from Yumi on the floor, half-eaten cinnamon raisin bagels in wrappers on the coffee table between them.

She shifted her gaze to Jeff on the other side of the

room, head in Daniel's lap, curled on the couch in the fetal position while he nibbled on a plain bagel like a toddler.

Yumi shoved a *Gobble Up!*–socked toe into Sam's ribcage. "*Carter!*" she pressed.

She frowned, breaking off a piece of her bagel and smearing off the excessive cream cheese the shop in town always added too much of. "Yes, I did," she answered in a tone low enough that Jeff wouldn't hear. "I told you that last night."

"Okay sure, use of the present tense and all that. But you really didn't give me enough details. You're a writer. I'm disappointed."

"I write nutrition articles about vitamin D deficiency and the best probiotics to shrink your gut. Not the fine details of a man's right dimple."

"You *would* know what side his dimple's on."

Sam shook her head, lowering her voice further. "Let's stop before he hears."

"Who, Jeff?" Yumi's face pinched in confusion. "Who cares? He's got a boyfriend now and he's happy, no?"

"Yeah, but last night, Nico and I—"

Yumi's eyes blew wide. "Last *night*? Oh my god, *I knew it.* 'I'm going to the bathroom' my ass."

"I *did* go to the bathroom. He was the one who followed me and pulled me into a dark corner and—"

Yumi fell back on the carpeted floor and squealed.

"What are you two gossiping about over there? I want in," Jeff declared. His face still looked a little green.

Sam tucked her hands inside the sleeves of her cable-knit heather-gray sweater and crossed her arms. "How's the hangover?"

He groaned. "I think this might be the end."

Daniel leaned forward and kissed Jeff's forehead. "I hope not. We've barely gotten started."

Yumi and Sam's *awwwww*s echoed across the house.

Mom popped in from the kitchen, hair in a tight ponytail at the top of her head, rouge flyaways running askew by her ears. "What, what? What did I miss?"

"Just Jeff and Daniel rubbing their cuteness in our very single faces," Yumi replied as she jumped up. Where she got the pep in her step after a night pounding six tequila sodas, Sam had no idea. "I think this calls for mimosas."

Jeff groaned again. "Please, dear god, don't make me drink more. I think I quit for life."

"Oh, be quiet." Yumi glanced at Sam and winked. "Besides, we have a lot to celebrate."

Sam scowled. "*Yu*."

"We do!" Her friend twirled, arms in the air. "We are the witnesses to budding young love!"

Sam knew her well enough to know she wasn't only referring to Daniel and Jeff. If she wanted Yumi to drop something, she had to be very direct about it. Otherwise she would *never* let it go—like the time Yumi bullied her into making a Nubo account, or during the brief period of her life when Sam thought she wanted bangs. Thankfully, Yumi's persistent comments had been welcome. Sam still cringed thinking about it.

But in the case of Nico, she needed Yumi to drop it. She needed Yumi to not mention it at all.

She followed her into the kitchen, grabbing the orange juice as Yumi popped open the bottle of Prosecco. "Nothing happened," she whispered. "We just...talked. He's mending his relationship with Jeff and I'm in a good place with my brother, and it was silently agreed that we don't want to ruin it again."

Yumi let out a *harrumph.* "I think it's crazy that the two of you are letting Jeff have such a huge say in all of this."

"Yu, he used to—"

"I *know.* I know the whole tragic tale. But you're grown-ups now. Do you even know how Jeff would react if you asked him about it?"

Her gut twisted. "I'm not sure if I even want to try."

Yumi's expression flitted into something soft and sad. She shrugged it off and turned back to the mimosas, filling each flute to the brim with sparkling wine. "Well...there's nothing stopping you from being friends."

Before she could respond, Mom barreled into the kitchen and demanded that the two of them start dicing up the celery for the stuffing.

Jeff stood up from the dining room table, declaring the meal was curing his hangover and he needed seconds. Sam half-listened to Yumi's story about the night a subway rat climbed onto her foot as she watched her brother leave the room. When Mom screamed with laughter, Sam chuckled along, then snatched her plate and escaped into the kitchen.

Jeff smiled at Sam's entrance, then picked up the metal tongs and pinched a slice of turkey. "Is it just me, or is this going really well?"

She scooped green bean casserole and dropped it on her plate. "It's going well. They seem to really like him."

"Thank god, because if they didn't, I don't know what I would do."

They prepared their plates in silence, listening to more laughter and Yumi's high-pitched voice that rang through the house.

Sam bit her lip. "Jeff?"

"Hmm?"

"Why didn't you tell me that you were talking to Nico again?"

Jeff frowned. "I didn't think that would be a big deal to you."

Sam put down her plate and placed a hand on her hip. "*Jeff.*"

He huffed. "Okay, *fine.* I didn't say anything because I needed the time to figure out what it was like being friends with Nico *without* having a spectacularly huge, embarrassing crush on him."

Her stomach twisted. "I get that. I do."

Jeff tilted the gravy boat and slathered his plate. "Plus, I figured you..." He trailed off, his cheeks turning pink.

"Figured, what?"

He calmly placed the gravy back down. "I don't know, Sam. I thought maybe you guys were still friends and just like, didn't tell me or something."

"You told me to stay away from him."

"I told you to not *date* him. I didn't say you couldn't be friends."

"Kind of weird to be friends with someone after all of that," she grumbled.

Jeff hung his head, then he put his plate down and squeezed Sam's shoulders. "Look, Sam, I'm sorry. I know I really screwed things up. I invited him last night because I want us to be a family again. I want my best friend back. I want us to spend holidays together and I want him to eventually be in my wedding someday." He exhaled. "Can we have that again? Or is it going to be weird between you guys?"

Her chest ached. "I don't know. But I want that, too. All of it. It's been weird not having him around."

"My thoughts exactly." He gave her shoulders one more squeeze then released her. "They'll actually be here for the holidays this year and I think Mom wants to invite his parents over for our Christmas Eve dinner, just like we used to."

"She should," she replied, the tone of her voice as soft as a whisper.

Jeff bumped her shoulder, careful to not tip over his very full plate. "I'm glad we talked."

Sam remained in the kitchen for a long moment, plate forgotten. Jeff was right—it was good they talked about it. Yet even if he apologized for his behavior all those years ago, why did she feel like there was more that needed to be said?

Chapter 5

Nico sat at his desk in the high rise on 15th Street, ignoring his laptop and watching the bustling Christmas market in Union Square outside his window. The place was swarmed with tourists eating waffles drizzled in chocolate and bags of mini doughnuts, gift givers buying ornaments and handcrafted bowls you couldn't find anywhere else. He grew up going to those markets with his moms and ice skating in Bryant Park with Jeff when he joined their family excursions into the city. He remembered the year Sam was finally deemed old enough to go. They ditched her on the ice and raced to the other end, leaving her to fall on her butt and cry in the middle of the rink. He and Jeff weren't allowed to have hot chocolate after that, the two of them watching with envy while Same sipped on her cup, big droopy tears falling onto the dollops of pillowing whipped cream at the top.

It felt weird being around them last week. He'd known his best friend as a kid, as a teenager, and even in his early adult years. It felt like a strange time warp watching Jeff so domesticated and responsible—besides the Jägerbomb and the excessive drinking that followed. It felt even stranger seeing Sam fully transformed, all soft edges and that prim and proper way about her. He only ever really saw her as the girl with scabby knees and a love for singing *Wicked* songs at the top of her lungs in her room. The girl who'd slept with the stuffed bunny in her bed that she'd won at the ring toss. He wondered if she still slept with it, or if she deemed it unfit for her new adult life.

Nico had never seen Sam and Jeff so comfortable with another. It made him sad that he'd missed their transition into friendship. It made him even more sad when he realized he was the catalyst for all of it.

Maybe Sam was right. Maybe he was the reason she'd never been close with her brother.

A *ping* came from his computer, the screen lighting up from the notification in OmniCorp's company messaging board. It was Jeremy, one of the lead engineers.

JEREMY

Test failed.

Nico groaned, running a hand through his hair. There weren't any signs of him losing his hair—the only thing he knew about his father was a set of numbers from his mothers' sperm donor clinic, and he had no desire to try to track him down—but Nico was convinced this job would be reason enough for it to start falling out. Especially if they couldn't get the new video integration underway.

He rubbed his face, then typed back.

NICO

What happened?

JEREMY

When you hit a video in the test feed, the whole thing breaks. We need to make some major changes to the core of the system to get user engagement working properly.

NICO

What kind of changes? Can we make it happen?

JEREMY

Nico, you know how much it takes to make that kind of change. Attempting to do it by New Year's? We probably won't get much sleep, let alone a holiday.

"Yoo-hoo, got a minute?"

Nico looked up to find Frank in his doorway, iPad in hand, take-out coffee in the other. Frank always wore a suit to work—a drastic contrast from the start-up tech types with their Marvel graphic T-shirts, flannels, and jeans. It wasn't that Nico didn't appreciate good clothes, he did. He figured out long ago that looking the part could also help you *get* the part—which was why he now had an office with a view. But his collared sweaters and navy-blue slacks did set him apart. It moved him from the category of *us* to the category of *them*.

He wasn't sure how he felt about it.

Nico stood and gestured to the seat opposite his desk.

Frank shut the door before taking a seat.

He exhaled quietly as he resumed his place in his ergonomic chair, a "necessity" deemed worthy by office management, along with a pool table and a soft-serve ice cream machine. More of a necessity than another week of paid time off or a proper eight hours of sleep.

Frank placed his tablet on Nico's desk, then leaned back and took a sip of his Americano. His order was clearly stickered on the side of his cup, the same coffee he grabbed every morning before barreling into the office at eleven in the morning with his high demands and little patience. Frank was the vice president of engineering. He was the one who pushed all engineering expectations from the C-suite, making sure deadlines were met no matter the cost. Nico was a director, but he wondered if "enforcer" would have been a more accurate title for the kind of work he did— pushing the lead engineers and their teams to make sure all projects were happening on time, while staying on top of any internal tickets sent from OmniCorp employees if there were any UX problems.

He didn't remember being this busy as an engineer, but at the time, the company was only Nubo. Now it was a multimedia conglomerate with thousands of employees, three different social media platforms, and a CEO with a penchant for buying off any competitors that threatened their top spots in the App Store. OmniCorp recently bought Snipbit, a video sharing social platform famous for their fast-paced, six-second clips. It had over a billion users, but that didn't mean much to CEO Theodore Nelson. Instead of adding it to their portfolio, Theo decided to merge it with Nubo for one massive media-sharing machine.

And he wanted it finished by New Year's Eve.

But this impromptu meeting, by the nature of Frank's ignored iPad and casual lean in Nico's extra chair, didn't seem like a "new demand from Theo" type of conversation.

Nico relaxed his shoulders.

"So." Frank slapped the desk. "The holiday party."

He nodded. The party was next Friday. Originally there were murmurs that the majority of their staff wouldn't be going, simply so they could have a peaceful night off away from the possessive claws of OmniCorp's deadlines. When Theo caught wind of it, he hired Kendrick Lamar to perform a couple of songs. Now everyone was going.

Frank sipped on his coffee. "Are you bringing anyone?"

Nico clasped his hands under the desk and squeezed tight, his knuckles going white. "To the party?"

"Yes. A girlfriend or boyfriend or whatever. I don't judge."

Nico never knew how to respond to comments like these. He knew Frank probably meant well, but why was the clarification needed in the first place? Wasn't the world past that point? Didn't the man remember that Nico grew up with two moms?

He let it roll off his shoulders and moved the conversation forward. "Why the sudden interest?"

Frank shifted in his seat, hesitating to continue. The man never hesitated. He was hiding something. "We are... hearing *rumors* that some employees are unhappy. We want to show them that a work-life balance is possible."

"What kinds of rumors?"

"Oh, you know. Some unnamed wannabe whistle-blowers looking to make their demands public."

"Which are?"

"I don't know who the whistleblowers are."

"No, what are the demands?"

"Oh, well." Frank paused, crossed his legs, then uncrossed them. He leaned forward. "Something about a union."

Nico's muscles tensed. "They want to unionize."

"Only a small group. They're posting demands on Nubo through undetectable accounts."

His use of *undetectable* made Nico pause. It made it sound like the company looked into the situation and weren't able to connect those accounts to the users. That meant they were using the company's data to track down whoever these employees were. It wasn't technically illegal...but it felt *wrong*.

"How do you know it's a small group of them?" he asked.

"There are only three accounts," Frank replied.

"With how many followers?"

"Followers could be anyone, and that doesn't mean company members."

"I'm more concerned with the engagement. How is the public responding?"

Frank remained silent, giving Nico his half-witted smile and bull's-eye stare. He knew that expression. It meant Nico took a step too far.

His boss tapped on Nico's desk. "We need to show these employees that a balance is not only *possible*, but that you can thrive at OmniCorp."

"By bringing a date to the holiday party?"

Frank snapped. "Exactly."

It wasn't even a Band-Aid for the problem. Neither was Kendrick Lamar or the soft-serve ice cream. But Nico knew the problem was too deep to fix in his office during an impromptu meeting on a Tuesday afternoon.

"Find someone on one of those dating apps or hire someone, for all I care," Frank demanded with a flick of his hand. "Just bring a date."

Nico worked his jaw, then nodded.

Frank slapped his chair again. "Good. Thanks for always being a team player. How'd the test go?"

He wasn't ready for full-on engineer recon from Frank yet. Nico needed a few minutes—maybe even a full evening—to think.

"I haven't received the results yet," Nico lied. "I'll let you know when I do."

Frank frowned, but thankfully stood up from the chair. "Then nudge them a little bit. We have less than a month to launch."

Nico didn't share his racing thoughts as he shook Frank's hand and watched him leave the office. Nudging his employees wasn't going to make the tech move faster or solve any of their worries regarding a union. Neither was bringing a date to a holiday party.

Which, evidently, he was now tasked to do.

Nico tapped on his cold glass, Negroni halfway gone, and scrolled the whistleblower accounts. Each square image was black with white text, with thorough demands that, to him, sounded reasonable. Fair wages. Flexible work location policies. Proposals for workplace culture improvements, particularly in terms of OmniCorp's abuse regarding harsh deadlines and working hours. One unnamed employee admitted to sleeping under a desk for a week straight because he didn't have enough hours in the day to get an integration ready before launch—and he hadn't been allowed to work from home.

It made Nico sick to his stomach.

"Sorry we're late."

Corrine plopped down in the seat across from Nico, her

large canvas tote from The Strand slipping off her shoulder and landing with a *thud* to the floor.

"You could kill someone with that thing," Nico joked.

Corinne rolled her eyes. "We're about to announce our top twenty-five books for the year, and I have a million different social posts I need to work on."

"Are you telling me there are twenty-five books in that bag?"

"No, because seven are in mine," Emory interjected. He placed two margaritas on the table, then shrugged off his backpack.

Corrine grabbed the front of Emory's puffer jacket and pulled him on for a loud smack on the lips. "Thanks, babe."

"Gross, keep it to yourselves." Leon took the seat next to Nico, frothy glass of Guinness in hand. He leaned in to see what Nico was looking at. "On Nubo while you're off the clock? Nico, do we need to have another conversation about boundaries?"

He sighed, then handed Leon his phone.

Leon read the screen. His face went serious. "Holy shit."

"Is this about the whistleblowers?" Corinne asked.

"You know about this?" Nico responded.

"Only recently," she replied. "Everyone at the shop was talking about it today."

He wasn't surprised. Corrine was the Strand's social media manager, and she seemed to always know the big drama happening across the island. The employees at the shop were well read. It's like they had a finger on the pulse of all five boroughs. She studied computer science alongside him and Leon at Berkeley, but decided against going into the industry after graduation. The three of them hadn't necessarily been close at the time—their cohort across all four years was made up of fifty students—but they grew closer when Nico reached out with the news that he'd be moving to the city. Along with Emory, Corinne's boyfriend of almost two years, their weekly nights out for beers soon transformed into weekend brunches, strolls through the farmers' market, and late nights at hidden cocktail bars.

"Are OmniCorp employees going to unionize?" Leon asked, sounding astonished.

He took his phone back. "It sounds like it."

"How do you feel about it?"

"I don't know," Nico replied.

"What do you mean you don't know? You're at the senior level, you *should* know."

"I'm a director. My voice barely matters."

"That's bull and you know it."

Nico rubbed his face with both hands, then perched his elbows on the table.

Corinne tilted her head. "Nico, you all right?"

He huffed. "Frank wants us to look like a unified front at the holiday party next week, a beacon of 'work-life balance.' He says I need to bring a date."

"That is multiple levels of fucked up," Corinne spat.

Emory rubbed the spot between her shoulder blades, a sign Nico recognized as his way of calming down his fiery, feminist girlfriend.

Leon tipped back his head and laughed, causing a few curious heads to look in their direction. "You, a date, in less than two weeks? *Impossible.*"

His eyes narrowed. "I could find a date."

"Dude, I never saw you land a date in the four years we spent at Berkeley. And you've been in a city with *prime* pickings for two months now, and still nothing."

"Women aren't cattle, Lee," Corinne deadpanned.

Leon held up his hands in surrender.

Corinne squared her shoulders. "I'll be your date."

Nico quicked a glance at Emory. The man's face pinched, then smoothed out. Even if he was supportive of Corinne and her progressive ways of thinking, he knew that face. The universal sign of *please don't touch what is mine.*

He shook his head. "We're too good of friends. Besides, if I'm going to make it believable, I'll need the person to be comfortable with me...*touching* them, in certain ways."

"And friends can't do that? How in the world are you going to get that comfortable with someone in one week?"

"You make it sound impossible." Nico pointed a thumb at Leon. "This guy can get that comfortable in one night."

Leon shrugged again and leaned back, slinging an arm around the back of Nico's chair in his casual *I know I'm hot shit* kind of way. He smirked, his dark mocha skin glowing underneath the low lights of the bar.

"That's because he has confidence oozing out of his asshole," Corrine quipped, followed by another laugh and an *eww, oozing* from Leon. She pointed to Nico. "You, on the other hand—"

"Do you have any other friends in the city?" Emory interrupted. "People you're as comfortable with?"

Sam.

He would be lying if he said the idea hadn't immediately popped into his head. He knew she lived in the city, in a tiny studio with Yumi on the Upper East Side. He got fragments of information about her life at the bar last week —whatever he'd been able to pick up in casual conversation. It was all he had after a year of emailing his best friend. Jeff hadn't mentioned Sam at all, and when Nico finally worked up the nerve to ask how she was after six months of correspondence, he'd ignored the question. He did his best to tamper down his anger from Jeff's lack of response.

He thought Sam's body language in the phone booth that night sent a clear message. But then she told him she likes her martinis *dirty*, and he wasn't proud of how long his eyes lingered on her as she walked away.

"I-I do," he admitted. "One."

"Would they go with you?"

The three of them stared at him, expectant. He'd never told them about Sam—or *anyone* for that matter. When people asked about his exes, he mentioned Hilary or Caroline or any other short-term relationship that didn't really mean anything to him. Yet somehow, even though things never developed between the two of them, those moments with Sam meant *everything*.

But what could he really share? That he kissed his best friend's sister and it ruined his desire to be with anyone else?

"I don't know," he answered honestly. "We lost touch until just recently, when I was home."

Emory shrugged. "Sounds like you don't have much to lose then."

Not much to lose.

The phrase felt so comical to Nico. If it weren't for Jeff and the way he'd reacted that night, things could have looked so much different. He'd missed his best friend after those years not talking, but deep down, he couldn't ignore the simmering anger beneath. How could Jeff have made such a fuss? Was he really so disgusted by the idea of his best friend and his sister getting together? Wouldn't he have wanted Sam to be with someone he fully trusted? Did Jeff not *trust* him?

He took a deep breath. It didn't matter now. Jeff was

with Daniel and clearly happy, and it seemed he and Sam were doing really well.

Would it really be so bad? Nico drummed his fingers on the table. Jeff was miles away and she was only eight subway stops, and it was one night, in the grand scheme of things.

He picked up his phone and opened his texts.

Chapter 6

Sam sat up on the couch, back straight, eyes wide, phone in hand.

"I know we're trying to taste test all the salad kits at Trader Joe's, but I have to admit"—Yumi pierced a forkful of salad in her bowl—"adding chicken nuggets makes all salads infinitely better. I don't think there's a fair assessment."

"He texted me."

Yumi's brows pinched as she chewed then swallowed. "Who?"

Sam looked down at the text on her screen—fresh on a completely blank slate of a text conversation—then blinked back up at Yumi.

Her mouth fell open. "Oh...my *god*."

"Yu—"

"*Ahhh!*" Yumi plopped the bowl down on the coffee table, then reached for Sam's phone with grabby hands.

Sam dutifully obliged, giving her friend enough time to evaluate the six words in silence.

Yumi covered her mouth, then placed it on her cheek. "Do you think his proposition is '*hey, let's bang and never tell anyone*'?"

Sam pulled her hair over her shoulder and began braiding it. Truthfully, she wasn't sure if the answer to that question would be a no. She had absolutely no idea what Nico was thinking. Her mind flashed to the way his body curled toward hers in the phone booth at the bar last week. She would be kidding herself if she said there wasn't any kind of heat there. Especially after the foolish way she told him she liked her martinis dirty and watched his brain short-circuit in real time.

"*Let's do it once, Sam. To get it out of our systems,*" Yumi added in a husky voice, attempting to mimic Nico's deep, steady drawl.

Sam shook her head. "If we couldn't get it out of our systems that night, I honestly don't think we'll be able to."

"That's *so* hot."

She took her phone back. "What do I say?"

"Something sexy and scandalous, obviously." Yumi smirked. "Or you could skip to the good stuff and send him a nude."

She rolled her eyes. "The fact that you even *think* I have a nude on here is a clear sign you don't know me."

Yumi giggled. "A girl can dream. You know I do it to rile you up."

Sam tapped her plastic phone case with the tips of her red nails, freshly manicured by herself because she didn't have the kind of budget to go to the salon. She'd gotten good at a lot of things in an effort to save money. Painting her nails and cheap Trader Joe's dinners and finding the best dollar books in the carts outside of the Strand. Apparently texting men was not a skill she'd acquired.

"You're a writer, Sam. Send what's at the top of your mind. It's probably your best idea."

She took a deep breath, then typed.

SAM

Sounds dangerous.

The *swoosh* sound followed after she sent it, then the two of them waited in silence, eyes on the screen, half-eaten salad bowls untouched on the coffee table.

A small bubble popped up, three dots dancing as he typed back.

"I am *so* enraptured," Yumi said.

"Is that the proper use of that word?"

"Don't ruin my fun."

Her phone dinged.

NICO

All body parts will stay intact, I promise.

Yumi sighed. "Darn. I was hoping he'd break your back."

Sam shook her head.

SAM

Hmmm. I believe I've heard this before.
Remember climbing up the backyard tree?

NICO

Hey now. That was not my fault. You fell
and sprained your ankle all on your own.

SAM

But it WAS your fault for pressuring me to
do it.

NICO

I promise, no ankles will be sprained. And I
will not pressure you to do anything.

She huffed. Yumi sat right beside her, salad bowl back
in hand, eyes glued on Sam's phone. She seemed far more
entertained by their conversation than the reality television
show she'd insisted they watch.

SAM

We'll see about that. What's the
proposition?

He typed, then stopped, then typed again. Then
stopped.

"He's fumbling, how cute," Yumi said.

"Why does this feel like a bad idea?"

"It probably is. Who cares." Yumi patted Sam's knee. "I
mean Jeff *did* say he wanted you guys to be friends again."

A text finally came through.

NICO

Could we meet for coffee tomorrow? It
would be easier to explain in person.

Sam held up a finger to silence Yumi. "Before you say it,
no. I will not be hooking up with him in a public bathroom."

"You know me so well," Yumi cooed.

SAM

I have to work tomorrow.

NICO

I'll meet you near your office, wherever's
convenient. You pick the spot. Thirty
minutes.

Please, Sam.

Her face grew warm. She pressed a palm into her cheek to try cooling herself down.

"Wow," Yumi breathed.

Sam turned to her friend, realizing Yumi was looking at her and not her phone. "What?"

"You *really* like him, don't you?"

She felt the heat shift underneath her palm. She was full-on blushing, and she couldn't control it.

"He's fumbling again," Yumi pointed out.

Sam watched the dancing dots that kept appearing and disappearing as he attempted to say something else.

She saved him from his misery and sent him an address.

She cozied up in the back of Ground Central coffee shop, next to the tall bookcases. She'd arrived fifteen minutes early, ordered a black coffee, then sat down and contemplated for the umpteenth time in the last twelve hours whether she was making a mistake.

It's too late now. I'm already here.

She scanned the spines of the books as footsteps approached, the floorboards creaking underneath.

"You already bought a coffee?"

Sam swiveled around to find Nico standing above her with a deep frown. He wore slim black slacks, a button-down, fitted perfectly to the toned muscles she couldn't ignore, with a long navy-blue wool coat. His hair was tousled from the early December wind, and he had a leather briefcase in hand. She caught whiffs of fresh air and lemon verbena soap and something spicy and woodsy from his cologne. He looked and smelled *good*, and it kicked her nervous energy to a whole new level.

"Yes, I got here kind of early," she replied, keeping her voice as calm as possible.

His brows pinched. "Sam, hot tip. When someone asks you to coffee, you let them buy you a coffee."

"It's fine, really—"

"Did you eat?"

"Um, no—"

"I'll get you something." He dropped his briefcase to the floor, then shrugged off his coat and folded it over the chair opposite hers before escaping to the counter at the front.

Her phone buzzed on the table.

YUMI

How's it going??

She scanned the space around her to make sure he hadn't returned before snatching it up and responding.

SAM

He carries a briefcase.

YUMI

Why does that make him even MORE hot?

A paper bag with a greasy bottom was placed in front of her, along with a black plastic gift card.

She flipped the card between her fingers. "What's this for?"

"For your next coffee order," he replied as he settled in his chair. He popped open the plastic lid, a couple strands of hair at his forehead curling up from the steam rolling off the top. She hated herself for noticing that very miniscule detail, and for noticing how much his body took up space in the chair. His long legs were bent, leather loafers planted on the ground, while the tips of her heels barely touched the wood.

"How much is on this card?" she asked.

"Fifty."

"*Nico.* I can't take this."

"Eat your breakfast, Sam."

She huffed, then peeled open the bag and pulled out the warm pumpkin spice muffin. She flattened the paper and placed it on top, then broke off a piece of the sugary top. "Please have some."

He smirked, fingers wrapping around his cup, his hand taking up the entire surface area.

"Eat your breakfast, Nicolas," Sam teased.

He chuckled, lips curving into a smile, straight white teeth gleaming in the low light of the back room—a stark contrast to his olive skin. Nico had a tanned complexion all year round. It used to drive her mad when she was a teen, watching her tan lines fade as the temperature dropped, when his didn't. She wondered if it drove her mad now...for a different reason.

He ripped off a chunk of the muffin top and popped it in his mouth. "How are you?"

"Is that why you summoned me?"

"No. But I would like to know how you're doing."

She shifted in her seat. "You know how I'm doing. I graduated college. I live in a studio apartment. I work at a magazine."

"Okay, *sassy.* Anything else going on?

"What do you want, Nico?"

He leaned back and held up his hands. "Forgive me. I figured it was polite to ask how you were before asking for a massive favor."

"How massive?"

"Massive enough to warrant some kind of pleasant conversation beforehand."

She sucked in a breath.

"Eat your breakfast," he repeated.

She glared, but followed his instruction, breaking off another bite. He smirked, breaking off an even larger chunk and shoving it in his mouth.

She kicked him underneath the table. "Hog."

His eyes widened, his expression lightening up in the playful way she'd always known. *Some things never change.*

Sam tapped the point of her heel at his calf. "What do you need?"

He chewed, wiped his hands, then propped his elbows on the table. "What are you doing next Friday?"

"Probably eating a Trader Joe's salad on my couch."

"Would you like to go to a party instead?"

She leaned back and crossed her arms. "Your big favor is a party?"

"The OmniCorp holiday party."

She tilted her head. "Why in the world would you want me to go to that?"

Nico heaved a deep sigh, a soft rumble escaping his chest as he rubbed his face then ran a hand through his hair. It seemed like a practiced motion. "Don't kill me, okay?"

Her chest ached, watching him like this. She nudged her toe into his leg again. Slower this time, like *I'm not going to kill you if you don't spit it out.*

He gave her a shy smile. "There are some internal struggles happening at the company. People are unhappy, and they're voicing their demands online. Work-life balance in tech has always been terrible, but at OmniCorp it's nonexistent."

Sam reached for her cup. "Okay..."

He leaned over and flicked her wrist. "My boss thinks bringing dates to the holiday party will be the solution."

She covered her mouth.

"Don't laugh."

"He can't be *that* stupid."

"He can, in fact."

"So he told you to bring a date."

"Exactly."

"And you texted me."

He waited a beat, eyes on hers. "Yes."

Her brows raised. "You seriously don't have anyone else?"

"I only just moved here, Sam."

"Two months is long enough to go on a couple of dates."

"I haven't been on any dates."

"Why do I not believe that?"

"Well, it's the truth."

"*Awe*, poor Nico." She leaned in, threading her fingers together. "Has it been hard for you?"

"Never." He leaned in as well, like it was a challenge. "I just haven't had the desire to. Or the time, for the matter."

"Then make the time. The party is in, what, ten days? You can find someone by then."

"I don't want to make the time."

"I also think you don't want to go with me."

"Yes, I think I really do."

He was close. *Too* close. She pulled back and placed her hands on the table.

"Please," he begged. "I could use a friend."

She didn't respond. After a few uncomfortable beats, he nudged her foot this time. He cocked a brow. *Still friends?*

She exhaled, then nodded. *Still friends.*

"If I go to this thing with you, I'm guessing it wouldn't be as friends though." She tapped her fingers. "I'm assuming you'll want me to pretend to be your girlfriend."

He nodded. "Does that freak you out?"

Nico touching her? Guiding her through a crowd with his hand at the small of her back? Kissing her temple? Gripping her waist during a dance?

"A little," she admitted. "Doesn't it freak *you* out?"

"All of this freaks me out."

She went to remove her hands from the table. He caught one of them, then squeezed. "Let me be clear. I'm freaked out about what's going on at work. I would never freak out about being around you."

She stared at their joined hands, thinking it through.

"At the end of the night, we can go back to what it was," he continued. "You living on the Upper East Side and me down in the Financial District, and we'll never talk unless Jeff forces us to during the holidays."

She pursed her lips. "You live in *FiDi?*"

He chuckled, a thumb sweeping over her knuckles. "Please, Sammy girl."

It's a bad idea. She could feel it, knew it as soon as he texted her last night. Even Yumi had thought so.

Still, it didn't stop her from pulling her hand away and squaring her shoulders as an even more terrible idea formed in her head. "I'll make you a deal."

He grinned. "Hit me."

She moved her hands to her lap, keeping this as professional as possible. "The *Nourished* holiday party is on Friday."

"*This* Friday?"

She nodded.

Nico's eyes narrowed, and she watched his expression shift as realization crossed his face.

"A party for a party," she continued. "A date for a date."

He swallowed. "Are we acting as friends at your party?"

She shook her head.

He let out a shaky breath. "Why? What do you need it for?"

"Do we have a deal or not?"

He bit the inside of his cheek, then held out a hand.

"We'll have to set some ground rules," she added.

"Of course."

"And after your party, we never speak of this again."

He wiggled his fingers, beckoning for her to take his hand.

She wet her bottom lip, then placed her palm in his.

Chapter 7

"Explain this to me again. Like I'm five."

Sam took a sip of her coffee—her second one of the morning, after Nico insisted he buy her *another* one before she went across the street and up to the forty-fourth floor. "He needs a date for his company holiday party. He asked me to go, so I'm going."

"Okay, but we're missing a key fact here." Yumi hopped up on Sam's desk and took a seat, crossing her legs. She was wearing Sam's long-sleeve knit black sweater dress that she'd conveniently forgotten to ask to borrow. "It's not just *going to a party*. He wants you to act like his fake girlfriend. *And—*" She held up a finger to emphasize her point. "You thought it would be a good idea to make him do the same in return."

Sam slunk into her desk chair.

"Honestly, babe. I've never been more proud."

"I don't know what came over me," Sam admitted. "It was like some kind of feral animal crawled out of my chest and was like, 'Hey, crazy idea. Why don't I make this impossibly dumb situation even dumber?'"

"*Feral.* Great word. I bet he is feral in—"

"Stop it," she grumbled.

Yumi smiled, the winged tips of her black eyeliner hiding between the creases of her eyes. "Why are you so upset about this?"

Sam sighed. "I'm not upset. I'm...nervous. All of it seems like a bad idea."

"You keep saying that, and yet, you keep going through with it." Yumi leaned in. "May I remind you that you technically don't need a date for our holiday party?"

"*I know.*"

"Then why did you invite him?"

"Samantha. Yumi."

Sam swiveled around to find Barbara in her cubicle. It was rare for the editor-in-chief of *Nourished* to make an appearance in her cramped work space. It was even more rare that she was doing so before ten in the morning.

Yumi scrambled off the desk and clasped her hands in front of her. "Barbara, good morning. How are—"

Barbara turned to Sam, ignoring Yumi. "Those SEO reports, did you finish them?"

Yumi pressed her lips together.

Sam pulled freshly printed paper from a pink file folder on her desk, then handed them to her. "It's still a little too early to tell for some of these, but we are seeing growth on some of our top keywords."

Barbara slid the glasses on her head to the bridge of her nose. "Which are?"

"*Detox juice cleanse* and *avoid holiday weight gain,* which are keywords that spike this time of here. We also noticed that *chia seed water* was taking off because of a social media trend, so Yumi interviewed a nutritionist and published an expert take on it."

Yumi twisted her head at Sam and mouthed a *thank-you* as Barbara scanned the sheet, not bothering to look at either of their faces.

"And the total numbers?" Barbara asked. "Are these moving the marker at all?"

"We added the totals at the bottom of the sheet," Sam said.

"But are these moving the marker? What's the comparison to last year's numbers? Were we pulling the same page reads this time of year, or are we seeing any kind of increase?"

Sam opened her mouth, then shut it.

Barbara pushed her glasses back to the top of her head. "This report is half baked. I need real numbers. I'll talk to Garrison about properly training you on how to do this."

Sam took the papers from her. "O-okay. Thank you."

Barbara walked away from them, the click of her Louboutins reverberating across the silent, empty cubicles. They were always the first ones to arrive, and the last to leave.

Yumi whipped her head in Sam's direction, eyes hardening. "You said *thank you*?!"

"What else was I supposed to say?"

"How about 'our editor is a sack of shit who pawns off all his work to us and doesn't teach us how to do any of it'?"

Sam slid the papers back in her folder, then tapped her computer mouse, waking up her screen. "This is how we learn. We mess up, we get corrected, we fix it, we improve."

"Maybe that's how *you* learn. I, on the other hand, would rather not be treated like garbage."

Sam shook her head. "She's not treating us like garbage. She's doing her job."

Yumi was silent for a moment, then she leaned against

Sam's desk. "That's why you invited Nico to the party, isn't it?"

She felt her heart skip as she turned to face her friend. "What are you talking about?"

"You want to impress them," Yumi continued. "You want them to think you have everything together instead of looking like a single twenty-something at the bottom of the totem pole."

Sam turned back to her screen and clicked open the report spreadsheet. "Is that such a bad thing?"

"Pretending to be something you're not? At a job that we both hate? Yeah, I think so."

"Maybe I don't like how it feels to be young and poor and naive," Sam admitted. The words rushed out of her mouth before she could stop them. She clamped her lips together and forced away the stinging sensation in her eyes.

Yumi hesitated, then wrapped her arms around Sam's shoulders. "We'll unpack that later over salad, yeah?"

Sam nodded, thankful her friend knew her limits and when to give her space.

Yumi kissed her forehead, then walked down the row of cubicles to her own desk.

Her phone vibrated on her desk.

NICO

So, what do I wear to this thing?

She rubbed her neck, embarrassed by the way her stomach dipped when she saw his name on the screen.

SAM

A Santa suit.

Oooh, do you still have that dog costume you wore when you and Jeff decided to be puppies for Halloween? Wear that.

NICO

Samantha.

SAM

Kidding. Wear something nice. Whatever you'd like.

NICO

If you're not going to give me any instruction, then at least give me a color scheme.

She bit her lip, then typed back.

SAM

You look good in blue.

Sam held her breath as he typed, then exhaled slowly at the response.

NICO

Blue it is.

She set her phone screen-down and focused on work. *No more of that.*

The apartment was unbearably hot when Nico got home from the gym. He dropped his duffel and hung his coat, then peeled off his dry-fit shirt as he made his way to the thermostat. He'd set it to seventy-two before leaving to meet Sam that morning, the apartment frigid thanks to the floor-to-ceiling windows that brought in a slight draft. But now he was boiling after an hour of lifting weights and doing every-thing he could to *not* think of Sam's black high heel digging into his calf—a thought that replayed over and over as he sat at his desk all day.

He turned the temperature back down, then opened the fridge, hoping dinner might magically appear. The only two things in there were a jar of mustard and a half gallon of two percent. He sighed, closed the fridge, and pulled up Seam-less on his phone.

After ordering a chicken shawarma plate from the shop around the corner, his phone rang.

It was Jeff.

He stared at the name on the screen, shocked that Jeff would actually be *calling* him. When he'd first reached out to Nico, it made sense that the beginning of their correspon-dence started through email. But as the year progressed, Jeff didn't seem to have a desire to move the conversation to the phone or even text, so Nico continued to play along.

But now Jeff was calling him, and Nico could think of only one reason as to why. *Sam.* Did she tell her brother about their agreement? Hadn't she been the one to insist on keeping their swapped dates discreet? Nico played through their conversation in his head, realizing that she didn't *explicitly* say to not talk to anyone about it. She simply said to not talk about it after.

The phone rang a fourth time. He swiped the screen to answer the call. "Hello?"

"Nico!"

"H-hey man, what's up?"

"Got a minute to chat?"

Oh god. "Of course."

"Won't be long, I promise." He heard shuffling, then the

closing of a door. "Are you planning on coming to our Christmas Eve dinner? Your Mama said something to my mom about you *not being there?*!"

Nico hesitated. He'd met with the lead engineers that afternoon to discuss testing the new change to the integration, and they weren't kidding—it was going to take a lot of work to make it happen before the new year. The thought of leaving his team and taking time *off* seemed selfish and unrealistic.

"Dude I...I don't know. There's this big project at work and I think—"

Jeff made a snoring sound. "*Boring.* Screw the project."

Nico sunk down on his couch. "I can't. OmniCorp wants this big integration launched by New Year's Eve and it's an all-hands situation. I'll likely have to pull some late nights."

"Aren't you past the point of late nights though? I thought getting promoted means you get to hand off the late nights coding in front of a blue screen to your little minions."

He sighed. "Generally, yes. But it wouldn't feel right dumping such a huge project on them during the holidays, especially when things are really weird right now at the company and I sort of feel like I'm failing them."

Jeff was quiet for a moment. "You doing all right?"

Nico felt the wind knock right out of him. After years of spending every waking minute together, long summer days outside and shared family holidays in the winter, hours suffering through homework after school and their stupid fights about games or sports or girls...The two of them knew each other *too* well. They'd experienced almost every phase of life together—from stealing each other's trucks in the preschool sandbox to awkward middle school dances with mouths full of braces. Jeff Carter had seen it all. They'd fought like an old married couple and there'd been plenty of times Jeff's inherent stubbornness had made Nico want to scream.

But, *this*. The moment when Jeff softened and cared for Nico in a way that he'd never experienced in the same way with another man. He loved both of his moms, but it wasn't like he had a male in his life to look up to. Any he came across were all hard edges, radiating masculine energy. Even in the tech world, and *especially* in the Omni-Corp board rooms. Yet Jeff was different. He'd held Nico's intimate thoughts and emotions and never made fun of them.

He missed those moments the most in the last four years of not having his best friend in his life, and it left him feeling disappointed and deeply sad.

Yet he wondered if he deserved the punishment. He hadn't been thinking about how Jeff would feel when he kissed Sam. He'd only thought about himself, and how much he'd wanted to taste her.

He let out a long exhale. "No," he admitted honestly. "I know a lot of the engineering team is unhappy with the workload and I feel stuck in the middle. Theo is insistent on this integration launching by New Year's and Frank follows him around like a dog and I—" He cleared his throat. "Well, I guess I kind of do the same thing."

"I doubt that. You make a terrible dog, remember?"

Nico chuckled, leaning his head back on the couch. Funny how both Carter siblings brought up the same memory on the same day.

"Nico, you're clearly different. Your boss sure as hell doesn't care about his employees around the holidays, but you do. That's what makes you a good leader."

"I can't help but think I'm failing though. If I feel this way, if I don't pressure them, then the work won't get done."

"But if you *do* pressure them, will the work be any good?"

He blew out a breath, his lips rumbling.

"Listen, I get it," Jeff continued. "You always want to do the right thing. It's one of the reasons I keep you around."

"*One* of the reasons? You sure it's not solely because you have a two hundred and thirty-seven *Smash Brothers* winning streak against me?"

"That, mostly. But also this."

His phone beeped. Nico glanced at the screen.

Sam. She was calling him.

His stomach dipped as he pressed the screen back to his ear. He wanted to answer—probably *needed* to answer so he could get more details about her company's holiday party this week. But Jeff was still rattling on about how Nico should also stick up for himself and his time around the holidays, and something about leading by example.

His phone beeped a second time. Then a third.

"Babe, I smell burning," Daniel called out from the distance on the other line.

"Shit, sorry, man. Gotta go. I forgot to flip the chicken thighs."

A fourth beep.

"All good," he replied in a rush. "We'll talk—"

"Yep, bye!"

Nico felt a rush of adrenaline as he tapped to answer the call. "Hello?"

"Oh!" Sam breathed. "Hello?"

He grinned. "You sound surprised, even though you were the one calling me."

"Yes, well, you weren't answering and I thought—"

"That I was ignoring you?"

She exhaled with a soft sigh. "Yeah. Something like that."

"Well, I wasn't." His doorbell rang. He hopped up from the couch, pulling his wallet from the pocket of his athletic shorts. "I was just on the phone with someone."

He swung open the door, then took the plastic bag with his dinner from the delivery guy.

"Sorry," Sam added. "I interrupted your call and it sounds like you have company now."

Nico handed the man a twenty.

The delivery guy's brows shot up. "Seriously?"

He reached for the doorknob. "Happy holidays." Then he closed the door and placed the bag on the empty counter. "Delivery guy, Sam."

She exhaled again. "Oh. Right."

He grinned as he propped the phone on his shoulder, then popped open the Styrofoam container. "Is someone jealous?"

"*No*," she replied in an annoyed huff. "You can talk to or invite over anyone you want."

He transferred the rice and chicken to a plate, licking the white sauce off his thumb. "I think it's time to set our first ground rule."

"Which is?"

He grabbed a clean fork. "If we are to make this believable, then we commit fully."

"Okay..."

"Which means we don't see anyone else until our deal is done."

She hesitated. He waited patiently for her reply, mixing his chicken and rice and sauce on his plate, contemplating if he should take it back—or continue to be this incredibly stupid.

"Why would that matter?" Sam's voice dropped low, almost to a whisper.

"Because if we want to make this believable, we should commit to it fully," he repeated.

"You mean at the parties?"

He placed a hand on the cool marble. "I mean the whole time. We don't want someone we know seeing us with someone else. New York is big, but...you never know."

He was ready for Sam to tell him how ridiculous that sounded, but was pleasantly surprised when she said "All right, that makes sense."

He was glad to have a place all to himself, so no roommate could see the embarrassing grin that he couldn't control on his face. He shoved food in his mouth, then carried his dinner to the couch. "Your turn. Make a rule."

He listened to rustling on the other line, like a chip bag being opened. "A rule," she repeated.

"You asked for ground rules, remember?"

"I did." Another pause. "You're not allowed to kiss me on the lips."

He held his fork up mid-bite. "Kissing is actually on the table?"

"You said make it believable, right?"

He put his fork down and cleared his throat. "Right. I did say that."

"Good."

He flexed and unflexed his thighs, loosening the tension that'd quickly built up in his muscles—and groin. "Where can I kiss you then?"

"*Hmm.*" He listened to the crinkling of a bag again. "I guess if there's skin exposed, then it's fair game."

He blew out a breath. "G-good. Sounds good."

More crinkling.

"Let me guess. Doritos Cool Ranch?"

She let out a soft laugh. "A pathetic excuse for dinner."

He sat up. "You're eating *chips* for dinner?"

"Y-yeah." Her voice dropped another octave, like she was trying to hide it. "We paid rent yesterday and I don't get paid until Friday—"

"What is your address?"

"Why, are you going to magically show up in that flashy Bronco of yours and share your dinner?"

"*No.*" His chest burned as he put her on speakerphone, then opened up Seamless for the second time that night. "I'm going to order you dinner."

"*Nico.* No. We're fine."

"Pizza, tacos, dumplings?"

"Nothing."

"Pizza it is. You still like sausage deluxe, right?"

"New rule." She huffed. "You can't keep paying for me."

"Request denied," he said. "Plus, it's not your turn."

"Okay, well, when it *is* my turn—"

"Good thing it's my turn, because I'm going to make a rule. We each get to deny one rule request."

She growled. It sounded like a baby tiger cub, so very unthreatening. *Cute.*

"Then fine. I request you don't ever pay for me," she said.

"Request denied. What's the address?"

She growled again. He bit his fist.

She rattled off the address details, then listened to Yumi cheer "*Our hero!!*" at an ungodly high decibel as he placed the order.

"You know, you could have said something else as a rule. You knew I would deny it," Nico said, feeling smug.

"That's why I did it. You've used up your one chance."

He rolled his eyes. "Well played."

She hummed. "Your turn, I think."

He returned to his dinner, now slightly cold, but he didn't care. "I think we should arrive together and leave together. No meeting at the party." He tapped his fork to his place. "I'll pick you up."

"I am *so* out of your way. That would be excessive. We could meet a couple blocks from the party or something."

"Samantha, would you really not expect your boyfriend to pick you up for a date?" He paused. "For the love of god, do not answer that with a *yes*."

"Yeah, but you're not my boyfriend—"

"I think we already agreed that I technically am for the next"—he craned his neck and peered at the calendar hanging on his fridge—"ten days."

There was a muffled *harrumph* on the other line. He grinned again and took a big bite of his food. This was going *much* better than he thought. "Anything else, dear?"

"Yes." A pause. "We probably need a time to properly terminate this contract."

"Seems fair."

"Midnight, after your party."

"Wow, we're not partying all night?"

She huffed again. "How am I supposed to know how late this thing goes?"

"But what if Kendrick doesn't show up until after midnight?"

"Kendrick...like, *Lamar*? He'll be there?"

"Mmhmm."

He heard an ear-shattering *"ARE YOU KIDDING ME?!?"* from Yumi and chuckled.

"I don't really listen to his music," Sam said, which Yumi quickly interrupted with *"Nico, screw Sam! Take me!"*

He laughed to himself. "Anything else, Sammy girl?"

Nico could easily imagine her expression: eyes narrowed, nose scrunched, cheeks pinched. Her usual look of disdain when she was annoyed at him. He used to love annoying her simply so he could see it. He wondered if maybe his intention hadn't always been to rattle Jeff's little sister, but something deeper he couldn't put a name to yet. A feeling he wasn't sure he could be able to control now.

Ten days. He had the liberty to be Sam's boyfriend for just under two weeks. It may be the only time he would ever get to be like this with her.

"No," she breathed. "I think we're good for now."

Yes, we are, he thought.

He was going to make these ten days count.

Chapter 8

He was going overboard. And there was nothing Sam could do to stop him.

She sat at her desk the following morning, reviewing last year's SEO data and providing year-to-year and month-to-month comparisons in her report, when a bouquet of red roses showed up at her desk.

The girls around her let out a chorus of *awww*s as Sam's face flushed. "From who?" she asked the receptionist who carried them from the front desk.

She handed Sam a white envelope with a golden flower emblem pressed into the center. "This came with it."

Sam flipped it open.

Just because. - N

Sam covered her lips, knowing her cheeks were blazing.

"Oh my god, Sam." Tally, the magazine's social media editor whom she shared a cubicle with, rolled up right next to her and examined the bouquet. "Who are they from?"

"My f—" She pressed her lips together, correcting herself. "My boyfriend."

"Wait, you're seeing someone?!" She placed her hands on her hips. "And you didn't tell me?"

"They're *very* secretive about it," Yumi butted in, slinking into their cubicle with a smirk. "He's always doing annoyingly cute shit like this. He ordered us pizza last night when he heard we were too broke after paying rent. You should have seen her on the phone with him. She looked like the human equivalent of a sunbeam."

Sam glared at Yumi as more coos circulated around her, followed by a few *I want that*s and *when will it be my turn*s as her coworkers crowded around to see the flowers.

"What are you doing?" she whisper-screamed to Yumi.

Yumi lifted her hands in defense. "Only speaking the truth, babe."

"Are you bringing him tomorrow, Sam?"

She folded up the note. "Yes. He's coming."

"Who's coming?"

Their group jumped at the sudden appearance of Barbara.

Yumi gestured toward the flowers. "Sam's boyfriend. He sent her these."

Barbara leaned in, looking at the gold detail on the card. "Flowers from Fleurs. Good man." She stood up straight, facing Sam. "He's coming to the party, you said?"

Sam nodded, tongue-tied.

"Good. I look forward to meeting him."

The girls watched Barbara walk back to her office, mouths agape.

"Damn, Sam. She's *never* nice to me," Tally said.

Yumi eyed Sam, then winked.

Minutes later, when she finally had her section of the

cubicle to herself again, she pulled up the texts on her phone.

SAM

Flowers, Nico? Really?

NICO

Anything for you, baby girl. ;)

SAM

Doesn't that seem excessive?

NICO

Never. I'm an excessive kind of guy.

...any comments in the office?

SAM

My editor-in-chief says she's looking forward to meeting you.

NICO

Excellent.

SAM

And I'm pretty sure the social media editor will want to date you after your display of...excessiveness.

NICO

Too bad I'm already taken.

She blinked and bit her lip, watching as he typed.

NICO

I'll pick you up at six. Your apartment?

SAM

No, the office. And you don't have to come so early. The party starts at eight.

NICO

New rule.

SAM

...fine.

NICO

I pick you up two hours before the date.

SAM

TWO HOURS?

NICO

Do you deny my rule?

SAM

You suck.

NICO

See you at six.

SAM

What are we going to do? The party is literally two blocks from the office.

NICO

You'll see.

She closed her eyes and pressed a finger to her temple. This is why Nico and Jeff always got along. The two were a powerhouse, using their collective stubborn energy to get their way. It used to annoy her to no end. *Nico and Jeff want to go ice skating. Nico and Jeff want to go swimming. Or play pirates. Or eat burgers for dinner.*

Yet, in this particular instance...she wasn't bothered by his stubbornness in the slightest.

Sam stood by the elevator banks outside the *Nourished* offices, listening to the soft crooning of Bing Crosby's "White Christmas." She looked down at her phone again, just to make sure.

NICO

I'm here.

She was about to go on a date with Nico. Sure, they were calling these evenings fake dates; a mutual agreement between *friends* to help one another navigate sticky corporate politics, or whatever excuse Nico originally came to her with. If that really were the case, then why did she have pesky butterflies in her stomach? Why did she go to the bathroom three times in the past hour to make sure her black leather skirt and charcoal sweater still looked okay, or check if her red lipstick needed touching up? Why, if it was all meant to be fake, did it feel kind of real?

The elevator swung open, and her stomach dipped from the anticipation of it all. She fidgeted with her black tote bag as she stepped in and pressed the button for the lobby.

A perfectly French-manicured hand stopped the elevator from closing. Barbara stepped in, blocking the door. "Samantha. I took a quick look at your updated report."

She stood up taller. "Yes? Anything else missing?"

Barbara shook her head. "Only wanted to say good work, and thank you for taking the time to redo it."

"It was a team effort," Sam quickly defended. "And Garrison—"

Barbara shot Sam a *Do not lie to me* look. "I know who's doing the work and who isn't."

Sam tightened her grip on the handle of her tote. Clearly Barbara wasn't blind to the nutrition editor's lack of...motivation. Specifically, his inability to answer emails or Slack messages in a timely manner, and his penchant for showing up late to editorial meetings. Any time Sam handed him a piece to edit, it came back to her days later with barely any corrections or notes on how she could improve her work. It infuriated her.

Barbara tapped her nails against the metal, still holding the door open. "Keep this up, and maybe we'll find ourselves doing some internal reorganizing next year." *Tap, tap, tap.* "Is your significant other still coming tonight?"

She swallowed. "Y-yes. He's downstairs waiting for me."

"Ah." Barbara's lips smoothed into a smile. "Off to do something fun before the party? Where are you going?"

"I'm not sure. He wanted to keep it a surprise."

"A romantic. Good." She released her hold on the door. "See you in a couple hours."

Sam nodded as the door closed. Her stomach dropped, but she knew it wasn't the fast-dipping motion of the elevator as it sped down to the lobby.

Yumi. Sam wasn't the only one who worked on the report. They'd pulled late nights this week trying to learn *how* to make the kind of report Barbara wanted despite the lack of guidance from Garrison. They collated the numbers and formed a concrete plan for tackling their new set of SEO terms for the new year, which was always the busiest time for *Nourished,* what with New Year's resolutions and claims for a "new year, new me." The two of them never did find the time to sit down to unpack Sam's confession. She felt embarrassed by it, about how much she wanted to seem put-together, and was secretly thankful that it hadn't come up with her friend again.

Yet now, with Barbara paying her more attention, she wondered whether this was the kind of attention she wanted at all. Especially if it meant using her best friend to achieve it.

The doors swung open. Sam's heels clicked on the tile as she tapped her badge and exited into the main lobby.

Nico stood by the twenty-foot Christmas tree decked out with purple and orange baubles to match the colors of Sigmond Media, their parent company. The colors seemed odd to have on a tree. Sam originally thought it would look silly to anyone who walked by the building, until she realized that almost every corporation down the street did the same thing. They decorated their lobbies with trees in company-appropriate colors, each one standing taller than the next, like every business was trying to compete for the title of Most Festive Company of Manhattan. It seemed a little overboard, but it certainly added to the city's charm this time of year.

She examined Nico as he stared up at the tree, unaware that she was approaching him. He'd followed her request, wearing navy-blue slacks and a matching collared sweater. His caramel-colored wool coat layered overtop sharpened the whole look and brought out the reddish brown tones in his hair. Even his *shoes* looked good, leather Oxfords that likely cost the same as Sam's monthly rent.

She stopped six feet from him and crossed her arms. "You clean up good, Giuliano."

He turned to her and his face brightened. "So do you, Sammy girl."

"I thought I was your *baby girl* now."

He grinned, then took two steps to close the distance between them. "You are."

She held her breath. He stood close enough for her to feel the warmth radiating off his chest.

His eyes danced across her features. "Samantha, if we want to make this believable, you have to actually act like you *like* me."

She licked her lips. "And how does one do that?"

"Well, for starters, you could touch me."

She lifted a finger, then pressed it to the center of his chest. "There. What else?"

"Next, I should probably touch you."

She nodded slowly. "Seems appropriate."

He slipped his hand inside her jacket, then wrapped it around the small of her back. He pulled her flush against him. "There," he hummed.

She nodded again, like this was a business transaction and not what it actually was: Nico's chest pressed up against hers while they stood next to a tall, glittering Christmas tree.

She traced her finger up the fabric of his sweater—cashmere, she was almost certain—then pressed her palm at his sternum. "Next?" she asked quietly.

He covered her hand with his free one. "I'm going to kiss this hand, because that's what a boyfriend would do, and it's the only limited amount of exposed skin you gave me to work with tonight."

She rolled her eyes.

"Then I'm going to hold your hand and lead you to the train and take you out for a drink, where we'll discuss your workday and anything I need to know for this party tonight." He brushed his thumb across her knuckles. "And I'll touch you some more, because that's what a boyfriend would do, and you probably shouldn't flinch when I do it."

"Have you seen me flinch yet?"

"Nah, baby girl. You're already doing this so well."

She huffed a laugh, a strand of hair brushing across her cheeks. "You really like calling me that, don't you?"

"If you don't like it, you could make a rule."

She scrunched her nose. "I think I can handle it for the week."

He smiled then lifted her hand from his chest. He kissed her pulse, his lips lingering at her wrist for a beat. Before Sam could thoroughly comprehend any of it, he dropped their hands, tucked the rogue strand of hair behind her ear, then threaded their fingers together and pulled her to the door. "Come on. Let's go."

She followed. And she did not flinch.

"Did we really have to come all the way down here for a drink?"

Nico placed his hands on his hips and turned from the entrance of the building on Pine Street to face her. "Samantha, what happened to your sense of fun and adventure?"

She crossed her arms. "Hey, I can be adventurous. But the party starts at eight and it's already seven o'clock."

"Everyone makes fun of the loser who shows up to the party on time. Did college teach you nothing?"

She squinted her eyes. "You'll be going to your party *alone* if you call me a loser again."

He hung his head, then pulled her in for a hug. "I'm sorry."

It was the third time Sam had suggested some kind of

change or questioned his plans. The 3 train was delayed and they sat on the plastic seats in the stuffy subway, listening to someone rap a raspy version of Mariah Carey's "All I Want For Christmas" on the other end of the car. Sam bounced her leg, asking if they maybe should get off at the next stop and find a drink near there instead. Then it was the way her eyes had grown wider and wider as they moved south into Manhattan, until they reached the station at Wall Street.

He was starting to think that he'd misread the entire situation.

He pulled away and placed his hands on her shoulders. "Do you feel forced to hang out with me?"

Her face softened. "No."

"Are you feeling uncomfortable because of Jeff?"

"Well, yeah..."

He cocked his head, attempting to remain calm as he patiently waited for the end of that sentence.

"...*but* none of this is actually real, and it's not like he'll find out. We're just having some fun."

His chest squeezed. "Right. We're having fun." He released his hands. "But are you? Having fun?"

She bit her lip, then checked the time on her phone.

It all clicked for him in a matter of seconds. He wrapped his hand around her neck and titled her head up to face him. "Are you nervous about the party tonight?"

"Yes," she whispered.

"Because of me?"

"No, not at all."

"Is there stuff going on at work?"

She nodded.

He massaged the back of her neck, watching her tense

shoulders loosen as she eased into his touch. "I think we need drinks for this conversation. Let's go upstairs."

"It's okay. We don't have to talk about it," she pleaded.

"Hey now." He pressed his thumb into the soft spot beneath her chin. "We might be playing around here, but I'm still your friend and I will always care about your well-being. I'm basically your second big brother."

"*Ew*, that is so weird. Do not ever call yourself that again."

He laughed and released his grip, then reached for the door. "Come on."

They made their way through the building lobby, donned with century-old art deco tiling across the walls and floor.

Nico nodded at the man behind the desk, skipping the line of people waiting behind the velvet red stanchions. He listened as she quickened her pace to keep up with his long strides.

"Please don't tell me you took me all the way down here just to go up to your apartment," she said, out of breath as she tried to keep up.

He scoffed and took her hand, the motion feeling natural between the two of them. "You really think I could afford this building?"

"Have you seen the watch dangling on your wrist?"

He pulled her into a gold elevator and pressed ROOFTOP, then leaned against the railing. "It wasn't *that* expensive."

"How much money do you have?"

The doors slid closed. "What an inappropriate question."

"You've said a number of things to me in the past seventy-two hours, but *this* is where you draw the line?"

He crossed his arms.

She scowled again, crossing her arms as well, strands of silky black hair falling in front of her face.

Cute.

The elevator shot north. Her eyes widened and she turned to him. "My ears popped."

"We *are* going to the top."

On cue, the doors separated, revealing a hostess stand planted at the center, gating their entry. "Hello, welcome to The Sixtieth," the hostess greeted. "Do you have a reservation?"

He nodded. "Giuliano."

"Splendid." The woman tapped on the screen in front of her, then grabbed two slender leather-bound menus. "Right this way."

Nico pressed a hand to Sam's back as they followed the hostess up a set of winding, narrow stairs, then into the octagonal-shaped room, lit with low, ambient lighting. Soft magenta velvet curtains were tied back with gold-threaded rope, revealing a glittering skyline view of northern Manhattan. The bar was situated at the center as men in salmon-colored coats shook cocktails in metal Boston shakers and stirred with gold-plated spoons.

The hostess led them to a small circular table by the window. Sam sat first, crossing her legs primly. Nico took the seat across from her. His legs swallowed up the minimal space they had, his thigh bumping into her calf, her sheer black tights rubbing against his slacks.

He watched her intently as she opened the menu, her mouth forming an O at the sight of it. "Wait, am I seeing this correctly?"

Nico leaned back in his chair and flipped open his menu with a smirk, browsing the page-long martini-focused menu. "If you're going to be a martini person, you might as well try the best in the city. Although fair warning, they will ruin you for life."

She hummed. "I think I'm okay with that."

He leaned in. "Are you, now? Done with the watered-down dive bar version?"

"That's because I live on a dive bar kind of budget instead of paying..." She scanned the menu. "Twenty-two dollars for a cocktail."

"Trust me, they're worth it. And don't worry, I'm paying."

"Yeah, I know you are," she replied, her tone soft.

They placed their orders—dirty martini for her; a specialty Japanese martini with yuzu and sesame oil for him —then settled into a comfortable silence, watching the mixologists throw together drinks. Sam's gaze kept drifting to the skyline: the glittering Empire State Building and the Rockefeller Center and Central Park and beyond.

Nico circled a hand around her ankle underneath the table, then squeezed lightly. "Sam...want to tell me why you want me to go to this party tonight?"

She scrunched her nose.

"Seems fair, yes? If you're going to throw me to the wolves, I should at least know what's going on with you."

She took a deep breath. "I hate being in my twenties."

He cocked his head, avoiding all of the easy teases that sat on the tip of his tongue. Something in her tone made him bite it. He'd only ever known Sam with her hard exterior, one he knew she probably built up after years of dealing with him and Jeff. He'd never experienced a vulnerable Sam though. He sensed that it might become one of his favorite sides of her.

"How come?" he asked gently. "Give me specifics."

"Well, for starters, I hate being broke. I hate that all of my money goes to rent and student loans, and I have to carefully consider how much I can spend at the grocery store—or if I can even afford it at all." She drummed her fingers on the table. "I hate that my job pays practically pennies but it's really the only thing I'm qualified to do. And it's not like changing companies will help, because all of them pay the same rate, which is *narrowly* above minimum wage. The only way I can make more is if I work my way up. So I'm doing everything I can to prove myself, even though I'm forced to write absolute garbage for the internet. But it's the only way I'll get recognized, and now...I think that might be happening, but it comes with a cost, and I'm not sure it's the kind of cost I'm willing to pay."

"What kind of cost?"

"The back-stabbing kind."

"Ah."

Frosty martini glasses were placed in front of them—hers with two olives, his with a yuzu peel twist.

She brushed the stem of her glass with her thumb, eyes on her drink. "I want them to think I'm put-together, not some young twenty-something running around the city wasting her life away. That's why I invited you. I wanted them to see me as responsible. Or at least responsible enough to have a steady relationship."

He massaged her ankle as she spoke and continued after she finished. She took a sip of her drink and let out a satisfied hum once she realized how a *true* martini tasted.

"Do your parents know how much you're worried about money? Or any of this?"

"I don't want to burden them, or make them think they have to give me money after contributing so much to my education. I just want—" She blew out a breath, and the defeated sound of it made his heart twist. "I want people to think I did it, you know? Made it work in the city instead of looking like a failure."

"People as in, people at home?"

She hesitated, then nodded.

He squeezed her ankle again. "You did make it, Sam. Look around you. You're *here*."

She eyed the glittering lights below. "Then why do I still feel like I'm failing?"

In his mind, it was quite obvious. Sam was impressive in so many ways. Her poise. Her determination. Her dedication to her work. Her love for her brother, and how much she cared about their born-again relationship. He grew up thinking he knew who Samantha Carter was, but this version, the one where she'd formed into the adult she was becoming, it was hard to look away. It was hard *not* to be in her orbit.

"Sammy girl."

She blinked and turned to him. He wondered if he would find tears, but instead he found flushed cheeks. Embarrassment.

"You are the furthest thing from a failure."

She gave him a reluctant smile.

"And I'm not just saying that to make you feel better," he continued. "Take Thanksgiving, for example. You smartly told that guy to get lost when he kept pestering Yumi for her number and she was clearly not interested. And how you made sure Jeff drank enough water so his hangover wasn't *too* painful. Your determination and loyalty to your friends and family is inspiring." He pressed his thumb into her calf. "And you're a great writer."

Her eyes widened. "You read my stuff?"

"Of course. And I don't think you're writing garbage for

the internet. I found a lot of what you wrote to be useful in my own life. There was this one article—" He pulled his phone from the pocket of his slacks, then opened up his browser. "It was about how eating a pre-workout snack with protein and carbs can help improve your overall workout. I've tried it this week, and my lifting has significantly improved. I even upped my bench weight this week."

She smirked. "Oh yeah? What are you benching now?"

He grinned. "Let's just say I could lift you no problem."

She rolled her eyes. "Of course you could."

"Hey, you give me sass now, but when it starts snowing outside and you don't want to ruin these precious little heels, you may want to consider an attitude adjustment."

She smiled and shook her head, then tapped the toe of her heel to his thigh. "You did say no ankles would be sprained."

"That I did." He knocked his chin, gesturing to her phone. "How much time do we have left?"

She looked down at it, screen facing down, but did not move to touch it. "Who cares," she replied. "Let's enjoy our drinks."

He lifted his glass. "Atta girl."

Chapter 9

SAM STEPPED into the restaurant forty-five minutes after the party started, Nico two steps behind her. She decided at the cocktail bar that showing up late wasn't going to make a difference for her image—and she'd been right. Barbara wasn't even there yet, and neither was Garrison. But Yumi was, and she was already two drinks in.

"The happy couple!" she cheered, giggling as she fell into Sam's arms.

Sam frowned. "Maybe cool it on the drinks, Yu?"

"Oh I'm fine. Plus, the drinks are *free*."

"Have you had any water?"

She scrunched her nose. "No. Tequila is better."

Nico appeared next to them holding a glass of clear liquid. He handed it to Yumi. "Here."

Yumi grinned. "Tequila?"

"Sure. Drink up."

Yumi drank the whole glass in three gulps, then pouted.

"Drink one more of those, and I'll get you a real drink," Nico said.

Yumi's pout deepened. "Sam never mentioned you were hot *and* mean."

Nico eyed Sam, eyebrows raised. "Hot, huh?"

Sam squinted at him. "Don't let it get to your head."

"*Definitely* too late for that."

She rolled her eyes.

"Hey now, that's not how you're supposed to do it." Yumi grabbed Nico's arm and tugged, then threw it over Sam's shoulders. "You're supposed to tell your boyfriend he's hot."

"He doesn't need the reassurance," Sam deadpanned.

Nico leaned in, his hand moving from her shoulder to her hair. "It is nice to hear every now and then, you know."

Sam blinked up at him. "Are you telling me Nicolas Giuliano feels insecure?"

"I merely want to hear you say it."

She hummed, turning away from him. "In your dreams."

He chuckled low, the warmth of his breath brushing against the exposed skin at her neck where he held her hair back. Despite the warmth in the bar, a shiver ran down her spine.

Yumi scrunched her nose. "Did you hear Garrison's not coming?"

"*Seriously?*" Sam asked. "Why?"

"No idea. He only told Tally that he wasn't going when he left the office tonight." Yumi frowned at the empty glass in her hand. "Who knows, maybe we'll find ourselves with a new nutrition editor next year."

Sam's chest tightened. "What makes you say that?"

Yumi shrugged. "He went into Barbara's office after you left and there was all this yelling, but no one could decipher what was actually being said."

Nico moved his hand to her nape and massaged her skin.

Yumi raised her glass. "We love the drama. More drinks?"

They followed her, "Last Christmas" blasting through the speakers as they made their way through crowded circles of other *Nourished* employees and to the bar. Waiters roamed the space, silver platters in hand offering jackfruit lettuce wraps and small cups of hummus with vegetables.

"Is this it for the food?" Nico whispered to Sam, eyeing the tray of chickpea fritters like he could devour all twelve of them at once.

"Probably," Sam mumbled back. "I highly doubt they purchased the full meal option."

Nico's brow furrowed as Yumi loudly ordered a round of tequila shots.

"Shots, already? Have we reached that time of the night?"

Sam whipped around to find Barbara behind her, black mink coat draped over her arm and a Prada clutch in hand.

"Oh, well—" Sam started.

"Yes, of course." Nico butted in. "Would you like to do one with us?"

Yumi's eyes looked like they were ready to pop out of her head.

Barbara smirked at Sam. "This is your partner."

She wanted to hit him. "Yes."

Barbara was silent for a beat, and Sam wondered if there was a black hole she could fall into. Then, to her shock, Barbara smiled.

"Why not? I haven't done a tequila shot in a decade," she answered. "Tonight feels like the perfect night for it."

"That's the spirit." He lifted a finger to the bartender pouring shots so he would add one more, then handed Barbara the first shot glass before passing out the rest.

"To feeling young and feeling alive," Nico declared, his gaze landing on Sam when he said it.

Barbara lifted her glass. "*Salut.*"

They all took their shots. Sam kept a close eye on the way Barbara did not flinch at the taste, then plucked a cocktail napkin and dabbed the corners of her lips. "I was impressed with the floral arrangement you sent Samantha the other day."

Nico smiled. "Only the best for my girl."

Butterflies. Pesky little butterflies.

"Very sweet," Barbara replied. "How did the two of you meet?"

Nico slipped a hand around Sam's waist. "We've actually known each other our whole lives. Sam's brother is my best friend."

She turned her gaze to Nico, shocked. *What is he doing?*

He ignored her, keeping his eyes on Barbara.

"Well, isn't that a wholesome story," Barbara responded. She paused and asked the waiter for a vodka soda. "When did you fall in love?"

Yumi coughed and turned away, pretending to choke on her food.

Sam reached a hand behind Nico and pinched the back of his thigh.

He continued, unfazed. "I kissed her when I was twenty-two and it was game over for me."

Sam froze. Nico's hand curled at her hip and squeezed.

"How special." A vodka soda was placed in Barbara's hand. "Well, you have a special one here."

She started to respond. "Th—"

"I know," Nico said at the same time. "I'm definitely the lucky one."

Barbara smirked at Sam, and it surprised her. She looked...pleased. More relaxed than Sam had experienced, or at least in the minimal time she has interacted with the editor-in-chief.

"I better make my rounds. Good work this week, Samantha." Barbara lifted her glass. "Yumi."

She took a sip, then walked off.

They collectively held their breath as Barbara made her way to Tally and a group of other editors and writers. When Tally saw Barbara approach, she covered her mouth before spitting out her drink.

Yumi blew out a breath. "Now that will sober a person up. Nice work, Nico."

"I barely did anything," he responded.

"You got our boss to take a tequila shot and say nice things. That is more than *barely*."

Nico squeezed Sam's hip again.

Yumi's phone buzzed in her hand. She looked at the screen and her eyes widened, then she cooled her expression. She twisted her charm bracelets as she looked up at them. "I need to take this. Be right back."

Once she was out of earshot, Sam stepped out of Nico's grasp and slapped his arm. "You told her the truth?"

Nico's brow pinched. "Yeah, why wouldn't I?"

"Oh, I don't know, maybe because this thing between us is meant to be temporary? And now when we eventually 'break up'"—she held fingers up to make quotation marks—"she'll—"

Nico grabbed her hands. "Sam, stop overthinking. When that day comes, we'll talk about how to handle it, okay?"

She hesitated, remaining quiet as Nico laced their fingers together.

"You promise?" she asked.

"Promise to eventually talk about our metaphorical fake breakup? Yes, Sam. I guess I promise."

She huffed. "And our story? What do we say to people who ask?"

"Simple. We tell them the truth."

She cocked a brow.

He grinned and leaned in, dipping his head so they were at eye level. "Come on. You know that story is far better than anything else we could come up with."

Nico's gaze dropped to her lips, then in a blink, he fixed his eyes back to hers.

"Yeah," she whispered. "I guess it's a good one."

He grinned again, and *god*, he really needed to stop doing that. That dimple was lethal.

Sam slowly made her rounds, Nico glued to her hip with each interaction. Her coworkers were enraptured by him, and Sam could understand why. Nico was *good* with people—especially in a corporate environment. He held himself with a cool confidence that Sam grew to envy. She started to take mental notes of his interactions—the way he asked questions and listened, then repeated what someone said to make sure he heard them correctly before continuing. She felt like she was experiencing a whole new side to Nico with each new conversation they had.

Yumi returned to them many moments later, cheeks flushed, bracelets jingling.

Sam frowned. "You okay?"

Her eyes widened. "Oh yeah! So good. Just...have lots going on."

"Was that your family?"

Yumi hesitated. "Y-yeah! Omma wanted to give me an update."

"And things are good?"

She nodded, brow furrowed.

Nico leaned toward them. "How long do we need to stay at this thing?" he asked. "Because while I don't mind the food, I will need dinner."

She smirked. "Let's get out of here."

His brows raised. "Yeah?"

She nodded and released her hands from his, then grabbed her coat she'd slung over the bar stool earlier. "We stayed for a while and saw who we needed to. Plus...I'm so hungry."

Nico took the coat from her hands and held it out to her, helping her put it on. "Thank god," he grumbled.

Sam tipped her head in Yumi's direction. "You coming?"

"And leave the free booze? Heck no." Yumi smirked. "Get out of here, you two fake lovebirds."

Sam shook her head as she followed Nico out of the bar. Halfway through the crowd, she reached for his hand and threaded their fingers together again.

He turned his head, that dimple fully on display. The sight made her heart flip. Until that point, Nico had been the one to make the moves, to make their "relationship" look believable. But now she was the one to make the move, and she didn't expect it to feel so natural.

Crap, I'm so screwed.

He squeezed her hand as he pushed the door open. The December chill cooled her heated skin and calmed her rapidly beating heart. They stood in silence, staring across Ninth Avenue at the dollar pizza joint that was still slinging slices after nine o'clock.

"Pizza?" she asked.

He tugged her hand, pulling her to the subway entrance. "I got something better."

They stepped into Russo's Deli, the windows decorated with string lights and dangling red, green, and white ornaments. It was late, but the place was still bustling.

She followed Nico to the woman behind the counter wearing a *Nonna's Favorite Little Meatball* apron.

"Only two meatballs left," the woman declared. "Are you the lucky winners?"

Nico tipped his head back in victory. "Yes. We'll take them."

Nonna's Favorite Little Meatball began loading a takeout container with two giant meatballs and heaping spoonfuls of marinara sauce.

An attractive man with wavy auburn hair appeared from a door in the back, then kissed the woman on the temple. "She's finally down, *mia bella*."

"Thank god," the woman grumbled. "I'm not sure how much I can handle running this place with her lack of sleep. Remind me again to give Mom shit for taking Nonna to Sicily in December."

He chuckled. "Can you blame Ro? She loves this place just as much as another beautiful woman I know."

She blushed. "Help me ring these customers up."

The man smirked. "Yes, chef."

The woman's face flushed a deeper shade of red as the guy looked up at Nico, then tilted his head, like he was evaluating something. Then he silently moved to the case of desserts and placed two cannoli in a box.

"Oh, we didn't order those," Sam said.

The man waved his hand. "On the house. I promise they won't disappoint. My friend Benji made them and he and his wife recently won a James Beard award for their pastries."

"Although Marissa's pretty adamant that *she's* the reason they won," the woman added, sliding the container across the counter to them. "One fork or two?"

The guy behind the counter looked up at Nico, brow raised.

Nico smirked. "One is fine, thanks."

Sam's stomach flip-flopped at the way this guy nodded in approval, then slid the box in Nico's direction.

Nico handed him a twenty in return. "Keep the change."

"Thanks." He placed the bill in the cashier as they turned to leave. "Date night?"

"Oh we're not..." Sam started.

"Yes." Nico grinned. "Holiday party."

She sputtered, words escaping her as Nico touched her back again and guided her out of the deli and onto Mulberry Street.

Nico took a seat on a nearby stoop and gestured for Sam to sit next to him, then popped open the lid. He held the fork to her. "You take the first bite."

She pinched the plastic fork handle. "Why did you say yes? We're not actually dating."

He shrugged. "Because for the next seven days, we actually *are*. Now, eat up."

She dropped it and took a bite. It was the perfect mixture of flavors—fatty pork and oregano and garlic and saucy tomato. "Wow," she said. "How did you find this place? I've been here for four years and I've never heard of it."

Nico stole the fork from her. "Jeff told me about it."

She shook her head, aghast. "What?"

"Well, technically Daniel did. When I told Jeff I was moving here, the two of them put together a list of their favorite spots for me to try." He chewed, then swallowed. "Apparently that dude in there is the executive chef of some big award-winning restaurant in Brooklyn."

"Then why is he here?"

"I'm assuming by the rings on their fingers that he married into the family?"

"I guess that makes sense." She stole the fork back.

Nico simply smiled at her, looking bemused. "So."

"So." She took a bite, taking a moment to gather her thoughts, now that the elephant was invited into the conversation. "Jeff," was all that she could say.

Nico sighed. "Jeff."

They ate in silence, listening to the far-off music playing at the Cannoli King.

"Tell me what you're thinking," Nico finally said.

"I'm thinking..." She tapped the fork on the edge of the aluminum container. "I'm thinking that Jeff said he wants us to be friends again."

"He said that?"

Sam nodded. "I'm also thinking that I don't want to hurt my brother's feelings."

"I don't want to either."

"And yet, here we are."

Nico bumped his leg against hers.

She went to eat another bite of meatball, but when she held up the fork, Nico swooped in and ate it instead.

"Hey." She shoved his shoulder. "Hog."

He laughed. "Sam, like you said, he wants us to be friends again. He wouldn't have set up for all of us to meet at Gilroy's last month if he didn't." He bumped his knee against hers again. "I've been having fun and enjoying hanging with you again. Do you feel the same?"

She pursed her lips. "Only when you're not stealing my food."

He beamed, then stole the fork from her. She growled at him, and he responded with another laugh. Then he held up the last bite of meatball to her.

She leaned in and took the bite, noticing the way his cheeks flushed pink as she backed away.

He pointed the fork at her. "You worry too much."

"Do not."

"It's okay, we can work on it," he teased.

"Oh yeah? And how will we do that?"

He winked. "You'll see."

She shook her head and closed her eyes, a small smile slipping across her lips. *Oh, I'm sure I will.*

Chapter 10

Nico picked up the phone on his desk to put it on silent, but other texts quickly rolled in.

He sighed, eyeing his office door, making sure Frank wasn't about to walk in on him texting at his desk.

NICO

She said yes.

CORRINE

SHE SAID YES!

LEON

SHE SAID YES!!!!

EMORY

Nice. Good for you, bud.

LEON

PICTURE! NOW!

His phone kept going off as Leon texted *PICTURE, PICTURE, PICTURE* over and over again. He opened up Nubo on his phone and typed in @SamanthaCarter. A few alternate-universe Samantha Carters popped up, but not his Sammy girl. He tried typing in other usernames he'd known her to use in the past, like @ReaderGirl325 and @SammyCarter<333, but nothing popped up. She really kept her username private and impossible to find. He felt equal parts pride for his engineers making that level of privacy possible for people like Sam…and equal parts hatred for not being able to find her so quickly.

Then he remembered the photos on his phone. He sent a picture from the other night. Sam was on the stoop, cannoli in hand, laughing at the dollop of creamy ricotta that'd fallen onto her skirt. Her cheeks were pink from an evening of drinking and sitting out in the cold, her hair windswept from the breeze.

LEON

...are you kidding me right now

CORRINE

NICOLAS

EMORY

Wow. How do you know her?

LEON

WAIT IS SHE SINGLE

NICO

She's my best friend's sister.

Lee, you touch her, I kill you.

LEON

Oh so THAT'S how we are playing.

You're sweet on her, aren't you?

He pressed his lips together, unsure how to respond. *Yes.* After Friday night, he couldn't deny that he was still "sweet" on Samantha Carter. He'd done his best to avoid her throughout the weekend, ignoring the fact that she hadn't texted him or anything. It wasn't like they were truly beholden to each other, but he couldn't help feeling the disappointment deepen with each passing hour. He'd attempted to brainstorm ways he could step in as her "boyfriend," maybe order her food again...But she clearly wanted to keep to herself, and he'd ultimately decided to give her that space.

But the space did nothing for him and how he was feeling. It only made things worse.

CORRINE

There's a story here, isn't there?

Nico sighed.

NICO

Yes. There is.

CORRINE

Debrief at Phebe's tonight?

LEON

Fuck, I can't. I'm meeting Mariah

CORRINE

You always cancel on her. What's one more
time?

LEON

I canceled on her the last two dates. It
would be a bad look. Tomorrow?

CORRINE

Strand Christmas party

EMORY

Strand Christmas party

LEON

CAN WE COME?

CORRINE

No

LEON

You sure you don't need a fake date? I hear
Nico is good at that.

NICO

I think I can only handle one fake date at a
time.

CORRINE

I have a feeling, based on this enlightening conversation, that Nico is probably horrible at fake dating.

EMORY

What about Thursday?

It continued that way—as it had since he'd moved back from the West Coast—with his friends trying to nail down a time and a borough at which they'd all agree to meet. It was getting harder as the holidays approached. The only day that was actually available was Saturday, the day after Nico's holiday party. At least he could debrief with them then, seeing as his and Sam's agreement would've wrapped up. Pour his heart out and maybe down a beer, or two. Or five.

A knock sounded at his door.

Nico straightened in his seat and fixed his tie, expecting Frank to walk in. Instead, Jeremy waved awkwardly as he stepped through the door. His lead engineer had seen better days—he was sporting a deep seven o'clock shadow and even darker shadows under his eyes. There was a crusty mustard stain on his red flannel shirt, and he attempted to smooth down his unruly hair as he stepped into Nico's office.

Nico stood and shook his hand. "Good to see you, Jer. How's everything?"

He shrugged. "It's not looking good, dude. Got a minute to talk things out?"

Nico checked his calendar. He was supposed to report to the board room in thirty minutes for one last end-of-the-year discussion to make sure they were still on track to hit their goals before the holidays. He knew it was important they all be there, but he also knew he would sit in that board room and not say a thing.

Plus, by the state of Jeremy's appearance, he had a feeling this meeting would be far more important.

He clicked on the meeting invite on his computer, hit *Decline*, then reached for his jacket. "Yes. Let's step out for a coffee and get some fresh air."

He looked panicked. "But we still have a lot to do."

Nico frowned. "Jeremy, when's the last time you left the building?"

His employee hesitated.

Nico sighed. "Grab your coat and meet me by the elevators in five."

He ignored the buzzing in his pocket, likely Frank wondering where Nico was and why he thought anything else on his calendar was more important than a Q4 check-in.

The two of them popped into the Irving Coffee Roasters across the street from the office.

"Have you eaten lunch yet?" Nico asked, ordering himself a black coffee.

Jeremy shook his head. "I was trying to solve a bug this morning and—"

"Order something. On me."

"Nico, you know we're not supposed to expense lunch on the company when we have the cafeteria."

"This isn't on the company, it's on me," he repeated. He gestured toward the sandwich menu. "Please."

Jeremy hesitated, then ordered a ham and cheese

baguette. Nico paid, then they took a seat at the table in the back, away from prying eyes.

He sipped on his coffee, waiting patiently as Jeremy ate. The whole interaction was making him sick to his stomach. Jeremy was a hard worker, but this? This was insanity. His lead engineer looked like the life had been sucked right out of him, and he was shoving the sandwich in his mouth at the speed of light.

Jeremy wiped his face with a napkin, then his hands. "So, I think we have the solution to get videos working in the feed."

Nico's eyebrows raised. "Well, that's promising. How'd you do it?"

"The algorithm now has a focus on watch time versus engagement. We took out the parts of the code that were competing with it."

"Does that mean Nubo photo posts will be lost in the mix?"

Jeremy shrugged. "Maybe initially. But at least this gives us the opportunity to actually launch that part of the platform by the deadline. We'll figure out how to boost static posts in the new year."

Nico tapped the table. "Okay. I know I don't have much of a say, but I don't want users getting upset that the plat-form is changing so much. There's a reason why we're successful—people come to Nubo for the posts, to feel inspired."

"I didn't think you cared so much about the users," Jeremy deadpanned.

Nico frowned. "Of course I do. That's why I work in UX. I want people to enjoy the experience."

"Yeah, me too. But I guess it doesn't seem like that from the rest of the higher-ups."

"I get that," Nico replied, voice low. "I do. And I'm sorry it's been hard."

Jeremy nodded, dodging the apology. "Here's the problem with this algorithm update. We can't get live videos to work, and I know that's the biggest driver for this project."

"How come they won't work?"

"The tech is still crashing the feed when we test it. On other platforms, you have to click into live videos. You don't exactly scroll through a feed and come across them. In order for us to have live footage, we would need some space on the screen that users can tap into."

He nodded, understanding the complexities that went into building a whole new part of the app. It was the kind of project that could take months or even years, not weeks.

Jeremy leaned in. "Does the New Year's project really have to be a live stream?"

The project was meant to be their big surprise moment to users—Ryan Seacrest live on Nubo in Times Square while the ball dropped. A splashy launch of their merger, hopefully soaring them to the top of the App Store. Merely posting a video didn't have the same shock factor, and he already could hear what Theo had to say. *Make it work, whatever the cost.*

But if the cost was watching his employees burn out, with unshaven faces and hollow eyes, Nico felt in his bones that the cost wasn't even close to being worth it.

"Let me talk to Frank and Theo," Nico started. "Maybe we can convince them to meet us in the middle. At least we know we can get the videos working by our deadline. That's already a huge deal."

Jeremy exhaled deeply, then rubbed his eyes. "*Fuck*, I'm so tired."

"Go home. You've done more than enough."

Jeremy shook his head. "I'm supposed to meet virtually with the Silicon engineers in an hour. Besides, I don't have any food in my fridge. At least there's free food in the cafeteria."

Nico bit the inside of his cheek. Yes, it seemed like a blessing to have a cafeteria full of free food for employees. A blessing, but also a curse. He noticed employees staying around the office later and later because of the free food, keeping to their desks and their work instead of leaving the office and enjoying their lives. Nico wondered when Jeremy last saw his friends, or if he even gave himself the opportunity to see anyone.

Nico tipped his chin. "Take a container of food to go, do your meeting at home, then sleep. And take the day off tomorrow."

"Nico, I—"

"*Please*, Jer. If there's anything that needs to be done, send it my way and I'll handle it. I don't want to see you like this again."

"He said *whatever the cost*." Jeremy pinched his shirt and lifted it to show off his mustard stain. "This is the cost."

"Well, that value is no longer on the table," Nico stated. "I'm not okay with it anymore."

Jeremy blinked at him. "Fine. I'll go home then."

"Good."

Nico sipped on his coffee, thoughts racing about how he was going to broach the topic of *not* going live to Frank and Theo. Especially after he'd blown off their board meeting this afternoon.

But after sitting here and watching the color return to Jeremy's face, Nico knew whatever met him back at the office would be worth it. He never wanted to see his employees look this grim and overworked ever again.

Nico leaned forward. "Can I ask you something?"

Jeremy balled up his napkin and sat back in his chair. "Sure, what's up?"

"Have you seen these posts about OmniCorp employees unionizing?"

Jeremy hesitated, then nodded. "Yes. Everyone's talking about it."

Nico swallowed. "Everyone?"

"What do you expect? People are overworked and angry. HR is overrun with complaints from employees and they're doing nothing to actually solve the problem. Omni-Corp's top priority is their product, not their employees. People are worried that if they're too loud about what they need, they'll lose their jobs to greenies that are cheaper and a lot more eager to stay all night and work."

"That's...that's a worry people are having? Has that happened?"

"Apparently it has in Silicon. Also, the marketing department here was wiped and they hired a swath of new employees all under twenty-five, with salaries at half the rate."

Nico was aware about the re-org happening within the company, especially after their recent merger with Snipbit, but he had no idea it was this bad. His stomach dropped when he realized how ignorant he was to everything going on.

Jeremy tilted his head. "Are you about to come at me with some company bullshit about how we all need to stick together and make this work?"

Nico hesitated, scanning Jeremy's determined expression. He couldn't know for sure, but he had a sneaking suspicion that Jeremy might be one of the whistleblowers—or at least knew who was making those posts online. Especially since the users for those posts were untraceable, pointing to the work of a skilled engineer. Or a whole team of them.

"No," Nico replied, surprising himself. "I'm not going to say that to you."

His expression relaxed. "Then what are you going to say to me?"

Jeff's words of wisdom from their conversation the other night popped into his head. *Your boss sure as hell doesn't care about his employees around the holidays, but you do. That's what makes you a good leader.*

"I'm going to say that you need to do what is right for you," Nico answered honestly. It was a vague attempt at an answer, but he wasn't about to sit here and tell Jeremy not to stand up for what was right. "I'm also going to say that you can communicate to your engineers that I will be discussing the project with Frank and Theo. Hopefully I'll be able to talk them out of going live on New Year's. I'm proud of the work you've put in to make this happen before the holidays, and I want all of you to get the time off you deserve."

Jeremy exhaled. "And if Theo tells you to fuck off and make the video happen? What then?"

"Then I'll figure out the solution myself. This is no longer something I want the team to worry about."

"That's *lunacy*. You can't possibly get a live stream working on Nubo by yourself."

He shrugged. "You're probably right. But at least the blame will fall on my shoulders and not yours. Understand?"

His face tightened, then he nodded. "All right, man. Th-thanks. For understanding."

Nico nodded, his head and his chest a whirling storm of emotions. He needed time to think about how he was going to broach this conversation with Frank, then Theo. Maybe he should rip off the Band-Aid and tell them both at once...

Jeremy cleared his throat. "Are you going to the party on Friday?"

"Yes. You?"

He rolled his eyes and nodded. "I know adding Kendrick was just a ploy to drum up attendance, but it worked."

He smiled. "It's kind of hard to say no to that one. Are you bringing anyone with you?"

Jeremy let out an exasperated *as if* kind of laugh. "What a funny joke. No. You?"

His phone buzzed in his pocket again and it took everything he had to mask his flinch. He didn't have to look to know who it was.

"Yes, actually," he replied.

Jeremy hummed. "Must be nice."

Nico's face pinched. "Nice?"

"To have enough time in your schedule to date. I don't even have enough time to get laid."

He sighed. "Promise me you're heading home after this."

Jeremy lifted three fingers. "Scout's honor."

He told Jeremy he needed a minute before heading back to the office, then watched him quickly leave the shop and jog across the street. He reached into his pocket for his phone, exhaled, then tapped the screen to see what mess he was about to deal with.

But it wasn't a mess. Instead, there were three text messages from Sam waiting for him. One of them was a selfie.

She was sitting at her desk, a deep frown on her face.

SAM

I had dreams about those cannoli last
night.

And now I want one.

Nico's lips peeled into a grin. He rubbed his mouth to
try to hide it, but it was getting harder and harder as he
stared at her adorable pout, and the tiny triangle of cleavage
in the photo.

He typed back.

NICO

They're on Seamless. Need me to send
some to you?

SAM

NO. You'll make my cannoli fantasies so
much worse.

Cannoli fantasies. He tried his absolute best to not let
his mind spiral into forbidden territory with that one.

SAM

BTW, what's the dress code for this thing
on Friday?

NICO

Formal.

I'm sorry. Don't kill me.

SAM

I don't mind. I never get to dress up fancy.

...want to give me a color scheme?

Nico leaned back in his chair and crossed his legs, the
music in the coffee shop aptly switching to "It's the Most

Wonderful Time of The Year." The image of Sam and her silky black skirt at Gilroy's weeks ago flashed before his eyes. Then he thought about her lips.

NICO

Wear red.

He watched the gray bubbles dance as she typed, impatiently waiting for her to say something snarky back.

Her reply was so much better.

SAM

Excellent. I have just the thing.

He bit the inside of his cheek. Feeling reckless, Nico saved Sam's selfie on his phone, then set it as his background image.

Chapter 11

Yᴜᴍɪ ᴘᴏᴘᴘᴇᴅ her head above the other side of Sam's cubicle, eyes wild with excitement. "Did you read the email?"

She frowned. "Uh, no. I've been trying to focus on this apple cider vinegar piece." She shook her head. "Why people would want to simply *drink* the stuff is beyond me."

"Check your email. It's *juicy*."

Sam saved what she wrote and opened up her inbox.

To: editorial@nourished.com

From: eic@nourished.com

Subject: *Emergency Staff Meeting*

Hello Nourished team,

Please free your calendars and meet in the conference room today at 4 p.m. for an emergency editorial staff meeting. Attendance is mandatory.

Thank you,

Barbara

Sam looked up at Yumi, wide-eyed. "What do you think it's about?"

"No idea, but let's pray it's a surprise week of vacation. Or free food."

She looked at the screen and checked the time. "The meeting is in ten minutes."

"Then we better go and get the good seats."

Sam closed her laptop and followed Yumi to the conference room. Every seat around the long center table was taken by staff members, all eager to find out whatever was going on for Barbara to call an emergency meeting, something she had *never* done before. What kind of emergency could possibly warrant an all-hands?

They settled into two chairs in the back. Tally sat beside them, firing off pre-made social posts on her phone as she waited for the meeting to start.

"Any idea what this is about?" Yumi asked Tally. She lifted her legs and sat criss-cross on the seat.

"Maybe someone's getting fired," Tally replied, not looking up from her screen as she wrote out a caption for another video.

"There's no way she would fire someone in front of all of us, that would be *so* dramatic." Yumi shimmied in the chair. "And delightful."

"Then maybe someone quit," Tally said.

Sam scanned the faces in the room, listing off the editorial staff in her head as she noted who was here. One person obviously wasn't.

She leaned in and whispered, "Garrison isn't here."

Yumi's eyes widened as Barbara swept into the room. She marched to the front, head held high, shoulders back. The woman was a serious force. Sam had to remind herself that this woman, as tough-as-nails as she tried to seem, had easily kicked back a shot of tequila with Nico.

Nico. Her hands itched to check the phone in the pocket of her blazer and see if he responded to her recent text. They had been messaging non-stop—well, more like sending each other photos as they documented their mundane workweeks. She almost didn't send the selfie at her desk earlier in the week, noticing the small dip of her chest that was evident in the photo and wondering if it was too much. But she concluded that it didn't matter much, because Nico was Nico and he had seen her in a bathing suit before. So she sent the photo, and he had been firing texts back at her ever since. Photos of him at his desk, photos of the Union Square Christmas market as he walked through it heading to the subway station, photos of him eating a slice of pizza on his way home, photos of him tucked into bed. *Good night, Sammy girl,* he wrote with his last one.

And she sent photos back, from her sad Trader Joe's salads to the small spill of her morning coffee on her blazer sleeve that morning, which she'd rolled up so no one noticed. Her last photo was a selfie of her at the desk again, frowning at her keyboard. *Writer's block,* was how she'd captioned it. She'd felt her phone buzz in her pocket as she made her way to the conference room with Yumi, but she refused to check it until the meeting was over. Not with the way Barbara's stern expression locked on hers from across the room before she spoke.

"Thank you for gathering on such short notice," Barbara started. She placed her hands on the table and leaned forward, not bothering to take a seat. Barbara didn't need to assert her dominance in this way, she already commanded a room with her sheer presence. But her tight body language and grim expression made it clear that something was wrong, and standing in front of everyone sent that message all the way home. "We are three weeks away from the new year, which as you know is our busiest period. The quarterly edition is still set to print, so for our print editors, breathe a sigh of relief. There is nothing wrong with the magazine."

A chorus of exhales sounded across the room. If the *Nourished* quarterly magazine had any issues going to print, Sigmond Media would have been looking at a major revenue loss. Although their efforts to build up their online presence was starting to make a serious financial impact, their print editions still drove a majority of the publication's —and the company's—revenue.

"However, we do have an issue that needs immediate attention. Due to some unsavory activities that have recently come to light, the Sigmond Media team and I have made the decision to let Garrison go."

Gasps echoed across the room.

"Unsavory activities?" Yumi whisper-screamed. "What the fuck did he do?"

"Makes sense, he kind of gave me the creeps," Tally added.

Sam held her laptop to her chest, still very aware of Barbara's attention, which continually focused in her direction.

"Because we are three weeks out from January, I am going to need everyone in this room to really step it up. We'll be expediting the process of finding a new editor, and I have every intention of promoting from within. I will be hosting interviews over the next week. Candidates will consist of team members who have proven themselves worthy of the position."

Sam felt like every sense sharpened as Barbara spoke. She was thrumming with excitement, and also very aware of the way Yumi tensed beside her and began playing with the charm bracelets on her wrist.

"Keep an eye on your inboxes for the next few days. Interviews will start on Monday," Barbara continued. "That is all. I will be very busy with this process, so if you have any questions, reach out to Bailey and she'll set time in my calendar." She shooed her hands. "Go."

Everyone swiftly gathered their things in silence, but that didn't last long. As soon as writers and editors left the conference room, chaos ensued, whispers of accusations about what Garrison did and predictions of who the next nutrition editor would be flew across the floor.

Sam turned around hoping to find Yumi, but instead saw her friend already taking a seat at her desk.

She returned to her cubicle and opened her laptop. Her heart skipped at the red notification bubble floating on top of her email app. She opened the app, her heart pounding in her chest at the sight of the email that'd come through following the meeting.

To: scarter@nourished.com

From: eic@nourished.com

Subject: Get your résumé ready

Monday, 12 p.m.

Barbara

Her mouth went dry. Three days. She had three days to polish up her résumé. More like two days, since it was Friday and she was set to spend the night with Nico and would likely be out late. *Two days.* That wasn't enough time. It was hardly enough time to get herself interview-ready. Was she too young for this kind of role? Was Barbara putting too much faith in her? Did she actually have what it took?

Yumi popped into Sam's cubicle out of nowhere.

She jumped and slammed her laptop shut.

Yumi lifted a brow, then held her hands out to Sam. "Come on, miss jumpy. Time to go make you hot."

"It's barely five o'clock."

"I don't know about you, but there's no way I'm getting any work done after that." She wiggled her fingers. "Come on. Barbara's too preoccupied with her hunt. She won't notice."

Or would she? Sam eyed Yumi's hands, wondering if her best friend had also received a similar email. Would they both be interviewing? If she got promoted, would she be Yumi's boss? Would Yumi be *her* boss? Plus, if Barbara was considering them for the role, shouldn't they stay as late as possible? Show that they're hard workers and all of that?

Yumi poked Sam's forehead. "I see that brain working overtime. Enough. Let's go. You have a fun night ahead of you, and I think it would be good to go out and stop thinking about all of this."

"But—"

"Samantha, I am five seconds away from stealing your date and going with Nico myself so I can see Kendrick, so you better get your cute ass out of that chair and come with me."

Sam rolled her eyes, then took Yumi's hands and let herself be pulled out of her chair. She promised to meet her by the elevators in five, then stuffed her laptop in her tote bag.

Her phone buzzed at her desk. She tapped the screen and found an image waiting for her. It was a photo of a chest; white button-down and black lapels with a matching black bow tie.

NICO

Ready for you, baby girl.

Picture for a picture?

She shook her head and smirked, then fired a text back.

SAM

Sorry, baby boy. You'll have to wait for the real thing.

Baby boy? Baby dog?

NICO

I don't hate it.

Which one?

You know which one, sassy.

You're right. See you soon, baby dog.

Nico arrived at Sam's apartment building on the Upper East Side at seven. She told him she needed time to go home and get ready, which meant cutting his two-hour rule short. It only gave him an hour with her before the time he decided he probably should show up to this thing, which certainly wasn't enough of a window to take her out for another martini.

His disappointment was quickly gone at the sight of Sam in her dress.

She stepped out in sky-high strappy silver heels, revealing a full-length silk red gown that flowed against her curves like water. Her hair was down, the strands tucked behind her ears revealing a pair of dainty teardrop earrings. But it wasn't the dress or the earrings or the heels that captured his attention. It was her skin.

The dress connected as a halter at the top and dipped into a generous V at her chest. She smiled and turned, tucking her hair around her shoulders. The silk dipped low, exposing miles of skin at her back.

So much skin. It's like she was trying to send him a message. Giving him permission to explore her, on the last night he would ever be able to.

She turned her face, and her smile was...*evil.*

What a wicked little thing. "You're going to freeze in that."

The front door of the building swung open. Yumi handed Sam her long black coat, then winked at her. "Good job."

"Thank you," Sam said proudly. She lifted the jacket to find the sleeve.

Nico jogged up the stairs. "Wait, let me." He took her jacket, then held it out to her.

Sam smiled again, and *god*, the things he would do to see it over and over again. Especially in that dress. He was *way* in over his head.

She slipped her arms into the sleeves. Nico watched the creamy skin on her back disappear behind black wool, and immediately regretted not touching it right away. Because he could. Because she was allowing him to.

He untucked her hair, and it felt like midnight velvet on his hands as he draped it down her back. Then he patted her shoulders, because he wasn't sure what else to do. He wasn't sure he would be able to properly function around her tonight.

She turned to face him. "So, train?"

Yumi glared at Nico from behind Sam with narrowed eyes. *Do not make her get on the train in those heels*, she appeared to threaten.

He tilted his head at her, then focused his attention on Sam. "Of course not, I already have a car waiting."

Sam looked around his shoulder, where the Uber Black sat idling at the bottom of the stoop. "Oh. Wow."

Yumi exhaled, sounding relieved. "Don't get into much trouble, you two." She pointed to Sam. "If you don't send me videos of Kendrick, I will kill you when you get home."

"Not in this dress, you won't," Nico butted in.

Yumi laughed as she closed the front door.

Sam shook her head, then touched the bow tie at his neck. "You look hot, Nicolas."

He grinned and puffed up his chest. "Thank you, Samantha." He backed down a step and held out his arm to her. "Shall we?"

Chapter 12

They rolled down Fifth Avenue, then took a right on 66th Street, following the curvy road through Central Park. A light snow had begun to fall, dusting the grass and the leaves with unexpected charm. Nico took a deep breath, hands in his lap as he scanned the people gliding along the ice rink.

Sam shifted in her seat and crossed her leg, the fabric slipping halfway down her thigh from the slit in her dress. A center console separated their seats, and he was glad for it. He wasn't sure he could trust his hands quite yet. He blinked at her leg then turned his attention to the front of the car as they cruised through the park heading for the West side.

She cleared her throat. "So. Want to tell me what's going on at work?"

He rubbed his chin, freshly shaved. "What do you want to know?"

She spun the silver ring on her middle finger. "Have things improved since the last time we spoke? How are the employees feeling?"

He exhaled. After his conversation with Jeremy earlier in the week, Nico had set a meeting with Frank to discuss their progress. But Frank asked to reschedule because he was out of office for the days leading up to the holiday party, and there was no way they would discuss anything tonight. The meeting was pushed to Monday, and the entire thing had him on edge.

On the bright side, his engineers seemed more at ease. The day off had done Jeremy well, and Nico made sure to watch him leave each night. He did, and he always returned the next morning in a clean shirt. The engineer team chat on their messaging board had relaxed back into their usual banter, with lots of *Arrested Development* memes and jokes and excitement about the holiday party. Things felt somewhat normal again, but Nico knew it may not last long. But he was going to do his best to make sure it stayed that way for his team as long as possible.

He rubbed the tops of his thighs. "Yes, in a way. I was able to make things comfortable for my team. Me, on the other hand..." He heaved out a sigh. He didn't respond for a beat, then two.

Sam reached a hand over the center console and brushed her fingers over his knuckles. "Are you okay?"

He eyed Sam's polished nails and silver ring, the metal warm against his skin as she cupped her fingers over his knuckles. "I have to have a hard conversation with my boss on Monday, and I have a feeling it's not going to go well."

"Does he suspect that? Will things be weird tonight?"

Nico shook his head. "He likely thinks I'm giving him the update he wants, but I essentially have to tell him that the project they're pushing for won't work in time and we'll have to make some adjustments."

She nodded. They sat in silence as the car exited the

park and made its way down the West Side Highway. OmniCorp may be stingy, finding ways to cut costs without cutting the amount of labor needed, but when it came to parties, the company never played it safe. They were always lavish, and this year they'd rented out the Glasshouse—an event venue with wall-to-wall windows and a view of the city far below, making them feel like unworthy gods among ants.

When the Uber pulled over to the sidewalk out front, Nico immediately hopped out of the car and jogged over to Samantha's side, buttoning his suit jacket before opening the door for her. He held out his hand.

She took it, eyes on the street as she stepped down carefully, wary of falling on the ice that'd started to form from the compact snow on the road.

Nico steadied her with a hand at her back, reaching into the car to grab her purse before thanking the driver and closing the door. He guided her to the building's entrance, making sure she didn't slip in those heels that were one hundred percent not good for this weather and one hundred percent not good for his heart.

They followed the throngs of employees—all dressed to the nines—to the coat check. He recognized a few people, but there were a lot of new faces among the crowd thanks to OmniCorp's recent expansion, many of whom had flown in from San Francisco—all on the company's dime. Nobody wanted to miss Kendrick's performance, it seemed. Even if the idea felt ridiculous to Nico, he had to admit it; it seemed to work to get employees here. He wondered if their other vision—of senior-level employees coming with *dates*—would also work in the ways Frank hoped. He assumed it wouldn't, but as he watched Sam slip out of her coat and hand it over, he didn't care. If it meant he could be *here*, then he would say yes to this lunacy. Over and over again.

Sam turned and blinked up at him with long, curling lashes and those bright honey-green eyes. A chill swept through from the revolving door, and he watched as goosebumps scattered across her shoulders and down her arms.

Nico sucked in a breath, then smiled. He kept his hands by his sides.

She grinned. "Nicolas, if we actually want to make this believable, you have to act like you *like* me."

He huffed and hung his head, feeling his cheeks go warm at the return of the words that'd come out of *his* lips only a week ago. "I'm sorry."

Sam stepped closer, pressing a hand to his chest. "Do you want to leave?" she whispered.

He shook his head, then gently gripped her wrist, guiding the inside of her forearm to his lips. But before he made contact, he blinked down at her and raised a brow. *This okay?*

She bit her lip and nodded.

He brushed his lips against her skin, her coconut and vanilla scent knocking him senseless. He lingered there, noticing the way her arm relaxed in his touch, the blush on her cheeks in his periphery.

Jesus.

"Hey, you guys want to move so others can check their coats?" someone asked behind them.

He dropped his hand and placed it on Sam's back. "Sorry, all yours," he answered.

They made their way to the elevators, his hand sliding down her skin then curving around her hip. They entered an empty, open elevator, the entire surface covered in mirrors. Nico leaned on the back railing as Sam stepped close to a mirror to check her makeup.

"Don't worry, you look good," he said.

She smirked. "I know. Just making sure I don't have any smudged makeup. I'm not sure if you heard, but I'm the engineering director's date."

He smiled at her as she continued to examine her lips and eyes. He liked this about the new Sam, the one he was still getting to know. There was a confidence when it came to her appearance, and he found it intoxicating.

Before the doors closed, a swarm of people rushed in to join them.

Sam stepped closer to Nico to make room, and eventually the two were pressed tight together as more people squeezed in.

She made herself comfortable between his legs, turning to face him. She played with the bow tie at his neck. "Gotta keep up appearances," she whispered as the doors finally sealed closed.

He grinned again. He had a feeling that by the end of the night, the corners of his lips would permanently be glued to the sides of his face. His hands found her waist as the elevator shot skyward. "I appreciate your dedicated work ethic," he teased.

Her smirk slipped. "Speaking of work, I would love your professional opinion on something."

He tilted his head. "*Professional* opinion, huh?"

She nodded.

"Well in my *professional* opinion, a man should always pick you up for a date."

She rolled her eyes. "Yeah, you made that one clear already."

He squeezed her hips. "Just making sure."

"I'm looking for your *actual* professional opinion. Stuff is going on at work that I need help...figuring out." She sighed, then patted his chest. "But not tonight. Tonight, we have fun."

His brow pinched. "You sure? We don't have to stay long at this thing, we could leave—"

"You heard what would happen if we left before Kendrick. My life is clearly on the line, Nico."

He chuckled as the elevator came to a stop and people filed out. They remained squeezed together in the back. "Does this make me your savior then?"

Her face pinched into that scowl as she stomped away from him. He tipped his head back and laughed, following her out of the elevator. Even as an adult, Nico still loved to tease Samantha Carter.

He caught up to her and grabbed her hand, pulling her to him.

She complied with a huff. "I still hate you, you know," she said, glaring up at him as their fingers interlocked.

"I wouldn't want it any other way, baby girl."

She shook her head. "I think it's time for a martini."

He pulled her through the tall, swinging black doors. "I agree."

The Glasshouse was a beacon of extravagance. Glittering light fixtures and panoramic windows and sparkling glassware as flutes of Champagne were passed among guests. Yet despite the grandeur of the space, Nico was really the one who made the space glow. A few moments by his side while she sipped on her dirty martini, and similarly to how he was at Sam's party, Nico charmed *everyone*. It was evident that he was good at what he did. Not just the coding stuff—Sam was almost certain after years watching Nico tinker with computers that he was still excellent at that—but leading people and making them feel welcome. He remembered intimate details about the different engineers he introduced her to and was sure to ask them specific questions.

"How's your mom doing?"

"Did you guys win your club soccer tournament?"

"What did you think of the Park Slope farmers' market?"

"I told you that spot was perfect for a first date. Did you land a second?"

It continued like that for at least an hour, and honestly, Sam didn't mind. She sipped on her martini—then a second—and listened alongside Nico as he floated through the room. With the way the different engineers or OmniCorp team members responded to him, it was clear the respect was mutual. People liked Nico, even if there was an obvious undercurrent of discontent amongst the employees and senior-level management—the latter not seeming to mind segregating themselves to a corner of sectional couches toward the back of the room, surrounded by bottles of Dom Perignon.

A waiter balancing a tray of mini–fried chicken sandwiches swept past them.

Sam held out an arm to try to stop them, but the waiter was too quick—likely trying to get to the other side of the room since anything leaving the kitchen was getting devoured immediately by employees lingering near the doors.

Nico hesitated in his conversation with someone from the content strategy team, noticing Sam's piss-poor attempt at getting food. He took two large steps, then positioned himself in front of the waiter, the tray almost bumping into his chest.

"If you don't mind me," he said. He placed a napkin on his hand, then balanced a sandwich in his palm. He handed it to her, oblivious to the waiter who left in a huff.

Sam smiled, pinching the little bun between her fingers. "I'm not sure I can elegantly eat fried chicken in this dress."

"Then don't eat it elegantly."

She gently kicked his ankle. "Not with the number of people you have me meeting. I need to keep up appearances."

He smiled, then reached for her glass, which was practically empty. "Here, I'll hold your drink while you eat."

"Are you not eating?"

"Oh I will, but I also didn't drink two martinis in less than an hour. And I'm going to assume you haven't eaten in a while."

She hummed. "Fine. You win."

"Always do."

She shook her head and took a bite, observing the room while she chewed. Some members of the management team were still in the corner, but many of them had dispersed.

She tipped her chin in that direction. "Do you need to go over there?"

Nico turned and eyed the couches, then sighed. "At some point, if they decide they don't want to leave their corner." He pointed to a man in a cerulean-blue suit with sunglasses on his head. "That's Theo, our CEO. And I'm assuming the blonde in the sparkly dress is his new girlfriend."

"And your boss?"

"*Hmmm.* I saw him earlier, but I'm not sure where he is now." His eyes swept through the room. Eventually they landed on someone, and his eyes widened. "Oh, he's actually coming this way."

Sam looked at her half-eaten sandwich, then at Nico's full hands. Panicked, she shoved the rest in her mouth.

Nico handed her glass back with a laugh. "That was *so* elegant."

"Thank you," she said, her mouth full. "I try."

He laughed to himself again, then took a step to the high-top cocktail table next to them. He placed his drink down, raising a brow.

She swallowed, then huffed. "I didn't see that there."

"That's okay. Your solution was much cuter."

She grimaced and touched her lips. "Do I look okay? No smudged makeup?"

He hesitated and his right hand twitched by his side. Then he gently cupped her chin and wiped his thumb underneath her bottom lip. "There. Better."

She felt her face go hot as Nico's name boomed from a deep voice beside them.

He wiped the lipstick on his thumb with a cocktail napkin, then held his hand out to his boss. "Frank, good to see you."

"Likewise!" He patted Nico on the back, then turned to the slender woman in a floor-length green velvet gown beside him, standing a foot away. "Nicolas, this is my wife, Serena. See, this is my east coast director, Nico."

Serena held out her hand. "Pleasure."

Nico took her hand and nodded his head. "The pleasure is all mine." He let go of the woman's hand and wrapped his arm around Sam's waist, tucking her close. "Frank, I'd like you to meet Samantha, my girlfriend."

Frank's brows shot skyward, his eyes wide with delight.

"Girlfriend, huh? Way to hold things close to the chest, Nicolas."

Sam noticed the way Nico smiled at his boss, tight and polite.

"Did you guys meet on one of those dating apps or whatever?" Frank asked, leaning in conspiratorially. "Now *that's* an idea for the OmniCorp profile."

"One thing at a time," he responded. He drew Sam closer, like he was holding on for dear life. "No. Sam and I have known each other since we were kids. Her brother is my best friend."

She sucked in a breath at the mention of Jeff.

Nico squeezed her hip gently in response to her stiffness. Then squeezed again.

To Sam's surprise, Serena smiled at that, the first time the woman genuinely looked like she was having fun at this party instead of scowling at a glass of Champagne in her hand, like she was earlier. "You're her brother's best friend? Now isn't that a story. How romantic."

Nico turned to her, his eyes softening. "Yeah, it is."

Then he dipped down and kissed her temple.

She blushed at the feel of his warm lips on her face, aware of the way Frank and Serena were watching them. Making a show of it, she placed her palm on top of Nico's at her hip and interlaced their fingers.

Frank turned to a passing waiter and placed his empty glass on the tray. "Time for another, right, dear?"

Serena's back straightened and she crossed her arms. "Don't you think we should call it a night? We only paid the babysitter until ten."

Frank flicked his hand, shooing away her suggestion like it was a pesky fly. "Text her and say if she can stay until midnight, we'll get her tickets to the Z-100 Jingle Ball."

"*Frank.*"

He grumbled something under his breath, then turned to Nico with a smile. "Great work today." He made a vague gesture. "The both of you."

Serena's eyes rolled so far in the back of her head, Sam wondered if the woman would hurt herself from the strain. Then Serena turned on her heel and walked off to the exit.

Nico shook Frank's hand. "Thank you, sir."

Sam noticed the way Frank squeezed Nico's hand a touch harder than before. "Monday. Good news, or bad?"

He hesitated. "Good. A promising update, but we need to discuss the possibility of a few changes."

Frank's face darkened, his hand still gripping Nico's. "Changes? Changes like what?"

Nico opened his mouth then closed it. He took a long breath. "Videos are working, I will say that. We'll discuss details on Monday."

Frank's face brightened again. He dropped Nico's hand. "Excellent! I knew I could count on you to push them to the finish line."

Nico closed his eyes and nodded. "Yes, sir."

His boss laughed, then pointed at Nico as he turned to Sam. "Does he bring that kind of diligence to bed?"

She looked back at the man in horror.

Frank laughed, then slapped Nico's shoulder. "I'm only kidding. See you on Monday, Nicolas."

The man walked off with a pep in his step toward his wife, who stood by the door tapping her foot. He made a brief stop at a waiter holding a tray of margaritas and downed the glass in one go.

Nico shifted his body, using his wide chest to shelter Sam from the party. He placed his hands on her shoulders. "Are you okay? Sam, I am so, *so* sorry."

She took a deep breath. "Is he always that inappropriate?"

"Unfortunately, yes."

"And you're okay with it?"

He shook his head. "But there's also not much I can do about it."

Sam worried her lip as she eyed the pockets of employees who either looked a little too drunk from the open bar, or bored as they waited for their private concert to start. Not a single person was on the dance floor.

"There are a lot of unhappy people in your company, huh?"

Nico tucked a hand behind her neck, his eyes on her white gold earring as he flicked it with his thumb. "Yes."

"And you? Are you happy?"

"I used to be."

She blinked up at him. "What changed?"

He exhaled. "I don't think taking a management role was the right move. I'm not very good at it."

She shook her head. "That's not true. I've watched you all night. You are an *excellent* leader."

"You haven't seen me at work, Sam."

"Yes, but I have seen your compassion. You care about these people, and in my opinion, that's what makes for a great leader."

She didn't mean for her words to ring so true to her own heart, to everything that was going on back at the *Nourished* offices. Garrison had been terrible at bringing a team together, at creating an atmosphere where employees could thrive. Yet watching *Nico*...It gave Sam hope. It made her want to be the kind of leader who inspired too.

"It's funny."

She tilted her head, pulling herself out of her thoughts

and landing her attention back on Nico and his tanned skin. "What's funny?"

"Your brother pretty much told me the same thing on the phone last week."

She backed up a step. "He did?"

Nico nodded. "I feel lucky, you know."

"Why?"

He shrugged. "I feel lucky that I have the two of you. I feel like I wouldn't be the kind of person I am if I didn't grow up with you guys."

"The kind of person you are, like, really stubborn and annoying?"

He chuckled. "Compassion. I think you and Jeff are really good at that."

She smiled. "I'll Be Home For Christmas" slipped through the speakers, like a smooth sleigh ride from one song to the next. She eyed the dance floor. It was still empty.

She grabbed Nico's free hand and tugged. "Come on, let's dance."

He grinned. "Dance? There's no one dancing."

"Exactly." She pulled.

He followed.

Once she got to the center of the dance floor, Sam turned and placed her hands on Nico's shoulders.

He smiled, then in one swift motion, slipped his hand around the small of her back and pulled her close, their bodies flush. He took one of her hands and brought it to his chest as he began to sway.

She tipped her head up to look at him. "When did you get so suave, baby dog?"

He grinned, then dipped low, kissing the soft spot

between her neck and collarbone. "When did you get so beautiful, baby girl?"

She twisted to face him, his head still dipped low enough so they were eye level. "I always have been."

He smiled, but this time, it seemed sad. "I know. And I hate that it took me so long to notice."

Those pesky butterflies were back. She wet her lips, trying her best not to pay attention to them. "Well, maybe it was a good thing."

He frowned. "How so?"

Sam scanned the area around them, realizing that other couples had joined them on the dance floor. "I wouldn't change our past. You and Jeff annoyed me, but you are also the core of some of my favorite memories." She smiled. "Remember that summer you got that basketball hoop and you spent hours teaching me how to shoot the perfect three-pointers?"

"*Hours,*" he groaned. "Are you still horrible at basketball?"

"Hey now, sorry I'm not *six-foot-three.*"

"I wasn't that tall when I was twelve, Samantha." He smirked and stood up straight. "Glad to know you remember my height, though."

She shook her head and smiled up at him. "If things were weird between us back then, then I'm not sure we would have all of those special memories."

"I get that."

"And I want us to keep having those moments." She wet her lips. "I don't...I don't want things to go sour between you and Jeff again."

His eyes shifted to the wall behind her. "Right. Neither do I."

They swayed for a few more moments.

Nico relaxed his shoulders and looked back down at her. "But tonight?"

"What about tonight?"

He smirked, then kissed her shoulder. "Tonight, Sammy girl, you're mine."

She bit her lip. "Oh yeah?" She read the watch on Nico's wrist. Ten thirty. "If that's the case, what shall we do with the little time we have left?"

He hummed, pursing his lips. "How keen are you on seeing Kendrick?"

"If I don't get a video—"

"Right, but if I got Jeremy to send me something... Would you be upset if we left?"

She smiled. "Not at all."

"Good." He stepped away from her, keeping their hands clamped. "Then let's go."

Chapter 13

THE PARTY WAS ALMOST OVER, but Nico did not want the night to end. By the time they left the Glasshouse, they had sixty minutes until midnight, when his fantasy would transform from the most magical night of his life back into a pumpkin, and he wanted to live in this storybook tale a little while longer.

"Where are we going?" Sam demanded.

He guided them down 50th Street, past the crowds spilling out of Broadway shows and the yellow cabs jam-packed into the tiny side streets, the honking horns and yelling voices a constant chorus over the distant holiday music echoing from Times Square.

"I did not wear the right shoes for this," she grumbled.

Nico turned and dipped low, then scooped a hand underneath Sam's knees and lifted her up. She squealed and fastened her arms around his neck as he weaved through the tourists toward the 50th Street station for the 1 line.

"Are you really going to carry me all the way onto the subway?" she asked as he took the stairs down.

"I did promise no sprained ankles," he stated. "And we're not getting on the subway."

She turned to him, her face pinched with confusion. *So damn cute.* "And yet we're currently heading into the station?"

Nico grinned as he pushed past the turnstiles, then veered sharply toward another set of steps. Deep, thumping music came from a door perched open, leading into a dark room backlit by red lights and illuminated by a disco ball that slowly circled at the ceiling.

He placed Sam down, holding her steady, then asked the bouncer if he had room for two.

The man sighed and looked back. "We *technically* don't have any more tables."

"No need for a table," Nico insisted. "Just a couple drinks."

The bouncer looked at Sam, his eyes scanning her silhouette. She seemed unaware of the interaction as she bounced on her tiptoes to get a closer look inside the bar. Nico felt the violent urge to punch the man, but instead, wrapped a hand around Sam's waist.

He sighed, then waved a hand. "Fine. Don't cause any trouble or I will kick you out."

"Noted," Nico deadpanned, and shuffled Sam inside. "Thank you."

The place was packed, but not with the usual tourists who swarmed the Times Square area. Instead, it was a mix of true New Yorkers. Local Manhattanites cramped in tight circles, still in their work attire or dressed in going-out outfits, ready for a long night ahead. Couples danced at the center, bodies pressed tight, some with locked lips.

Magic.

"You would know about a hidden bar in the subway,"

Sam commented, flipping an abandoned menu perched on the ledge beside a table. The name of the bar—Nothing Really Matters—was printed in discreet letters at the top.

He ran a hand down her arm. "Martini?"

"*Hmmm.*" She scanned the menu. "I'm kind of in the mood for something different."

"Oh yeah? Like what?"

Sam scanned the room, taking in the scene bursting with energy. She removed her coat and draped it over a chair. "I'm in the mood to dance."

The tempo of his heart picked up speed. "Nothing to drink?"

She tipped her head at the bar. "You pick something and I'll sip on it with you."

He nodded and turned from her, biting his bottom lip as he approached the bar. "Manhattan," he told the bartender.

Sam hugged his torso from behind as he watched his drink being made.

This can't be it, he thought to himself. He kept his eyes trained forward, afraid to face Sam and show her all the emotions he wore too easily on his sleeve. *How can this possibly be all we get?*

The bartender dropped a bright red cherry in the glass, then slid it over to Nico. He felt Sam loosen her grip, then she slipped a bright blue card across the counter.

Nico reached into his pocket. "Samantha, no."

"*Yes*," she insisted. "Please, Nico. Let me treat you."

He glared and picked up the drink. "You better drink half of this then."

Sam plucked the glass out of Nico's hand and took a long sip, keeping her eyes on him. She smacked her lips. "See? Now stop feeling so bad."

He shook his head, taking a sip of his own, keenly aware of the stain her lipstick left on the rim.

Sam stepped closer and unhooked Nico's bow tie. His eyes darted across her face, unable to speak as she adjusted it to hang loose around his neck. It was like he was under some kind of spell, one that only Sam knew how to cast.

She tugged on the lapels of his jacket. "Dance with me?"

"Always."

He followed her, watching as she maneuvered them to the middle of the dance floor, perfectly hidden among bodies of people they didn't know. Perfectly hidden from the rest of their world.

She slid her hands up, up, up, until they hooked around his neck.

"When did you get so suave, Sammy girl?" Nico asked, his free hand finding her waist.

She smiled and twirled a finger around the hair at his nape. "Probably that night, long ago, when I realized what I was capable of."

He quirked a brow. "So...you're this way because of *me*?" He grinned, half-lidded eyes dipping down to her lips "Not surprised."

She scoffed. "Cocky."

He chuckled. He traced the tip of his fingers up her bare spine, feeling the gooseflesh on her skin as he made a slow trail up, then back down.

She swayed, and he followed. She was so close, her legs slotted between his as they moved to the bass reverberating from the speakers. He took a sip of his drink, then, feeling bold, he held it up to her. She pressed her lips to the glass and he poured the liquid into her mouth, a red hue glowing on her skin from the low lights of the bar. His pants grew tight, but how could he be expected to control himself around her? With that dress and those lips, and the way she licked them when she polished off the rest of his drink... Eventually his boner was pressed tight against Sam's stomach, and the way she *didn't* back away made it clear she didn't mind.

Nico kept one hand tight around Sam's waist as he abandoned his empty glass on a nearby high-top, checking the time on his watch as he went. Instant regret flowed through him. It was 11:55. They had five minutes, and then it was time to call it a night. Back to friends. Back to not being able to touch her or feel her body pressed against his, letting all of his fantasies run wild in a dark bar tucked away in a subway station.

"Samantha, I have another rule I would like to propose."

Nico noticed the way Sam's eyes drooped low, down to his lips. "What's the rule?" she murmured.

"Let's extend this. Let's keep doing...whatever this is, until we go home from the holidays. Then we'll call it quits."

She pressed her lips together tight, then shook her head. "No."

His heart fell into his stomach. "Wh-what?"

"No. I deny your rule."

His mouth fell open, then he snapped it shut. "*This* is what you'll deny?" He dropped his hands. "Am I...Am I crazy right now? For thinking that we should keep going? For feeling the way I'm feeling?"

Her honey-green eyes locked with his. "What are you feeling?"

He hesitated, then reached for her neck, cradling the back of her head with both hands. "That none of this feels fake, baby girl. That this entire time, when we said we were doing all of this for show…That none of it felt like a show to me. That every moment of it felt real."

She closed her eyes.

"You can't tell me you don't feel it too, Sam. There's this…*buzzing* between you and me, and it's hard to deny. Nothing in my life has felt like this. No one has ever made me feel like this."

Sam exhaled.

"I know Jeff wants us to be friends but *god*," he growled. "I can't be friends with you anymore. I can't go back. *Yes*, I want special moments, but I want them to look differently this time. I want *you*, in all the ways a man wants someone."

Eventually, Sam blinked her eyes open. "Nico."

He swallowed. "Yes?"

"I denied the rule because, at midnight, our agreement will end and all of our other rules will be gone."

"R-right. But I think we should—"

She smirked at him. "You're not listening to what I'm saying. All of our other rules *will be gone*."

He held his breath, then it hit him. *All our other rules will be gone.*

Nico checked his watch. 11:59.

He grinned, then brought her face close to his. Foreheads sealed, noses brushing. "Are you sure about this?"

She exhaled, a low hum escaping her throat.

"Sam, I'm going to need you to answer, because in thirty seconds, I am going to ruin everything again."

Her hands found his waist, her breath warm against his skin, the smell of coconut, vanilla, and her sweat more intoxicating than the booze coursing through his veins.

"Ruin it," she pleaded.

He didn't bother checking the time, because Nico didn't want to waste any more of it. He pulled her mouth to his, crashing his lips against hers. They were as soft as he remembered, but this time, Sam was confident as she kissed him back. She was the one to open her mouth and slip a tongue into his mouth. She was the one to bite his bottom lip before plunging back in, her hips grinding against his as she pushed herself closer and closer to him. He was consumed by her, the room a blur of music and clinking glasses and loud voices and many other things that didn't matter except Sam's lips on his and the dips of her curves in his hands.

She broke away, then slowly dragged her lips down his chin and neck, nipping at his earlobe.

He groaned. "Samantha, I would prefer not to destroy these suit pants."

She stopped, a giggle escaping her lips. Her cheeks flushed as she examined his throat, then backed away from him, heading for the bar.

He reached for her. "Hey, I didn't say *stop*," he teased.

She returned with a stack of clean, black napkins, then wiped at his face and neck. "I may have left my mark."

"In more ways than one."

She ducked her chin, then wrapped her arms around his shoulders. "What now?" she whispered.

He pressed another kiss to her lips. Because he could. Because she was letting him. "Now, we leave."

She pouted. "Already? We only just got started."

He shook his head, his smile probably way too dorky to seem cool. He didn't care. "We leave and I'll take you home, but we're not going to do anything. Not until we talk things out."

Her pout deepened as she stared at his lips. No denying it now. Nico knew what she wanted. "Then let's talk. Right now."

"You're killing me, baby girl," he groaned, slipping his hands down her back and tucking them into the silky fabric, right above her ass. "I think we should be sober for this conversation, don't you?"

She flushed and whispered, "Okay."

"Hey." He dropped three quick, soft kisses on her lips. "We'll figure it all out. I'm not going anywhere, okay?"

She hesitated, then nodded. "Okay," she repeated.

He gripped the back of her neck, tilting her face up, making sure she was looking directly at him when he spoke. "I want this. I've *always* wanted this. I have wanted this since the day I asked you to go to this dumb party with me. I honestly used it as an excuse, to finally have my chance with you."

She traced a finger down his cheek, then brushed a thumb across his lips. "I think...I think maybe I asked you to also go to my party because..." She trailed off. Nico saw the way she swallowed, the words stuck somewhere between that gorgeous throat and the brain likely telling her to retreat. To not say it.

They were already so close, bodies pressed together, but still he pulled her in, making sure his lips brushed against hers when he said "Tell me. Whatever it was you were about to say. Say it."

"Because I want this too," she admitted.

He grinned, then pressed in, this time taking his time as his lips rolled against hers, keeping a firm grip as her body went soft, reminding himself over and over that this was real. *This is real. This is real. This is real.* That in the end, his perfect night wouldn't disappear, and the pumpkin would never show.

Chapter 14

"Leaving" became a rather loose term, since their process of getting to their respective homes was a deliciously long, dragged-out process thanks to Nico's insistence on kissing Sam at every corner they turned. He kissed her as they walked out the bar, then molded his body against hers as they squeezed through the turnstile of the subway together, then kissed her up against the tiled wall on the platform. On the train, their mouths locked as they zipped northward, New Yorkers around them not seeming to mind. Just another couple kissing on a late Friday night, none of them aware of what was truly happening. That after all this time, Sam had Nico in the ways she wanted, even if she'd tried convincing herself otherwise over the years.

Eventually, when they came up for air somewhere between the Natural History Museum and Morningside Heights, they realized they had no reason to be on the 1 train, since neither of them lived off of this line. So they exited at 103rd Street and got in a cab.

Nico curled an arm around her frame, a hand firmly gripping her thigh as he pulled her *closer and closer*. Like he was holding on for dear life. Like at any moment, she might disappear.

She kissed his nose. "Nico. I'm not going anywhere."

He huffed a laugh. "I know. I'm just...still in shock."

"I get it. I'm a pretty *unbelievable* woman."

"You have no idea."

She laughed out loud, the cab turning at the corner at 3rd Avenue and 82nd Street, then rolling to a stop in front of Sam's apartment building.

She pressed a hand to his cheek. "Thanks for a fun night."

He looked at her like she might have slapped him in the face. "Do you seriously think I'm not going to walk you to your door?"

"But the meter is still on for the cab—"

"Sammy girl, seriously. I do not care." He told the cabbie he would be right back, then opened the door and hopped out. He held his hands out to her. "Come on."

She obliged, letting Nico pull her to the sidewalk, then letting him kiss her deeply before closing the door and walking her up the stairs, one hand on her back, the other threaded with hers.

When they reached the top of the stoop, he tucked her into the small alcove next to her front door and trailed kisses down her cheek and neck. "I don't think I'll ever get sick of this."

"Kissing me in the freezing cold?" she teased.

"Kissing you *anywhere*."

She giggled as Nico came up for air.

He pressed his thumbs into the dip at her hips. "So. Here's what's going to happen."

She licked her lips. "Tell me."

He smiled and kissed her gently before continuing.

"You're going to go upstairs, and you're not going to overthink any of this."

She felt her body go cold, reality slowly slipping in.

He shook his head. "No. Don't do it. You're going to sleep and you'll probably dream about me because who wouldn't."

She rolled her eyes. "*Cocky*."

He grinned. "Then you'll text me when you're up, and we'll set a time to chat tomorrow. Because the last thing I will do is go another four years without you. We make this work. No matter what."

She bit her bottom lip, staring at the dimples on Nico's cheeks instead of looking him in the eyes. It all seemed… nice. Like they could actually make it work. That somehow this little fantasy they were living in could be a reality, that things with Jeff would be okay and they could all be happy and move on. *Happy.*

But would she really be happy if she knew she'd broken her brother's promise?

"*Sam.*"

She blinked up at him.

"Don't. Please. We'll figure it out."

She sighed, then nodded. "I'll text you tomorrow."

"You better," he growled. Then he devoured her mouth again before backing away with a wink and getting back in the cab, leaving her breathless and a little too hot for such a cold December night.

Nico stepped into Phebe's at noon the next day, feeling on top of the world, despite his complete lack of sleep. It was hard to snooze when *reality* felt like a dream. He replayed moments with Sam over and over in his head, and eventually saw it was three o'clock in the morning before he forced himself to get some sleep, pushing thoughts of Sam and all the little sounds she made kissing him out of his mind. He had to count sheep to finally get her out of his head. *Count sheep.*

He was like a lovesick teenager. Or something far worse.

Corinne jumped out of her seat at the booth, arms wide. "The man of the hour."

Nico grinned, tucking a hand to his stomach and bowing low.

She cheered as he made his way to the booth and slid in next to Leon.

"Now that's uncalled for," Leon pointed out, eyes narrowed. "I relayed my crazy night and you say *he's* the man of the hour?"

"We're here to debrief his night, not yours," Corinne answered.

"His date was fake! Mine wasn't!"

A waitress came to the table, unfazed by Corinne and Leon's bickering as she poured Nico a cup of coffee and took his brunch order.

Emory held up his mug. "Cheers."

Nico did the same, the two clinking mugs in silence as their friends rattled on.

Corinne held up a hand to shut Leon up, settling her attention back on Nico. "So. Details, Nicolas. *Details.*"

He smirked and leaned back in the booth, taking another silent sip of coffee.

Leon's jaw dropped. "Oh my god. You got *laid.*"

Nico coughed, spits of coffee landing on their table. He wiped at the dribbles on his chin with the sleeve of his black hoodie. "*No.* I did not get laid. Jesus."

Leon sank half an inch in his seat. "Damn."

"Did *you* get laid?" Nico teased.

Leon pepped right back up. "Oh, dude. I met this *insane* girl on the apps last night. And I think I'm in love."

Now Nico was the one with a jaw open, staring at his friend as he laughed out loud.

Corinne snapped her fingers. "Nico, *focus*. We're not done having this discussion."

"But Lee says *he's in love*," Nico replied. "I don't know, this sounds pretty serious."

"He falls in love every week," Emory bantered.

Leon pointed at Emory. "Okay, smart-ass. That might be true. But this one is *different*."

The waitress arrived with a tray of their food—eggs benedicts and omelets and waffles.

Corrine held up a finger. "No. They do not get to eat until this one"—she pointed to Nico—"finishes telling us about his night."

Leon pouted. "But *Mommmm*."

The waitress looked confused, eyes darting across the table.

Nico shook his head. "Don't make her do that, you know that's annoying." He gestured for the waitress to place their food on the table. "I'll talk while you eat."

"Fine," Corinne said through gritted teeth.

Once the plates were on the table and Leon's mouth was stuffed with a sufficient amount of waffle, Nico finally told them the story, starting with that summer night four years ago. Then the blow-up fight he had with his best friend, and how he hadn't spoken to either of the Carter siblings until recently.

"Jeff and I have been talking for about a year now, and we're working on being friends. But seeing Sam recently..."

He blew a raspberry. "It brought up all of these old feelings, and I realized...maybe the feelings were never really old. Maybe I've always felt this way and I got good at stifling them all these years."

"Wow," Emory replied.

Corinne wiped her hands with her napkin and picked up her mug. "Fast forward to now, and your horrible friends decide to make matters worse for you and push you to fake date the woman that you've been holding a torch for all these years."

Nico shrugged. "It's not like it took much convincing."

She pursed her lips, her mouth twisting in concentration.

"So how was the fake date?" Emory asked.

"Technically it was our second fake date."

"*Second* fake date?" Corinne squealed. "What are we, chopped liver? When was the *first* date?"

Nico took a bite of his omelet, then told them all about their "fake date for a fake date" arrangement.

"We decided to go all in with the ruse," he finished. "Play it out like boyfriend and girlfriend for ten days. It was supposed to wrap up last night, after the OmniCorp party."

"How'd that go, by the way?" Emory asked.

Nico shrugged. He liked Emory and the care he had for the three of them, how he always knew the right questions to ask, to follow up on the hard things and listen with care. He could see why Corinne was so into him. It reminded him a little bit of Jeff and the way his best friend cared for him too.

Jeff.

He immediately pushed the thought aside. *Not now.* He needed to wait to talk to Sam.

Nico instinctively checked his phone. No text from her

yet. He hoped she was merely sleeping in, and not ignoring him. Because if she was ignoring him, he didn't have any qualms about taking the train up to 82nd Street and buzzing her apartment until she couldn't ignore him anymore.

"Don't change the subject, we're not done here," Corinne reminded him. "Okay, so you've been fake dating your unrequited love and last night was the finale, and you come in here...smiling? I'm lost."

Nico grinned, then rubbed at his face, hoping to hide it.

"Oh, it ain't fake anymore." Leon pointed a syrup-covered fork at Nico. "This mo-fo sealed the deal for once in his goddamn life."

He merely took a sip of his coffee, letting the silence speak for itself.

Leon cheered, then high-fived Emory from across the booth.

Corinne crossed her arms. "This feels like a bad idea."

His face fell. "How so?"

"Well, for one, you just mended your relationship with your best friend, who is clearly adamant about you *not* being with his sister."

"That was a long time ago, Corinne."

"Four years isn't *that* long. Do you really think he would be okay with it now? Do you have any idea *why* he reacted that way in the first place?"

He hesitated, unsure how to respond. In truth, he *didn't* know why Jeff had reacted the way he did all those years ago, and it still bothered him that they'd never properly talked it out. For the longest time, Nico blamed himself for everything that happened. Yet now, as he looked at the situation from a whole new angle, that persistent question of *why* kept coming up. Why was Jeff so adamantly against them then? Would he still feel the same way now? And why hadn't they truly talked about it yet?

Nico rubbed at his chest, like he could rub off the realization that maybe his disappointment toward the situation had nothing to do with *his* ruining the friendship by kissing Sam, but everything to do with the fact that maybe it was his best friend who'd actually been crappy to him.

Emory reached across the table and patted Nico's hand. "Dude. You're spiraling."

Nico hung his head. "Yeah. I think I am."

Leon flipped Corinne off. "You're ruining Nico's fun, Corinne. Let the man get laid."

"Oh, I don't think *that* will be a problem." She picked up her fork. "I just don't want his heart to be broken if things fall apart again."

His phone buzzed on the table.

Thankful for the distraction, Nico snatched it and flipped it over, finding a text from Sam on his screen.

It was a GIF of a kitten, looking grumpy with slitted morning eyes and crazy ruffled hair. Like it woke up from a nap that should have lasted a little longer.

"Dude, do you *see* that smile?" Leon pressed a finger into Nico's dimple. "This man is smitten."

"Maybe a little," he admitted as he typed a message to her.

NICO

I take it the sleep in wasn't effective?

SAM

Pounding head.

Need grease.

NICO

Uh oh. Is someone hungover?

SAM

Stop.

He chuckled, then motioned for the waitress to return to their table.

Leon held his chest like a scandalized Regency-era woman. "Is Nicolas Giuliano about to ditch us and *finally get laid?*"

When the waitress arrived at the table, Nico ordered a coffee and a bacon, egg, and cheese sandwich to go.

"Oh, *definitely* getting laid," Leon hollered, causing a few heads to turn in their direction.

"She's hungover. I'm not pushing for anything until she's ready," he replied, polishing off his breakfast as he waited for his second order.

Emory's mouth fell open. He covered it with his hand, looking rather bemused as he turned to face Corinne, then tilted his head in a *Stop being boring and have fun with us* kind of way.

She sighed and placed her hands on the table, like they were in an important meeting. "So, when do we get to meet her?"

Chapter 15

SAM BURROWED DEEPER into the mountain of blankets on her bed. The apartment was freezing with the window open, but it was a necessity unless she and Yumi wanted to be thoroughly roasted in their four-floor walk-up shoebox of an apartment. They didn't have any control of the radiator temperature, which constantly blew hot air into the apartment and gave them no option but to leave all of their windows wide open in the winter—including the window right above Sam's bed. It sat in the middle of their living room, divided by an ugly lime green partition they found on sale at the antique shop down the street. She twisted her head to get a look at the stack of books she used as a nightstand, hoping she was smart enough to at least put a glass of water there before she stripped off her dress and fell into her bed last night. She was not.

She groaned, throwing her blanket over head, the light through her white duvet too bright to block out the sun and dull down her pounding headache. Her nose was cold from a sharp crispness in the air that felt like the promise of snow.

A knock sounded at her door.

"*Go away*," Sam said, her voice groggy, a pitiful attempt at trying to get whoever was there to get lost. Probably someone from the new Chinese restaurant down the street, who somehow always got in the building and kept slipping menus underneath their door.

A deep voice rumbled from the other side of the door. "Let me in, Sammy girl."

Her eyes blew wide at the sound of his voice. She stood up swiftly, the motion making her feel dizzy and a little bit sick. She groaned and wrapped herself up in her duvet, then pushed the partition aside and shuffled to the entrance.

She cracked open the door, finding a bushy-tailed Nico on the other side. His black hoodie and Carhartt jacket were dusted with white flurries, a few stuck in his ruffled mop of hair. Somehow, even dressed down in a hoodie and a pair of charcoal-gray joggers, Nico looked *hot*.

Sam wrapped the duvet tighter around her frame, aware that she was still in only her underwear. "What are you doing here?"

Nico held up a brown bag. "Grease. As requested."

She squinted at the bag. "And coffee?"

He held up his other hand, revealing a large black cup and a dangling plastic bag at his fingers. "And painkillers."

She hummed.

He tipped his head. "Is Yumi here?"

She shook her head. "She texted me twenty minutes ago and said she was meeting up with some guy."

He smirked, then raised a brow. "So...does that mean you're going to let me in?"

"I think I like this view. Let's stand here for a while."

"*Samantha*."

She growled. "Fine."

Sam swung the door, but kept a firm grip on the knob as

Nico stepped in. She shuffled and closed it behind him, aware of the way Nico eyed her appearance.

She blushed. "Can you, um, turn around or something for a moment?"

He grinned and followed her orders, placing the coffee and bags on the vinyl-wrapped counter, then shrugged off his coat.

Sam threw her duvet to her bed, then snatched a large T-shirt and checkered sleep shorts from her dresser before slipping them on. She turned in Nico's direction, noticing how he kept his back to her as he sneaked a sip of her coffee.

"So...what's in the brown bag?"

Nico turned his head, a teasing smirk on his face. "Am I allowed to look now?"

She crossed her arms. "Only if you give me what's in the bag."

He chuckled and pulled out a sandwich. Steam swirled from the top as he unwrapped the aluminum foil, then held it out to her.

She shuffled up close and peered down at the bacon, egg, and cheese. Her stomach growled, but her pounding head made her groan. "Oh god," she breathed. "How can something smell so good but also make me feel so sick?"

He placed the sandwich down and took both of her shoulders. "You okay? I didn't realize you drank so much last night."

She scratched her head. "I don't drink much. Like, ever," she murmured.

Nico hesitated, then brushed a hair from her face and tipped her chin up in his direction. "Did it, um...do you remember—"

She gently squeezed his wrist. "Nico, I remember it all."

His shoulders relaxed. He spun her slowly and moved

her back in the direction of her bed. "Okay, good. Now get back under the covers."

"But, food—"

"I'll take care of it, baby girl."

Nico helped her as she crawled back under the covers, then moments later, returned with a plate and a glass of water.

He dropped medicine into her hand. "Take this, then eat."

"Okay," she whispered, watching as he left her. "Wait, where are you going?"

"Nowhere. I'm staying right here."

She melted into her sheets, then did as Nico said, swallowing the medicine with two large gulps of water. As she took a bite of her sandwich, grease dribbling down her chin, Nico returned with her cup of coffee and a stack of paper napkins.

He set the cup on her books, then leaned in, wiping the grease on her face. "Make room for me," he whispered.

She balanced her plate on the windowsill, then held up the duvet without hesitation.

Nico smiled and climbed in. She tucked the duvet around him as he placed his hands on her waist and pulled her close, her butt practically in his lap. He kissed her neck, then reached for the plate and handed it back to her.

From the moment Nico had stepped into her apartment to the effortless way he'd crawled into bed and wrapped his arms around her, every single movement between the two of them felt natural. There wasn't any early relationship awkwardness between them. They moved seamlessly around one another, a kind of comfortability you really could only get with time and history. Sam supposed that, with Nico, she *did* have history—years of growing up beside him. She watched all the phases of Nicolas Giuliano over the years. They didn't need time to move in the ways they already did with one another. They already had it.

She polished off her sandwich, then wiped her hands with a clean napkin. "Thank you," she said, finishing her bite.

He dropped the strand of her hair he was playing with and kissed her temple. "You're welcome. Technically it's my fault you're in this state."

"Yeah, it's all your fault, how dare you do this to me," she teased. She rolled over and placed the plate with left-over crumbs down on the floor. Nico took that as an opportunity to wrap an arm around her waist and seal her to his chest. She flattened her hands on his sweatshirt and propped her chin on her knuckles.

He went back to playing with her hair, twirling a strand around his ring finger. "No regrets?"

She shook her head. "None."

"Good."

They remained there for a few moments in silence; Sam lightly tapping the pads of her fingers against his chest, Nico twirling her hair. Even if things felt familiar between the two of them, unspoken words still hung stale in the air. She knew the sandwich and the coffee and the medication weren't the only reasons for Nico's surprise visit to her apartment.

We don't do anything else, he'd said last night. *Not until we talk this out.*

But the hurdle, it seemed, was too high of a jump. Or at least initially. The two of them remained content, keeping each other warm under her duvet.

Nico cleared his throat. "Yesterday, at the party, you told me you needed my professional opinion on something."

She sucked in her lips and closed her eyes. After everything that happened in the last twelve hours, she'd completely forgotten about *Nourished* and her meeting with Barbara on Monday. She needed to update her résumé and maybe go over her reports, or at least have *something* prepared to talk about, even if she had no idea what their conversation would be like.

And then there was Yumi. When Sam got home last night, she was still out with whomever her latest victim was from the apps, and she'd already left by the time she woke up.

Sam tugged on his sweatshirt string. "Barbara had to let my editor go this week. No one really knows why, but she held an emergency staff meeting at the end of the day yesterday to let us know she would be interviewing internally and promoting someone for the position as soon as possible."

Nico's brows raised.

"Before I left to get ready for the party, I saw she emailed me and told me that I should brush up my résumé for my interview on Monday at noon."

"Holy crap, Sam," Nico replied.

She grimaced, which made him frown.

"Are you not happy about it?" he asked.

"I'm...*ugh* I don't know." She pulled herself away from him and sat up. "Doesn't it feel weird though? To be promoted to such a huge position less than a year into my time working there?"

"Not if you've proven that you can do the job," he answered confidently. "Which, it seems you have."

She shook her head. "But I don't know if I'm right for the role, I mean it just...*feels* weird."

"Does it feel weird because you think you can't do it, or because you're afraid of what other people will think?"

She bit her lip.

He sat up and placed his hands at her hips. "Whose opinion are you afraid of?"

She sighed. "I'm not afraid of opinions. But I *am* afraid of becoming someone's boss. Someone who's been in the same position as me for a little while now. Someone who..." She turned her head to the designated bedroom space in the studio, separated by a curtain. "Who I kind of live with?"

She turned to face Nico. A crease formed between his brows. She traced a finger down the line, smoothing it out. "What was it like for you? When they promoted you so young at OmniCorp?"

He sighed. "Odd. I feel like an imposter all the time."

"But you're good at your job?"

He sighed again, then nodded. "Yeah, I guess you could say that."

"So you're not really an imposter."

"And you won't be either."

She pursed her lips and turned back to the curtain and the unmade bed she knew was behind it.

"Is she going to interview as well?" Nico asked.

Sam shrugged. "I don't know. I'm not sure if she also got an email. I tried to bring it up last night, but she quickly changed the subject to eyeshadow and perfume. She seemed way more excited about getting me ready than the possibility of a promotion."

"Sam."

She flicked his ear.

He trapped her hand, then threaded their fingers. "I don't think this should be a reason not to take the job if you get it."

"But what if it ruins our dynamic? What then?"

"Then the two of you will figure it out." He tilted his head. "Have a little faith in yourself. Your boss clearly thinks you're capable enough to handle this, and I think you need to let yourself believe the same."

She exhaled. Her phone buzzed on her makeshift nightstand. She reached for it, then realized it was a call from Jeff.

Her eyes widened as she flipped the screen to show Nico. When he read the name on the screen, he frowned.

"Do I ignore it?" she asked.

He shook his head. "You know your brother. He'll keep calling until you pick up."

She groaned. "Do not make a *single* sound."

He used his fingers to zip his lips.

She swiped it open to answer the call. "Hi, Jeff."

"*Sammy!*"

She slammed her eyes shut. "Please with the loud noises. I'm nursing a pretty awful hangover."

Nico chuckled silently. She glared at him and covered his mouth. *Do not make a sound,* she mouthed.

She could feel his grin inside her palm.

"Hungover? Oh my god, were you on a date last night?" Jeff squealed. "I want to hear *everything*. Did you finally do the deed?"

"*No,*" she quickly replied. The last thing she wanted was to talk about her lack of "doing the deed" with her brother, while sitting in Nico's lap. "Holiday party."

"*Ah,* well that will do it, I guess." He laughed. "Aww, Sam. Electrolytes and chocolate chip pancakes are the cure."

"Noted."

Nico kissed the inside of her hand. She attempted to

pull away, but he caught her wrist, then kissed the top of her hand and up her arm. She held her breath, afraid of making any kind of noise as Jeff rattled on.

"Okay, I won't keep you long then, since clearly you're a grumpy shit and dying right now," he said. "But I wanted to confirm that you're coming home for Christmas?"

Nico wrapped his arms around Sam's waist, his kisses trailing up her shoulder and to her neck.

She coughed in an attempt to make him stop. She felt his lips form a grin on her skin.

"Why would I not be home for Christmas?" Sam replied.

"I figured, but just had to make sure," Jeff answered. "And what day are you getting home?"

Nico's tongue made contact with her skin, drawing small circles above her collarbone. She leaned her head back, forgetting everything except for the way he tasted her.

"Sam?" Jeff asked.

"Um." She tried wiggling free of his grasp. Nico's laugh was silent, his chest rumbling against hers before he leaned back on the bed, hands on her thighs. He looked deliciously ruffled, the hood of his sweatshirt askew, his hair sticking up on the left side.

Sam cleared her throat and looked away. *Focus.* "I'm not sure which day yet. I may have this thing happening at work—"

"*Booo*, work. You sound like Nico."

She bit her lip. "Is that a bad thing?"

"It is if you won't be home for the holidays." Jeff dropped his voice to a softer decibel. "Especially *this* holiday."

Sam hesitated. *What does that mean?*

"Just promise me you'll be home for our Christmas Eve dinner," Jeff continued.

Sam focused on the feel of Nico's hands as they leisurely ran up and down her thighs. *I'm not very good at keeping promises.*

"I promise," she whispered. At least she could keep this one. It wouldn't be so hard.

Jeff cheered, then said he had to go and quickly hung up.

Sam stared at the screen for a moment, then dropped her phone in her lap and looked at Nico.

Nico opened his mouth like he was about to say something, but his phone rang in his pocket. He looked confused as he grabbed it, then rolled his eyes when he saw who it was calling him. He turned his phone to face Sam.

Jeff.

Sam's mouth fell open as Nico answered. "Hello?"

She crossed her arms and remained still and silent.

"Hey, man, yeah, doing good." He listened, then laughed, a brow raised. "She was hungover, huh? That's hilarious. I didn't think I would ever see the day."

She slapped his arm. Nico snatched the front of her shirt and pulled her to him, smashing his mouth against hers. She could hear Jeff, the phone so close to their mouths and ears. Nico kept quiet as he slipped a tongue between her lips.

She pushed up and away from him, noticing the way he frowned when she created distance.

Then his attention moved elsewhere, his frown deepening as he listened to Jeff. "Dude, I already told you, I'm not sure if I can—" He stopped as Jeff talked over him. Sam couldn't get every word, but she got the gist. He wanted Nico at their annual Christmas Eve dinner, along with his moms. *Just like old times,* she heard. *It will mean a lot to me. Please be there.*

Nico looked at Sam. "Yeah, of course, man, I'll make it work."

More cheering on Jeff's end, then a quick *can't wait to see you* before he hung up.

He looked at his screen, then placed his phone on Sam's books. "Enough of that."

Sam pulled on the strings of his hoodie gently. "What do you think that was about?"

Nico sat up. "Well, let's think. He told me that Daniel would be there."

"I assumed as much," she replied.

"And he really...*really* wants us all to be there."

Sam tilted her head, then it hit her. "Oh my...do you think he's going to propose?"

Nico's smile was shy, and if she wasn't mistaken, a little sad. "Yeah. I do."

Sam covered her mouth. "That's—well, that's—" She wasn't sure what to say. "I don't really have the words."

"They seem to make each other really happy," he reassured her.

"Yes, of course, it's clear they're meant to be." She rubbed her face. "I just don't know what to say. About this." She pointed between her and Nico. "What do we do?"

He traced a knuckle down her cheek. "I want to tell everyone that you're mine."

"*Nico.*"

"I know, I know." He cupped her face. "You're going to tell me we have to keep this a secret a little while longer, aren't you?"

Her chest sank, because even if she didn't want to admit it, he was right. If her brother was planning on proposing, the last thing she wanted to do was ruin his moment. Especially when she had no idea how he would react this time around. Would he be over what happened in the past? Would he be happy for them?

"Maybe until after the holidays," she whispered. "We'll tell him after, when there's time and space for him to cool off."

Nico's brow furrowed. "Do you really think he's going to be that mad?"

"I don't know how he's going to be," she replied. "But I can't help assuming the worst."

Nico's exhale was long, deep, and sounded a little frustrated. "Okay," he relented. "I'll wait. Although I'm not sure how I'll manage being so close to you without being able to touch you like this."

She rolled her eyes. "You'll survive."

He shook his head. "No. I don't think I will."

Chapter 16

THE APARTMENT DOOR shut with a slam.

Sam blinked her eyes open, noticing her home was blanketed in darkness, except for the soft glow coming from the city lights through the window and her laptop screen propped up at the edge of her bed, still playing the last few minutes of *The Holiday*.

A heavy arm was slung around her stomach, a nose pressed into her neck. Nico's breathing was warm and heavy. He was fast asleep.

"Oh my god, Samantha Carter, do we have so much to talk about," Yumi chimed from the other side of the partition. "You are not going to *believe* my last forty-eight hours. I splurged on some two-buck chuck for the occasion because this discussion requires *wine*."

Before Sam could comprehend what was happening, Yumi was pushing back the partition. "I even have Mister McStuffin, because he is *keen* to find out about—" She stopped when she took in the sight before her. "Oh...*oh my god*."

Sam gave her a shy smile. "Hi, Yu," she whispered.

Yumi looked at Mister McStuffin, then covered his eyes and turned the stuffed bunny around. "You don't need to see this, little one."

"I think he's seen far worse, given that he now permanently lives in *your* bed."

"Yeah, well, the poor thing is so *bored* in your room." Yumi held out a hand, gesturing to the sleeping body next to Sam. "Samantha, a warning, maybe? Even a *sock* would do."

"We weren't doing anything," Sam whispered.

"Yeah *now*, but who knows what I could have walked in on." She patted the stuffed animal. "Poor Mister McStuffin. I'm sure he's a little traumatized."

"It's okay, we're old buds," Nico mumbled, his lips grazing against her skin as he spoke. "I can't believe you still have that thing."

"Don't you dare make fun of Mister McStuffin," Sam quipped.

"I wouldn't dream of it."

Yumi's eyes blew wide as Nico stretched, then sat up and leaned against the back wall. She patted the stuffed animal like a baby, bouncing him back and forth. "Nico, hello."

Sam saw Nico smile in her periphery. Big. Goofy. Unashamed. "Yumi, hello."

Her friend nodded in response, like it was all very cordial. "I'll just, um, be in my room." Her eyes narrowed. "But hurry up, because I have quite the conundrum, and we have lots to discuss." She waved a hand between her and Nico in the bed. "I mean, clearly."

Nico threw an arm around Sam as Yumi retreated to her side of the studio. "I'll go," he whispered, kissing on the cheek. "I hear there's lots to discuss."

She frowned. "But I like having you here."

"I know." He tipped her chin in his direction and kissed her on the lips. "I'll be back."

"Promise?"

"Always."

They took their time getting out of bed, with slow movements and lingering touches. Eventually Sam shuffled behind Nico as they made their way to the kitchen. When they reached the front door, she threw her arms around his shoulders.

He tucked his hands underneath his black sweatshirt that she'd stolen, his fingers gripping her waist as he pulled her in for a kiss. "You're going to do great on Monday," he whispered.

She tilted her head. "We'll see."

"No, *you'll* see. Remember all that stuff you told me at The Sixtieth? About wanting to work your way up?"

She silently nodded.

"Do you still want that?" he asked.

"Of course I do," she whispered.

"Then go for it. Don't let anything hold you back."

"I'll try," she breathed, aware of Yumi's presence in the apartment. She was currently in the bathroom and likely couldn't hear any of what they were saying, but still.

"Good." Nico dipped his head to kiss her. The kiss was sweet, like honey in iced tea. But it didn't take long for it to progress. Nico's thumbs dipped into the side of her shorts as he pressed her up against the wall.

"*Ahem*, Nico." Yumi interrupted.

Sam detached her mouth from his and pushed him away.

Nico's hands remained firm at her hips. He turned his attention to Yumi. "Yes, Yumi?"

She held out her phone. "Kendrick video, please."

Nico chuckled as he reached for his phone in his pocket, then scrolled through his videos until he found the one he'd saved from Jeremy. He held out his phone to her. "Here, I'll Airdrop it."

Their phones both lit up as the video shared from one phone to the other.

Nico put his jacket on. "You should also have my contact info now. Do me a favor and share your location."

Yumi reared back, spluttering. "Share...my location?"

Nico nodded, his attention back on Sam. "Yeah. I have to make sure my girls are okay."

Sam noticed the way Yumi's mouth fell open, then her friend coughed and left their vicinity.

She crossed her arms. "Protective much?"

He shrugged. "Does that bother you?"

She leaned against the wall. "I feel like it should, but...it doesn't."

Nico placed a hand near her head, bracketing her in. "Do what makes you feel comfortable. I only want to make sure you're safe."

She lifted a brow. "You sure it's not to keep an eye on me?" she teased.

He twirled a piece of her hair between his fingers. "Sam, I don't *need* to keep an eye on you. I trust you completely."

She exhaled. "I trust you too."

Nico grinned as he leaned in and kissed her again. Then his face grew serious. "This week is probably going to be awful for me."

Sam sighed. "I don't know what it's going to look like for me either."

He cupped her neck and angled her face up to his. "We'll figure it out."

She shrugged. "At least we know we'll see each other on Christmas."

Nico's eyes slammed shut. "Yeah. There's that."

She rubbed his arm. "You okay?"

He nodded, then leaned in for a kiss. "Bye, baby girl," he whispered.

She felt her face flush. "Bye."

He kissed her on the lips again, then again. He opened the door and left, but before the door closed all the way, he burst back in and grabbed her face, kissing her long and deep.

"Oh *my god*, Nicolas," Yumi whined behind them. "Let the woman breathe!"

They laughed as Nico kissed her one more time and left, this time closing the door fully behind him.

Sam turned slowly to her friend, expecting her to seem pissed or confused by the whole situation. Instead, Yumi was biting her bottom lip, controlling a huge smile on her face. After a couple of seconds, she screamed with joy.

Thirty minutes later, the two of them sat on opposite ends of the couch, Mister McStuffin in between. The coffee table was covered in heated frozen pizzas and mason jars full of two-buck chuck.

Sam took a careful sip of her very-full jar. "You really went all out tonight," she teased. "Your news must be good."

Yumi smacked her lips after a long sip of her wine, then pointed to Sam. "No, you're deflecting. You first."

She scoffed. "I'm deflecting? Who was the one who

came into the apartment like a wrecking ball and forced my guy to leave?"

Yumi's brow raised. "Your guy, huh?"

Sam dropped her face into her hand. "Ugh. Stop."

"So what does that mean? Like, your *official* boyfriend? Just a holiday fling? The love of your life?"

"I don't even know myself! Stop asking such impossible questions."

Yumi set her glass down and crossed her arms. "Did he tell you what he thinks?"

Sam bit her lip. "He said he wants to tell everyone that I'm his."

Her mouth fell open, then she squealed and fell back on the cushion, kicking her feet in the air.

Sam hugged her knees and leaned against the couch backboard. "I feel like I'm kind of in a daze."

"Tell me every detail. Leave nothing out."

She launched into the story, starting with Nico's nervous glances and touches at the beginning, to the way he'd slipped back into his confidence by the end of the night. She also touched on the weird corporate dynamics at the holiday party, and how they ended up leaving early so they could go to the cocktail bar.

"Wait...so you didn't actually *see* Kendrick?" Yumi asked.

Sam shook her head. "One of Nico's engineers sent that video. We only had ninety minutes left until midnight and we kind of wanted to—"

"Make out with each other's faces?"

Sam hit her with a pillow. "That didn't happen until *after* midnight."

Yumi rolled her eyes. "Oh, come on. By that point it was

clear what was about to happen. I'm honestly not surprised by any of this."

"Really?"

"Samantha, did you see the way his eyeballs almost *fell out of his head* when he saw you in that dress? He looked like a real-life version of that big-eyed monkey meme."

Sam rubbed her neck. "You're being dramatic."

"No, I'm not. Seriously, Sam. If that guy hasn't told you he's in love with you yet, he will soon. It's very...*very* clear."

She bit her lip and glanced out the window, eyeing the trickles of snow still floating down.

Yumi placed a hand on hers and squeezed. "How do *you* feel?"

She closed her eyes. "I feel...I feel..." She sighed. "Happy. And scared. All at the same time. Scared because I don't want to upset Jeff when he and Nico are trying to fix things after I ruined them."

"You didn't ruin them."

"I did. Their friendship falling apart was all my fault."

Yumi tugged on her hand, forcing Sam to look in her direction. "Come on. You know it wasn't you. Sure, that kiss might have been the catalyst for the fight. But based on how we know Jeff felt about Nico...I have a feeling that fight would have eventually happened, just in a different context."

Sam's mouth twisted into a frown. She knew what Yumi was saying made sense. But why couldn't she believe it herself? "Isn't this considered lying?"

Yumi made a *stop being stupid* face. "You haven't even had the opportunity to lie to Jeff. And you said you guys are planning on telling him after the holidays, yes?"

"Yes. That's the plan."

Yumi poked Sam's cheek. "Good. You'll just have to try

and keep your hands off each other for a few days. Can you do that?"

"I can. Him, on the other hand..."

A wide grin spread across Yumi's face. "Oh, he is *so* obsessed with you."

Sam rubbed her forehead, then hugged her legs again and pressed a cheek to her knee.

Yumi's grin slipped into a knowing smile. "Happy, you said?"

Sam smiled back. "Yeah. Really happy."

"Good. I'm so glad this little holiday party ruse finally did what the two of you couldn't so long ago."

"Which is?"

"Bang, obviously?"

Sam chuckled and shook her head. "We haven't done that yet."

"But...will you?"

She felt her face flush.

Yumi squealed.

Sam's chest twisted as she thought through the past two weeks, starting with Nico's attendance at the *Nourished* holiday party. "Yumi, I have something to tell you. About work."

Yumi's face pinched. "Why? Work sucks. Let's not."

"But it's kind of important."

Yumi waved her off. "Not as important as me telling you about *my* insane night."

Sam sighed. "Okay. Okay. But promise me we'll talk about it soon?"

"I promise." She snatched the empty jars. "We'll need more wine for my story."

Sam smiled. "Can't wait."

Yumi shuffled to the kitchen, the *glug, glug, glug* of the

wine being poured into the jar reverberating from the kitchen.

Sam snatched her phone to turn on some holiday music, then noticed she had a text.

It was a selfie of Nico. He was at the holiday market in Bryant Park, a large hot cocoa in his hand, piled high with whipped cream.

NICO

Should I cry all over it?

SAM

I hate you.

I want one.

NICO

It might be cold by the time I deliver it...

SAM

I don't mean now, baby dog.

Take me there? Soon?

NICO

Of course. Anything for you.

Her chest swelled at the sight of his last text. With a smile plastered on her face, Sam opened up Find My Friends, then shared her location.

Yumi shuffled her way back to the couch with jars filled to the brim. "Okay. So I met this guy on the apps, and *oh my god*, wait till I tell you the positions he got me in last night."

Sam laughed out loud as her phone made a *ding*. She glanced at the screen, noticing Nico sent his location as well. She smiled, then shoved her phone in between the couch cushions, giving her friend and what was sure to be an insane story her full attention.

They would talk about work. Soon. Her friendship with Yumi was too important to screw up, and as she listened to her friend talk about meeting who she deemed "the perfect guy," she decided that if this job was going to come between them, she wouldn't do it. Sam felt a desire to climb her way to the top, but backstabbing would never be her way to get there.

Chapter 17

Sam woke up to an abrupt body tackle from Yumi. Her friend scrambled to the window after screaming at Sam to wake up, then opened the panel fully so she could stick her head outside.

Sam tapped Yumi's leg with her toe. "Oh my god, stop that. You're making me nervous."

Yumi folded her legs into a perfect criss-cross sitting position. "Samantha, it's going to snow."

"It's been snowing for *days*, silly."

"No, but like, it's going to *snow*." Yumi lifted her hands up in the air, like a toddler. "*Big* snow. A huge storm is heading this way."

Sam sat up. "How huge?"

Yumi bounced up and down. "Like, they're estimating a foot, maybe more. Sigmond emailed us and said if we wanted to stay home today, we could."

She unplugged her phone and tapped open her email. Sure enough, an email from HR had come through earlier that morning, giving employees the opportunity to work from home. An email from Barbara followed that one, asking Sam if she still was planning on coming in for the interview, or if they should reschedule. *If you decide to come, you're more than welcome to head home right after,* was right there in black and white, above her signoff.

"This is *so great.*" Yumi continued bouncing, and Sam knew that it was too soon for the caffeine from her morning matcha to be kicking in like that. "Let's go to the store and get some provisions. And we could just like, stay in our pajamas all day and put on holiday movies, maybe snag another bottle of wine."

Sam swallowed. "That sounds so fun, Yu, but...I have to go to the office today."

She stopped bouncing. "*No!* Stay. They literally told us we're allowed to."

"I-I have to." She clasped her hands together and squeezed. "I have an interview today."

Her friend blinked once, then twice. "An interview at Sigmond?"

Sam nodded.

Yumi exhaled, then her brow furrowed. "For what position? *Wait,* did Barbara ask you to meet her?"

She hesitated, squeezing her hands tighter as she slowly nodded again.

"*Seriously?* But I thought we hated this job?"

Her eyes widened. "Hated it? Did I ever say that?"

"No, but..." Yumi pinched the bridge of her nose. "Sorry, I assumed we both did."

"You hate it?"

"*Fuck* yes."

"Oh." Sam loosened her death grip. "I didn't know that."

Yumi looked up at Sam. "How could you possibly not know that? I literally complain about it all the time."

"Well, yeah." She bit her bottom lip. "I guess I just thought it was like, part of the job for you, while you secretly wanted to work your way up to an editor."

Yumi waved her arms. "Don't get me wrong, I *do* want to be in editorial. Just not at *Nourished*. I am so sick of working in health content."

"Oh." Sam scratched her temple. "So you're not sad about me interviewing for the job?"

"Literally not at all." Yumi tilted her head. "Though I'm shocked that you would want to. Do you really want to be a nutrition editor? To work under the satanistic demand of search-engine optimization and having to 'hit those numbers' all the time?"

Sam folded her arms in her lap. "I do," she said calmly. "I know there are parts of the job that are not ideal, but I want to at least be high up enough to try and make any changes I can. I have ideas for new systems that could make the magazine money *and* produce good content."

"But I thought you loved to write?"

Sam shrugged. "I do, but...I don't know. Is it weird to say that I think I like this part more? And I'm not gonna lie, Yu. I want to make more money. I can't be eating Trader Joe's salads and frozen pizzas my whole life."

Yumi held her chest in shock. "You mean you don't *love* our dinners together?" she asked in a mocking tone.

She shoved Yumi's arm. "You know I do. But I would like enough money to buy a nightstand. Maybe even afford an apartment with an actual *bedroom*."

"So fair, bestie. So fair." Yumi tapped her lips. "So you're gonna interview."

Sam nodded. "Yes. Will that be weird for you, if I get the job?"

"Not at *all*. I'd be so proud of you. Although, can you promise me one thing?"

Sam held up her hands to Yumi. "Anything."

Yumi took them, then squeezed Sam's palms. "Can you *please*, for the love of Ariana Grande, not give me another SEO explainer assignment ever again?"

She laughed out loud. "But what if it makes us money?"

Yumi poked Sam's nose. "This is why you'd be perfect for the job, and I'd suck."

"I don't think you'd suck."

"Stop being a liar." Yumi jumped up from the bed. "Okay, as your personal stylist, I have the perfect thing for your interview outfit."

She smiled. "What would I do without you?"

"Not get the job, obviously." Yumi winked. "*Or* score Nico."

Sam blushed. "I think I could do that fine without you."

"Yeah, given that he's *obsessed* with you, you're probably right."

Nico sat in Frank's office tapping his foot, his laptop open on his thigh. It was 11:35, over thirty minutes after Frank was supposed to be at work, and five minutes past their scheduled meeting time. Despite the warnings for a snow storm, everyone had shown up to the office that morning, though you wouldn't know it. Employees were quiet at their desks, and Nico wondered if they were all still nursing hangovers three days after their free-booze fest.

His laptop began to ring. It was a video call from Frank.

Nico sighed, then answered it.

Frank popped up on the screen, wearing a sweatshirt

and sitting on his couch. "Nicolas, look at you! Sitting at the office. Good for you."

"Why wouldn't I be at the office?"

"Well, I'm not sure if you saw the weather, but a major storm is supposed to come in. You could have stayed home today."

Nico glanced through the glass doors behind him, eyeing the very full office. "But everyone is here."

He shrugged. "So? I would have understood if you told me."

"And would you understand if they did?"

Frank frowned. "Nicolas."

Anger simmered underneath his skin, but he took a deep breath to calm himself before he said anything he would regret. "Do you want to reschedule our meeting?"

"No, let's talk now. I want that update. It's why I called."

Nico nodded, then coughed to clear his throat, stalling. *You can do this.* "As I mentioned, the engineering team was able to merge the technology so we could have videos in the feed for Nubo."

"*Excellent* news. When can we launch?"

"We are ready to release the update for beta testing now, if that's what you want."

"*No.* No, no. Let's wait. I think we should have it all go live on New Year's."

Nico was taken aback. "You want to launch a major new feature without beta testing?"

Frank waved him off. "I trust you and the team. If you say it's good to go, it's good to go."

He sucked in a breath. Nico knew it was a terrible idea. Even if he and the team were confident that the feature would work—he'd tested it himself a number of times over the weekend to make sure there weren't any bugs in the coding—that didn't mean something wouldn't come up that they hadn't seen yet. But this also wasn't his company, and if Theo didn't mind a sloppy launch, then so be it.

"How about the live feature? That's also ready to go?"

Nico cracked his knuckles. "Unfortunately, after testing a number of different options, we do not feel this feature will be ready in time for New Year's."

Frank's face tightened, his eyes going dark. "How come? This is unacceptable."

Nico explained the complications of creating a new user interface that would work for live streaming on Nubo, something that would take more than a couple weeks to build. "Snipbit didn't have this feature, so it's not like we have any code to work off to make this work. It needs to be built from the ground up."

"So? Make it happen. Don't let them sleep, if that's what it takes."

He could feel the anger bubbling hot. "Frank, do you hear yourself? These are human beings we're talking about. Do you really think we should be pushing them like this if there are threats of unionizing? Don't you want your employees to be happy?"

"Sure, I want that. But I want this live feature more." Frank sat up taller. "I want Nubo to get to number one in the App Store, and I want Theo to know that it was me who did it."

"But it won't be you. It wouldn't even be me. It would be the engineering team who should get the credit."

"Which is led by me."

What a prick. He wanted to say all kinds of uncorporate-like things to this man he called his boss. But Nico had given up vulgar language a long time ago, when he had the girl of his dreams in his lap for the first time. Instead, he closed his eyes and thought back to his lunch with Jeremy. *No, never again.* He'd promised that he wouldn't push them this holiday. Even if it meant getting fired because of it.

He blinked his eyes open. "Frank, I'm sorry. It is not going to work. Please tell Theo that the video launch will not go live on New Year's. If he would rather wait to launch video on Nubo until it's ready, then we can circle back in the spring."

Frank's nostrils flared. "Are you saying *no* to me?"

"Yes. I am."

Frank let out an exasperated laugh. "You really think you can talk to me that way, kid? Absolutely not. We *will* go live on New Year's, even if it means I have to take matters into my own hands."

Nico didn't like the sound of that, but his position remained firm; it was his job to look out for his employees. "I'm s—" He stopped himself. He didn't need to apologize to this man again. Once was more than enough. "Please tell Theo that we can regroup as a team after the holidays about working on a proper live video platform for Nubo."

Frank shook his head. "Unbelievable." Then he hung up.

Nico closed his eyes and took a deep breath. Then a second. Then a third. Feeling calmer, he closed his laptop and left Frank's office, then made his way to the table of engineers. The office was open concept, but the engineers were tucked into a dark corner in the back, giving them silence to work—and larger table space for the three or four monitors they each used to evaluate code.

He stepped in front of the table, a number of his engineers hard at work, each with a pair of massive headphones covering their ears.

When Jeremy spotted him, he removed his headphones. His face was beet red. "Nico, what in the actual fuck is going on?"

"I spoke with Frank," he started.

"Yeah, no shit. He just sent us an email."

Nico's lips pursed as Jeremy motioned for him to look at his monitor.

To: engineering@omnicorp.com

From: frank@omnicorp.com

Subject: Let's reach the finish line.

Team,

I was informed that our live video function will not be ready by New Year's, but I believe a team as smart and capable as ours can get us to the finish line. So as an incentive, I will be offering a $500 end-of-year bonus to each of you upon completion. I have informed Theo of your hard work and our desire to have this feature ready, and he has agreed to this plan.

I look forward to seeing Ryan Seacrest live on Nubo come January 1.

Onward,

Frank

Nico stood up and ran a hand through his hair.

"Does this fucking fartbag think five hundred dollars is enough to lose three weeks of sleep and miss the holidays?"

"I could sell pictures of my feet online for more money than that," said Todd, one of the engineers.

"Please, don't do that." Nico shook his head. "And don't bother with the live platform."

"Sounds like the perfect time to strike," said another engineer in the corner.

Nico blinked. "Strike? The union?" He glanced at all of the engineers. "All of you?"

They nodded, heads held high. Except for Jeremy, who slumped in his chair and rubbed his neck.

He blew out a breath. "Ignore this email and please take the rest of the day off. Get home before the storm hits."

"L-leave? For the day?" Todd asked, sounding surprised.

"Yes. And don't log back on. I'm going to figure something out." He sounded more confident than he felt, but at least his employees no longer looked at him like they were about to breathe fire.

Without hesitating, they began clearing the wrappers and empty energy drink cans at their desk, then grabbed their coats and bags.

Jeremy stepped closer to Nico. "How are you going to figure it out?"

Nico sighed. "Not sure yet, but I will."

"That doesn't sound convincing at all." He shook his head. "Are you heading out for the day as well?"

"I'll be right behind you."

Jeremy rolled his eyes. "Yeah, right. Don't get snowed in here. We completely cleaned out the vending machines earlier."

Nico bent down and placed a hand on Jeremy's shoulder. "I promise I'm leaving tonight."

Jeremy's voice dipped low as the engineers dashed for the exit, like they were afraid Nico would change his mind. "About the strike comment," Jeremy started. "I'm sorry. They're all just...really angry."

"Don't be sorry. And they have a right to be."

"You're not mad about it?"

Nico pressed his lips into a thin line. "I don't know how I feel about it."

"What if you felt...*positively* about it? Would you consider joining us?"

He didn't answer that. Instead, he dropped his hand and straightened.

Jeremy held his hands up in defense. "Hey, man, maybe I overstepped. But from where I stand, we're not the only ones who get abused." He dropped his hands, then smirked. "But we are the only ones who don't have time to get laid."

Nico glared. "Drop it."

Jeremy grinned. "She's gorgeous, by the way."

A flash of red lips and midnight-black hair came to mind. His fingers tingled with the memory of a silky red dress. "I am very, *very* aware."

"Of course you are." Jeremy whistled as he grabbed his backpack and coat. "All right, man, I'm out. If you're not out of here in an hour I'm going to DoorDash you a pizza. And maybe a sleeping bag."

"*Goodbye*, Jer."

His lead engineer laughed again as he made his exit, leaving Nico alone in the dark corner of the OmniCorp offices, his mind still on one thing. He reached for the phone in his pocket, then opened up his texts.

Sam's name was next to a new avatar he didn't recognize. It was a cartoon of a puppy—a baby dog. He smiled and shook his head, thinking she must have changed it while he was asleep in her bed the other day.

He noticed her location next. *8ᵗʰ Avenue*. She was at work.

Her interview. He'd been so stressed out about his conversation with Frank this morning that he completely forgot to text her and wish her luck. It was past noon at this point, which meant she was likely sitting in Barbara's office, showing the editor-in-chief how absolutely brilliant she was.

He tucked his phone back in his pocket, then decided he too would leave early for the day.

Chapter 18

Sam knocked on Barbara's door a minute before noon. She pulled at the cropped vest Yumi insisted she wear, her high-waisted black trousers tucked neatly underneath the hem. She felt smart—professional. The outfit made her look like she could handle the job. Actually *feeling* like she could was a whole different sensation. Her stomach was in knots, the imposter syndrome screaming loudly at her. *You're not old enough for this. You don't have experience. You are not smart.*

"Come in."

She exhaled, then opened the door.

Barbara was at her desk, clicking at her computer, glasses perched at the bridge of her nose. "Samantha, so thankful you came in today. Thank you for making the effort. I know the snow storm is coming."

"It's no problem. I was looking forward to this interview."

Barbara removed her glasses and folded them neatly. "Good, I'm happy to hear that. Please take a seat."

Sam sat and placed her folder on Barbara's desk. She

opened it, then slid a document across the oak. "My updated résumé, as requested."

Barbara nodded and glanced at the sheet, then she looked back up at Sam. "I will admit, there isn't much here that I don't already know."

Sam nodded. "I figured as much. My media experience has solely been in this office."

"Which, if I'm being honest, is the reason I wanted to talk to you about this position. I prefer to promote internally before looking for a new hire. Our employees already know the brand well and it gives them opportunities to succeed. From the work I've seen you do, I recognize that you know this brand well."

Sam threaded her fingers together and placed them in her lap. She kept a straight posture—no slouching, no crossing her arms, no positions that would make her seem unfit for the job. "I am honored to discuss the position with you."

"Tell me." Barbara leaned back in her chair and crossed her legs. "Do you think you can do it?"

"I—" She hesitated.

Barbara sliced the air with her hand. "Forget your lack of experience or your age. Do you think you can do it?"

She sat up taller, Nico's words coming back to her at that moment. *Have a little faith in yourself.* "Yes."

Barbara smirked. "Tell me more."

Sam nodded, then reached for her folder and picked up the other sheets she'd printed, laying them out one-by-one in front of Barbara. "I've been doing some digging into our numbers for our digital nutrition content, and I've thought through a strategy that I think we should consider for the new year."

Her boss leaned in to view the reports, a single brow raised. "Go on."

She pointed to the bar chart, and the spreadsheet beside it. "As you can see, we had spikes in traffic this year in March, July, and November. When you look at those months historically"—Sam paused for emphasis, pointing at the charts from previous years she'd printed on another sheet—"those have been our lowest site traffic months. It seems odd, until you look closely at the data."

Barbara tilted her head. "You have my attention."

Sam smiled, then went to her second printed spreadsheet. "Our top three articles for the site last year were long-form pieces we did on unique topics, unrelated to our search-engine optimization efforts, our quick news pieces, or our sponsored articles. These pieces focused on original reporting, with topics other publications hadn't thought to cover. Each piece was published in these three months."

"Of course, I remember." Barbara leaned her elbows against the desk. "I also remember those pieces taking more time to produce, and costing us more money."

"Yes, but look at the numbers." Sam pointed to her spreadsheet. "The number of page reads each piece individually brought in was the equivalent of twenty-five pieces of search content we produced on average in each month alone. It also quadrupled the amount of time on page, and a higher conversion of newsletter subscribers. We also have data to prove," she said, pointing to her fifth and final paper, "that these pieces converted into higher revenue from our advertisements."

Barbara smiled. The last time Sam saw that smile, it was at their holiday party when Nico asked her to take a tequila shot. She knew her boss was enjoying this. Her chest swelled with hope.

"What are you saying, Samantha?"

Sam relaxed back in her chair, hands returned to her lap. Poised. Confident. "What if we put more effort into longform original reporting? Obviously our volume of content would decrease. But if we doubled or tripled the number of longform pieces we produce in a month, if you do the math, that would be more traffic compared to what we are bringing in now."

"But what about search? Would we stop that altogether?"

She shook her head. "There is indisputable merit in creating that content, as people are searching for answers that we provide all the time. But I think we slow down and be a little more choosy on the type of content we decide to write, giving us the financial cushion to pursue these other projects. A search piece on pre-workout snacks can be beneficial for people who love to lift." Her mind flashed to Nico and what he had to say about her article. "But a quick piece about Miley Cyrus's body? I think we could pass on it. That type of content can be really harmful for people who struggle with body dysmorphia or eating disorders."

Barbara slowly nodded, her eyes on the papers before her. "So let me ask you again. Do you think you can do this job?"

"Yes." This time Sam answered without an ounce of hesitation. The little voice in her head telling her she couldn't do this was gone, swallowed by the confidence that she clung to.

Barbara smiled again, tilting her face up to meet Sam's gaze. "Thank you. I appreciate you coming in today."

Sam's brow furrowed. "That's it? No more questions?"

"I've heard what I needed to." Her boss was still smiling, and Sam had a good feeling about it. "Please head home and stay safe tonight. This storm is escalating."

She relaxed and nodded. "I will. Thank you."

Barbara nodded, and Sam took that as her cue to leave. She reached out to gather her papers.

"No." Barbara placed a hand down on the spreadsheets and charts. "Leave these. I want to take a closer look."

Her heart soared. "Of course. Let me know if you have any questions about them."

Sam exited the elevator bank and tapped out of the gates, her heeled boots echoing across the Sigmond lobby. She was the only person there, except for a tall man sitting on a bench near the entrance with his face in his hands.

As she got closer to the door, she recognized who it was. "Nico," she breathed.

Nico leaned back against the tall glass panel behind him, briefcase by his shoes. His hair was askew in every direction, and he looked *tired*. "Hi, Sammy girl."

Sam frowned as she made her way to him.

He reached for the backs of her thighs and pulled her close, positioning her in between his legs.

She was ready to make a quip about the way his shirt looked a little ruffled and his hair being an absolute mess. Then she noticed the dark circles under his eyes and the crease in his forehead.

Sam placed a hand on his cheek. "Everything okay?"

Nico sighed, then shook his head.

"Rough day at work."

He closed his eyes and leaned his cheek into her palm, gripping her wrist. It was as good a yes as any.

"I'm so sorry." She rubbed a thumb across his cheek-bone. "What are you doing here?"

"I had to see you." His voice sounded gravelly. "I *needed* to see you."

Her phone dinged in her free hand.

YUMI

Hunkering down with Hottie McHottie Pants because my #1 hottie ditched me for work! Left a carton of ice cream for you. How'd the interview go?

Sam tucked her phone in her tote. "Nico?"

He blinked his eyes open.

"Do you want to come over?"

His smile was soft and serene. "More than anything."

It was only three o'clock, but with the dark clouds that loomed over the city, it seemed like the middle of the night. And it was snowing. *Hard.*

Nico and Sam rounded the corner onto 82nd, laughing at the heavy dusting of snow that already covered the square box in his hands after walking two short blocks from the pizza joint.

He popped open the lid. "Maybe we should eat it now while it's hot. It's going to be cold by the time we get to your place."

Sam hopped over to him and slammed the lid shut. "*No!*" When she placed her other heeled boot down, she slipped on a patch of ice.

Nico swiftly caught her waist and held her steady, the

pizza box wobbling in his other hand that was also holding on to his bag.

She looked at him with wide eyes, then the two of them burst out laughing.

"Your hair is covered in snow." She laughed.

He smiled, noticing the snowflakes that sat on the tips of her long lashes. *So, so beautiful.*

He dipped low and kissed her lips, her cheeks cold. "Come on," he whispered into her mouth. "Let's go get warm."

At that moment, the streetlight above them went off.

Nico widened his eyes, realizing that even this close, he couldn't see much of Sam. They were blanketed in darkness.

They let go of each other and glanced up and down the street. All the lights were out, decorated Christmas trees in windows completely off, businesses gone dark.

"Oh my god," Sam whispered. It was so dark Nico could see her breath. "Did the city lose power?"

They waited a beat, then two. No power resurged. Everything was still off.

"Yeah," he finally replied. "I think so."

He reached for Sam in the dark, tucking her under one arm, pizza box and work bag still in the other. They slowly made their way to her stoop, listening to loud sirens and a chorus of honking horns.

"Stoplights," Sam said. "Could those be out too?"

"If the power is out like this, then yeah, they could be."

They made it to Sam's apartment, and Nico followed her up the stairs of a pitch-black hallway and staircase. He smirked and reached in front of him, then grabbed her butt.

She screamed, then turned around and slapped his arm. "Not cool, Nicolas."

He laughed and grabbed her with his free hand and kissed her. His lips missed hers by an inch, the stairwell too dark to properly see anything.

She shook her head and pushed away. "I'm sorry you have to climb my stairs."

"Are you kidding? The elevators are probably out right now in my building, and I live on the thirty-fourth floor."

"Oh, so you're only here out of convenience?"

"I'm here because I can't seem to ever get enough of you."

Nico didn't need the lights to know he made her blush.

He continued to follow her up to the fourth floor and into her apartment.

Sam instinctively went to her lamp to turn it on, only to realize it was pointless.

Nico placed the pizza box and briefcase down, then peeled off his wet coat. "Candles?"

She snapped her fingers. "Yes. We have lots of those."

Ten minutes later, they had the place glowing with candlelight in every possible corner of her apartment.

Sam rung out her wet hair with a towel. She had stripped out of her wet clothes and was back in her oversize T-shirt. "Should we warm up the pizza in the oven? Wait, crap, would the oven even turn *on* right now?"

Nico blinked at her. He couldn't tell if she had those little shorts on, and it was driving him mad. He wanted to strip off her shirt and find out.

Her brow crinkled at him, waiting for him to respond. "What? Do I have more snow on me or something?"

Nico fisted his hands and released them. Then, slowly, he made his way to Sam. He removed the towel from her hands and draped it over the arm rest of the couch. Then he reached the bottom of her T-shirt and *tugged*, bringing her closer to him.

They sucked in a breath at the same time.

He pinched the hem of the shirt, pausing to look her in the eyes.

She bit her lip, then nodded.

Nico smiled and exhaled, and for the first time all day, he felt like he was doing something right. He pulled the shirt off of Sam, revealing miles of creamy skin.

She wasn't wearing the shorts.

Chapter 19

Sam stood there in nothing but her white bralette and thin cotton underwear. He held the T-shirt loosely in his fingertips before letting it drop to the floor, his eyes roaming her skin. They landed on her face, and he smiled.

Feeling bold, Sam took a step closer, then slowly unbuttoned his collared shirt. She could feel Nico's gaze on her as she unfastened each one, his hands still by his sides. When she finished, she reached for his collar and pulled it off him, revealing an undershirt and tan, muscular shoulders. Once the shirt joined her own on the ground, Sam slid the pads of her fingers up Nico's arms, following the slopes of his biceps up to his shoulders, then his neck. Nico lifted a hand between them and traced his knuckles down her cheek, to her collarbone, then down the center of her chest. Both hands found her waist. They were still cold from the storm as they slid across her skin.

"Still so soft," he whispered.

She smiled. "These are quite the muscles you have, Nicolas."

He smirked. "They have a purpose."

"Oh yeah? And what's that?"

His smirk widened as he crouched low, then wrapped his arms around her thighs, his hands landing on her ass. He lifted her up like she weighed nothing, her legs instinctively wrapping around his torso, her arms around his shoulders.

"Okay." She giggled. "I guess that's a good purpose."

He chuckled, then his smile shifted into something soft and wistful. "You make everything better, Sam."

She played with his hair. "Do you want to talk about it?"

He shook his head. "Not right now." He kissed her neck. "I have far more important things to do at the moment."

She grinned as Nico's lips found her neck again, then his tongue was on her skin. He licked his way up her neck, then nibbled at the tip of her ear.

Sam leaned her head back, a soft moan tumbling from her mouth.

"That's what I like to hear," he murmured against her skin.

"Do it again," she pleaded.

She could feel his smile as he turned and carried her to the bed. He placed her down gently, one hand at her back, the other gripping the entire circumference of her ankle. He kissed the inside of her ankle, then dropped kisses up her calf to her knee and the inside of her thigh. She knocked her head back onto the pillow when his mouth found the crease of her hips, the sensation making her tingle all over.

"Right there?" he whispered.

She nodded.

"Use your words, Sammy girl."

"Yes," she breathed. "Right there."

Nico hooked a finger beneath the sides of her underwear and lifted the fabric. She felt a jolt of cool breeze before his warm tongue made contact, dragging up the inside of her groin to her hip.

She moaned softly again.

"*Mmm*," Nico hummed. "Give me words. Tell me what you're feeling. Be the creative girl I know you are."

She bit her lip. "That feels so good."

He kissed her skin, low, just above the spot between her legs. "More."

Her lips parted. "That...makes my skin tingle, and makes me feel warm and gooey. Like my blood is molten lava. And I want...I want more of it."

"Warm and gooey, huh?" Nico traced a single knuckle along the fabric of her underwear, then between her legs, his knuckle dipping down the crease against the damp fabric. "Already wet for me. You are such a tease, baby."

She closed her eyes and fisted the duvet under her.

Nico unhooked his hand from her underwear and stood up.

Sam blinked her eyes open and watched as he slowly undid his belt, then slid off his trousers. She perched her arms behind her head at the sight of him in his black boxer briefs.

Nico chuckled. "What's that little smirk all about."

"Just enjoying the show."

He shook his head as he pinched the bottom of his tank top and stripped it off, revealing toned abs and pecs and even more of that olive skin.

She bit her bottom lip again.

"You drive me crazy when you do that."

She crossed one leg over the other. "Do what."

"When you bite your lip like that, all sweet and innocent."

She tilted her head and bit her lip again.

He leaned a knee against the bed, chuckling, then traced his thumb up her leg and pressed at the inside of her knee. "Open your legs for me."

Her face flushed as she did what she was told. Nico smirked as he crawled on top of her, positioning himself between her legs. He bracketed one arm next to her head, the other hand finding the inside of her thigh. He pressed his thumb into her soft skin, so close to the spot that was still concealed by her underwear.

She let out a sigh as Nico dipped to kiss her cheek, then down her neck. He released all of his weight on her, his hips finding contact with hers, the hardness inside his underwear finding the perfect sweet spot in between her legs. He pressed even harder, and she could *feel* every part of him. Her hand found his waist, and she dipped her thumbs into the elastic of his boxers. Then lower. And lower.

"Do you want these off?" Nico teased.

"*Mmhmm,*" she hummed.

He tucked a hand under her neck and tilted her head. "Words, Sam," he whispered into her ear.

"I want to see all of you," she blurted.

He huffed a laugh as he lifted himself off her, now kneeling above her. He grabbed her arms and lifted her into a seating position as well. "I want to see you too." He ran a pinky up the elastic strap of her bra, then hooked it and dragged it over her shoulder.

She hitched a breath. "Wait. Stop. I have to tell you something."

He froze, then fixed the strap back on her shoulder. "Too much?"

She shook her head. "No. I just...I have to be honest with you."

"Okay."

Sam scrambled to a kneeling position as well. "I..." She hesitated, feeling like it was impossible to say what she needed to. But this was Nico, and she trusted him. Completely. She calmed herself by tracing a finger down his skin, running it along the creases of his abs.

"Samantha, that tickles."

"Oh, does it?"

He shook his head in amusement, snatching her hand and kissing the inside of her wrist. "What do you need to tell me?"

She exhaled. "I've never done this before."

He peppered more kisses on her skin. "Done what?"

"Th-this." She circled a finger around them.

He froze, blinking slowly. "You haven't had sex before?"

She felt her face go hot, but this time, it wasn't a gooey kind. It was the red-hot, embarrassing kind. She nodded.

Nico's eyes widened as they scanned her body. When he looked at their joined hands, he smiled.

"Don't make fun of me," she whispered.

His head snapped up. "Make fun of you? Why would I do that?"

"Because I'm...*inexperienced* still."

"Oh screw that." He tugged on her arm, forcing her to lift up and onto his lap. She wrapped her legs around his waist. Back in the position they were in when everything began.

She raked a hand through his hair. "Then why are you smiling?"

He smiled, his eyes on her lips. "Because I am beyond thrilled that it's going to be me."

"You are?"

"*Yes.*" He kissed her chin. "I don't think I could be stoic if I found out that another man touched you in all the ways I've always, *always* wanted you."

She frowned. "Not always. You didn't know you liked me until that night."

"Maybe," he breathed. "Or maybe a part of me has always liked you, and that night made me face what I think I've felt all along."

She pressed her lips together and leaned her head back. "Nico."

"It's true, Sam. I've spent a number of years thinking about that night, thinking about how everything changed between you and me in an instant. And the only conclusion I can make is that I've always felt these things for you, and when I finally got the chance to kiss you and you said *yes*, my brain caught up with what my heart knew all along."

She snuggled close, pressing her forehead against his. "And what did your heart know?"

"That you're mine, and no one else's."

She closed her eyes and shook her head, her nose brushing against his. "You really know how to smooth talk, Nicolas Giuliano."

"I'm not just saying smooth words, baby. I mean it."

Sam leaned in and kissed his lips. She parted hers, opening herself up to him, letting her body become pliant against his.

Nico obliged, but then slowed. He gripped her neck and forced her to look him in the eyes. "Are you sure this is what you want?"

She nodded. "Yes. I'm ready."

"And with me?"

She smiled and tilted her head. "I couldn't imagine it not being you."

His grin was wide as he looked up at her. She shook her

head at that goofy look she knew so well, then bit her lip, just to make a point.

"Naughty." He laughed. Then he kissed her and flipped them around so he was on his back and she was straddling him.

His fingers drew a line on her skin right underneath the lace of her bra. "Take it off."

She flicked the elastic strap. "You want this off?"

"Yes."

"Say the magic word."

He shook his head. "Evil."

"*Use your words*, baby dog."

He growled. "Will you *please* take it off? Right now."

"Good boy."

He chuckled at that, then his laugh fell silent as he watched her peel off her bralette and toss it to the side. His lips parted, and for the first time, Sam had rendered Nicolas Giuliano completely speechless.

She placed her hands on his chest and leaned forward, pressing her breasts closer together with her arms, her hair falling in sheets, hugging her face.

He whimpered. "You are...*My god*, Sam."

She dug the tips of her fingers inside his boxers. "Your turn."

His thumbs found her underwear. "But you're not finished yet."

Before she could respond, Nico gripped her hips and flipped her over again, making her squeal. He ripped off her underwear, then tipped her legs open with his thumb, licking his way up her thigh and to the crease at her right hip, the spot he knew she couldn't handle.

She moaned so loud it made *him* moan.

"Can I taste you, Sammy girl?"

"Y-yes."

He grinned, then at an excruciating pace, he parted her slit with his tongue, dragging it slowly up the middle. When he found her clit, he licked small circles, then bit it at it gently.

She screamed, and his answering hum made her legs shake as he nibbled at her clit and sucked on it.

"*Nico*," she moaned.

"Words."

"You're making me...I think I'm going to..."

He stopped, then kissed her stomach. "Not yet. I want you to when I'm inside you."

She blinked her eyes open, the words *inside you* floating her back down to reality. Nico was about to be inside her. "C-condom?"

He nodded and sat up, then reached for his wallet, tucked inside his pants on the floor. He retrieved a square black wrapper, then handed it to Sam. "Time to put that Willow High sex education to good use."

"*Oh my god!*"

He laughed out loud as he crawled back on top of her, cradling her body under his. He kissed her chin. "Put it on me."

"Yeah? You like that?"

He nodded. "Especially when it's your hands doing it."

Nico rolled to his side, then Sam watched as he removed his boxers, his dick swinging out and upward, already hard.

When he noticed her staring, Nico grinned. "Touch me, Sam."

Sam shimmied closer, timidly brushing her thumb up his shaft, from the base up to the tip, then back down. She wrapped a hand around him, feeling the hard ridges in her palm.

She blinked up at him, noticing that he was watching her, that wistful look in his eye.

She smirked, then rubbed her thumb at the soft spot just under the tip.

He groaned, his face falling forward. "Samantha."

"I want this inside me, Nicolas."

"*Holy—*" He shook his head, then looked at her. "Get that condom."

She ripped open the wrapper, positioning the rubber at his tip. Nico closed his eyes and inhaled with each roll of the condom until she reached his base. Feeling bold, she cupped his balls and gently squeezed.

"All right then," he growled. He gripped her wrists then pinned her against the bed, rolling on top of her. "Enough of that."

She frowned. "Did you not like it?"

"Oh I liked it, maybe a bit *too* much." He bit her lip and sucked on it. "But I want so badly to come inside of you."

She wiggled underneath him. "Do you think...do you think I'll even be able to?"

"To come?" He gave her his cocky smirk. "Sammy girl, don't fret. I'm going to make you feel good."

"Yeah?"

He nodded, shifting his hands so he kept her wrists pinned above her, the other moving to hook her thigh around his leg. "Yes. Making you feel good will be my pride and joy." He paused, his face serious. "But it might hurt a little first."

She nodded. "I know."

"I'll be gentle with you."

"I know that too."

He smiled and kissed her cheek, then pressed his forehead against hers, positioning himself at her entrance.

"Still so wet," he whispered. Then he pushed in an inch, maybe less.

Her eyes slammed shut. "*Oh.*"

He kissed her cheek again, and this time his face angled so he could watch her. "A good *oh*?"

"As in, *oh*, you're so big."

"Thank you."

She laughed. "Even now you are so cocky!"

"You like it."

"Unfortunately."

He smirked, then pressed another inch in. Her eyes flew open, the pain like nothing she'd experienced before. She felt her mouth twist.

"Too much?" he whispered.

"I...no, keep going."

"That's my girl."

She smiled as he pushed in again, then again, and again. His strokes were gentle and slow. Sam watched as Nico's eyes closed, noticing the way he was holding back, barely restraining himself. The next time he pressed in, he was fully inside her, the stretch around him feeling unbearable.

"You're so tight," he breathed. "I think I'm going to lose my mind."

She whimpered.

His eyes blew open. "Does this hurt? Should we stop?"

"It hurts a little," she admitted. "Or maybe a little more than a little."

Nico began to pull out, releasing her wrists. "We should stop."

"*No.*" Sam gripped his shoulders, making sure he

remained there. On top of her. Inside her. "Just, give me a minute."

He nodded and kissed up her neck, then slipped a hand between them. His fingers found where they were joined, sketching a circle at her softest spot.

"*Oh*," she moaned.

She felt his teeth on her skin as he grinned. "Now that sounded like a good *oh*."

He continued, and the fire built in her abdomen. Suddenly, the feel of him inside of her went from painful to...something else. Something so much better.

She bounced, feeling every single ridge, loving the vibration of his hands and the movement of it all, feeling that familiar thrumming in her blood she recognized from the times she'd touched herself. But this feeling...This was beyond what she could accomplish on her own. She hadn't felt this kind of electricity in a long time.

"There we go," he murmured. "That's what I like to see."

Nico began to move, his hands still working, his tongue on her neck. "You're all I've ever wanted," he whispered in her ear, moving in and out, methodical and gentle. "I only ever think about you."

"*Nico*," she whispered.

"I'm so glad it's me," he continued, his hand moving from between her legs as he pressed a thumb to her hip. "I'm so glad you're mine."

She whimpered again, this time because she missed the feel of his hand, the way it drove the crescendo in her blood higher.

Nico caught on, moving his hand back and picking up the pace. He bit her bottom lip. "Sam, I'm not...not going to last much longer."

"Wait," she pleaded. "Please."

"Come for me, Sammy girl."

Her mouth parted.

Nico removed his hand, then hooked his thumb into her mouth. "See how we taste together. See how *perfect* we are together."

She sucked on his thumb.

He groaned and slipped his thumb from her mouth back to her groin, now wet from her tongue. "Let go, baby. Let go for me."

The sound of his demanding voice, the feel of his wet thumb, had Sam careening over the edge. She screamed, shocked by the violent way her body reacted to her orgasm with Nico filling every inch of her up.

"*Yes*, that's it." He pumped in and out, faster and faster. He moved his wet hand to her breast and squeezed her nipple, coaxing another scream from her. He crashed his mouth to hers as he slammed into her. Then he cried out, his head at the crook of her neck, his cock feeling even bigger inside of her now.

He moved his mouth to her breast and sucked it gently, then kissed his way between her breasts and up to her mouth. They looked into each other's eyes, silent for a moment.

Sam reached a hand to his hair and combed it back.

Nico smiled, returning a knuckle to her cheek.

Eventually he moved, removing himself from her. He quickly snatched his pants and tucked them underneath her.

"Um, why did you do that?"

"I don't want to ruin your white sheets." Nico stood up, removing the condom then snatching the towel they'd left on her couch.

Sam perched up, noticing the blood that was between her legs. "Oh gosh," she whispered, covering her mouth.

Nico returned and leaned over her, then gently wiped the towel between her legs, cleaning her up. "You may be sore tomorrow."

"I...think I still have those painkillers somewhere."

"Good." When Nico was finished, he neatly folded the towel and placed it on the floor, making sure no blood was in contact with the wood.

Sam went to move his pants. "Nico, I'm probably going to ruin these—"

"Sam, seriously, leave them. I could care less. I care way more about these white sheets."

"Why?"

He leaned in, then kissed her on the mouth. "Because they will live forever among my best memories."

She hooked her arms around his shoulders. "Should we do that again?"

He laughed, then climbed beside her and tucked her close. "After that, I think I'm going to need a minute."

"Or five?"

"Perhaps fifteen."

Sam looked around. "Pizza in bed?"

"One hundred percent."

Chapter 20

Nico popped open the pizza box. The slices were now cold, but neither of them minded. The distraction was more than worth it.

Sam sat beside him wearing his button-down, the sleeves rolled up and a couple buttons fastened at her chest. She was smiling as she typed something on her phone.

He leaned in and kissed her neck. "What's that smile for?"

She hummed. "Yumi wants to know if we did it."

"Send her the eggplant emoji."

Sam laughed out loud. "Oh my god, *no*. So vulgar."

He blinked up at her and gave her an evil grin. "Do it. I dare you."

She pinched her lips, the corners still turned up in a smile. "*Fine.*"

The *woosh* alerted them that it went through, and seconds later, her phone *ding*ed with a response. Then another. And another. *Ding. Ding. Ding. Ding.*

Sam's face flushed at whatever was being said. She silenced it and tucked her phone under her pillow.

Nico lifted a slice of pizza from the box and held it up to Sam. She took a big bite.

"Wow." Nico laughed. "Work up an appetite?"

She nodded as she chewed, her cheeks stuffed full like a chipmunk. It shouldn't have been as cute as it was, but to Nico, everything Samantha Carter did was cute.

Except for all the things she let him do earlier. That was *hot.* The memory of them together would be etched in his brain chemistry till the end of time. He wanted more memories like that. Even mere moments after he'd taken her, he wanted her *again.*

Samantha snatched the rest of the slice in his hand and took another big bite. He smiled to himself as he reached for one of his own. He'd been ridiculous to think he could get Samantha Carter out of his system all those years ago. *Just one kiss.* What a joke. One would never be enough. Ever.

"I can't believe the power is still off," Sam said between bites.

Nico sat up and looked out the window above her bed, clouded over from the heat no doubt the two of them caused. The windowsill was covered in white, and if they opened it, a pile of snow would flop down on Sam's bed.

Sure enough, the street was still dark. Nico checked his phone and opened the news, scrolling through the latest updates. "They're saying it's a blackout for all neighborhoods north of Houston Street and south of 92nd."

Sam's eyes widened. "That is such a huge chunk." She reached for another slice. "That would mean the Christmas markets *and* Times Square are out right now."

"Plus the Rockefeller tree."

"And Saks Fifth."

"This is nuts." Nico shook his head.

"How long do you think it will be out?"

"I hope a long time," Nico replied. "I want to stay right here with you for as long as possible."

She shoved his arm, and he laughed.

"Well, you're at least going to stay the night." She smirked. "Although if the blackout is north, then it sounds like the elevator in your apartment building is working."

"I see how it is. You use me for my body then kick me out to walk over a hundred blocks in a foot of snow."

"I also use you for the free food." She folded the slice in her hand then stuck out her tongue. "Besides, the subway could be back up and running."

"Brat."

She threw back her head and laughed. Nico clicked his tongue, shoving the box aside before tackling her. She screamed as he climbed over her, then took a bite of her pizza, eating half of it in one go.

"*Monster!*" she scream-laughed. "This is a good reminder that I actually find you so annoying."

He chewed with a big smile on his face. "You like it."

She glared at him.

He poked her nose. "Admit it. You do."

She growled, but still didn't say anything.

Nico threw an arm around her shoulders and pulled her close, kissing her on the cheek. She rolled her eyes, her face softening, then held up the rest of her slice so he could take another bite.

He chewed, then swallowed. "How'd the interview go?"

She picked up another slice. "Really good. I think Barbara liked what I had to say."

"Of course she did. You're brilliant."

Sam rolled her eyes again. "Stop that."

"I'm serious, Sam. You've always been smart. Used to drive Jeff crazy."

She tilted her head. "Seriously?"

"*Yes.* He said it was all your fault for taking 'the smart juice' when you were in utero, which sounds so weird to say now."

"That literally makes no sense. He was born before me!"

Nico shrugged. "You know Jeff. Always loves an excuse to complain."

She sighed. "Yeah. You're definitely right about that."

They ate in silence for a beat.

"And your day?" Sam asked, her voice soft. "Want to talk about it?"

He grimaced. "Not really."

"Nico, talk to me."

"See? You're so bossy. You're going to be perfect for that job."

"Nicolas."

He groaned and leaned his head back, closing his eyes. "I don't know what to say. All I know is that I'm scared if I don't fix everything, I'm going to lose my job."

Sam brushed a soothing finger down his cheek as a *ding* rang out in the apartment.

Nico opened his eyes and tilted his head. "I thought you silenced it."

She hesitated. "Um, I don't think that was mine."

Nico extricated himself with a sigh and went to retrieve his phone from his coat pocket, then froze at what he was seeing. It continued to go off as more messages trickled in.

CORINNE

Nico, give us the TEA!

EMORY

You doing okay man?

LEON

STRIKE STRIKE STRIKE STRIKE!

He felt his heart sink to his stomach as he opened up Nubo. The posts were everywhere—black squares declaring that eighty percent of the employees at OmniCorp were officially going on strike.

Not sure what else to do, Nico opened his email to see if anyone contacted him. There was a generic email from HR, letting employees know they were aware of the strike and would be contacting the people in charge of the union movement to work on negotiations. Then there was another email from Frank.

To: nguiliano@omnicorp.com

From: frank@omnicorp.com

Subject: <no subject>

Fix it, or you will find yourself without a job come January.

F

His mind was spinning. How could he possibly fix it? This wasn't just his engineers, this was *eighty percent* of the company. Employees were going on strike in every single department, including some in HR. Frank's demands were certainly a part to blame, but there was so much more going on at OmniCorp than Nico had realized.

There wasn't a way he could fix it. He would probably lose his job.

He shuffled back over to the bed where Sam was nibbling on a crust and scrolling through her texts, giggling at whatever was on her screen. He stood there, wondering what in the world he should do next.

Sam looked up at him and her face fell. She dropped her phone and threw the crust in the box. "Nico?"

He couldn't even stop it if he tried. Nico ran a hand through his hair and started to cry.

He wasn't sure why he'd initially felt like he couldn't talk to Sam about what was going on. Part of him wanted to shield her from the messiness of corporate politics, which he knew was useless given that she was looking at a promotion herself. Another part of him felt like his emotions were a burden and he wanted to keep things simple between the two of them. Being with Sam was fun, something he could look forward to. An escape from his reality.

But as he climbed into bed with her that night, as she combed his hair while he talked through tears about work and how everything felt too overwhelming to handle, he also knew trying to keep things light between them was useless. Jeff was who he used to turn to when he needed to talk through his feelings, but with everything going on between the two of them, his best friend didn't feel like his safest place. But *Sam?* She had always been a safe space. She'd been there for him all along.

When the power finally came back on, Nico was half asleep, exhausted from the day. The highs of being with the woman of his dreams for the first time, the lows of seeing his career implode in a single moment. He watched Sam through heavy-lidded eyes as she powered down his phone, placing it far from them on the other side of her apartment. She threw out the empty pizza box, blew out the candles, then climbed back into bed.

Nico ran a hand up her bare leg, tucking his fingers at her hip, beneath her underwear. "Thank you," he whispered.

"Of course." She cuddled him close, letting his head rest on her chest. She kissed his hair. "Hey, Nico?"

"Mmm?"

"I think crying is hot."

He smiled. "Thanks, baby girl."

They decided to have a snow day.

Without a proper boss at the moment, Sam was in limbo. And with a majority of his company not showing up for work, Nico decided it was useless to even attempt traveling to OmniCorp. Especially when the snow was piled high and cars were slipping and sliding on the streets.

Hooky it was.

After inhaling the coffee and bagels Nico retrieved from the shop around the corner, they bundled up to go to Central Park. Sam begrudgingly handed over his black sweatshirt—the one she'd gotten in a habit of sleeping in because it still smelled like him. He promised to return it with fresh *him* smell, then slipped on the joggers he kept in his bag for the gym, which he'd never ended up going to after the weather took a deep dive yesterday afternoon.

She lent him a scarf and gloves and a very pink knit hat, which she apologized for.

He laughed. "My masculinity is not threatened by wearing pink, Samantha."

Manhattan was heavily dusted in crisp, white snow—like a mountain of powdered sugar. It'd yet to be tainted by the city—no yellow pee stains or charcoal splatters. The city seemed pure—untouched and quiet. The streets were covered in sheets of ice, and besides a couple of cabs that rolled slowly down 5th Avenue, there weren't many cars in sight.

It seemed they weren't the only ones who decided to have a snow day.

Nico kept a firm hold on Sam's waist as they went, taking careful steps to make sure they didn't topple over. When they reached the park gates at 79th Street, he let go, then took off in a run, disappearing behind a set of trees.

"*Nico!*" She ran after him, the snow firm on top of the grass as they sunk deeper into the park. When she turned the corner at the trees, a hand snatched her waist and pulled her close. Nico crushed his mouth to hers, his lips warm compared to the chill. She slipped her arms around his shoulders and opened up to him, letting his tongue explore her mouth, listening to the satisfied rumble escape his chest.

She detached herself. "Did you really take me all this way just to make out under a tree?"

He rubbed her nose, then pulled on her hand. "Obviously not. Although I will take any chance I can to make out with you."

They made their way south in the park, occasionally stopping to throw snowballs, wrestle, kiss, and pretty much avoid anyone who looked in their direction. Nico certainly didn't care, and Sam—despite her efforts to *always* seem calm and collected—didn't either. The last time she'd had carefree fun like this, it was a steamy summer day, and she was sneaking sips of hard seltzer with Nico, Jeff, and a swath of other friends who lived in their neighborhood. Everything in her life had always been serious and focused, with a singular goal in mind. *Get the highest marks. Get the job. Work your way to the top.*

Yet now, as they made their way closer to the southern edge of the park, her throat sore from laughing, her cheeks permanently stretched into a smile, she wondered if maybe her *focus* was more about distraction. She took those parts of herself, coupled with her disappointment, and hid them away all these years. And now that they were free, she wondered if she would ever be able to tuck them away again.

Instead of exiting the park, Nico tugged on her arm and forced her in the direction of Wollman Rink, where a number of skaters were gliding across the ice despite the heavy amount of snow around them.

She pulled back like a child. "Nicolas, no. I will not ice skate with you."

"Oh *come on*," he whined. "It will be fun!"

She forced her hand back and crossed her arms, glaring at him. "I promised myself *years* ago I would never ice skate with you after the way you and Jeff completely embarrassed me at Bryant Park."

"*Awwww.*" He grinned and stepped closer to her, tackling her in a hug. "Is someone embarrassed?"

"Oh my god, yes! I fell on my butt and the two of you laughed like it was the funniest thing in the world."

"But it was so cute," he teased, kissing her on the nose.

"You didn't think that then," she grumbled.

"What if I hold your hands the whole time and I don't laugh a single time you fall?"

She pursed her lips. "Promise to get me that amazing hot chocolate after?"

"Duh?"

She shoved his chest, then walked around him. "Fine. You laugh once and we're done."

He cackled, then mumbled *wait, crap.*

She quickened her pace but could hear him chasing after her. He caught up and snaked his arms around her from behind, walking with her.

"I think it's hot when you fall on your butt," he teased.

"Are you about to make a joke about taking care of my butt if I fall on it?"

"Well, I wasn't, but now that you say it…"

"Cocky!"

He laughed again, and this time, Sam smiled with him. He threw an arm around her shoulders as they walked to the rink.

True to his word, Nico didn't laugh once. He held her hands as he guided her onto the rink, swaying with her as she skated along, avoiding the grumbling skaters around them, clearly annoyed that Sam and her horrible skating skills were in the way.

"Ignore them," Nico persisted. "Eyes up here, on me."

Her legs wobbled as she looked up at him. The tops of skyscrapers peeked over the trees surrounding the edges of Central Park, their branches parting to reveal a glistening view of the Plaza in the distance. It was like looking at a postcard; the perfect photo, with Nico and that silly pink hat in the center of it all.

Not paying attention, she lost her coordination, the skate slipping underneath her. Nico grabbed for her, then they both tumbled over.

He turned to look at her, lips sucked in, like he was trying not to laugh.

"You suck, Nicolas," she growled.

Then he burst out laughing. Before she could scramble away, he grabbed her waist and kissed her hard on the lips. "Want to try again?" he whispered.

She frowned. "I want chocolate."

He grinned, nuzzling her nose. "Then chocolate is what my baby gets."

Chapter 21

NICO

Snow day beers?

LEON

Fuuuuuuuuuuck yes.

EMORY

So down.

CORINNE

Snow day?? Did you losers work at all today?

NICO

No

EMORY

No

LEON

Absolutely not

CORINNE

EMORY?!

EMORY

How often is this city covered in a foot of
snow?

CORINNE

Well I'm working, have fun being
irresponsible.

NICO

I'm going to, um, bring someone, if that's
okay.

CORINNE

Never mind, I'm coming.

EMORY

More than okay.

LEON

YEESSSSS

NICO RETURNED TO THE BOOTH, a beer in each hand and
a smile on his face. Sam's hair was tied up in a bun, her
cheeks pink from being outside in the cold. She was
scrolling through all of the pictures they took. He slowed,
unable to take his eyes off her, the sight stealing his breath.
Even in jeans and a sweater and puffy coat, Samantha
Carter was stunning. He felt the sudden urge to ditch the
effort to see his friends and take her home, remove her
clothes, and never return to civilization ever again.

Then she blinked up at him and beamed.

His smile brightened. "I can't believe you actually told

me to get you a *beer*," he said, placing the pint down before her.

"You know, sometimes martinis just aren't the right move." She sipped at the frothy top. "Although after I ordered this, I instantly regretted not getting the mulled wine. I still can't feel my hands."

Nico hung his coat then sat on the same side of the booth as her, taking her hands in his. He pressed them together, then rubbed them hard, warming them up.

They'd spent the majority of their day outside, leaving the rink and leisurely making their way down 5th Avenue. Luckily the snow slowed New York down and kept away the endless tourists that flooded the streets during the holidays, so it almost felt like they had the place to themselves—besides the occasional yellow cab and fellow crazy Manhattanites taking advantage of a quiet city during the busiest time of the year. They stopped at the Rockefeller tree and took pictures, until Nico grabbed her waist and rocked her back and forth as "I'll Be Home for Christmas" played through a fuzzy-sounding speaker in the distance. Then they walked further south, hitting Bryant Park where they stopped at the holiday market, hot chocolates topped with pillowy whipped cream in hand. Nico watched from a distance as Sam took a sip, exploring a booth full of twinkling holiday ornaments, the reflecting crystals and lights making her skin glow. A thin layer of whipped cream was on her upper lip when she returned to him, and he kissed it away.

"How was your snow day?" he asked her.

"Perfect," she whispered.

He grinned. "Mine too." He kissed the tips of her fingers. "Thanks for being cool about meeting my friends."

Sam tilted her head. "You know, for so long, I thought

you and Jeff were weird because you only had each other as friends."

Nico chuckled. "I thought the same thing for a while." Then his face grew serious. "Although I didn't really make new friends until after, well…" He paused, then shook his head. "These guys were all in the same program with me at Berkeley, but we only got close after I made the move in September."

"I think it's healthy, you know? To have other friends. They help you see things differently."

"Are you telling me that Jeff and I are close-minded?"

"Again, for so long, I would have said *yes*." She shrugged. "But now? Maybe not so much. I've learned a lot more about my brother these past few years, and I think there were a lot of things he was suppressing. His sexuality being one of them."

Nico nodded. "Yeah. I kind of agree."

She sighed. "What do you think he'll say, when we tell him?"

He frowned, eyes on their joined hands. "That he's happy for us."

"Do you think he'll really say that?" she asked, her voice dropping to a whisper.

Nico blinked up at her, staring into those gorgeous honey-green eyes. Eyes that looked a little frightened. "I'm not going to lie, Sam, I don't know." He sighed. "But I do know that I want you, and I'm not willing to let you go. If Jeff tries fighting me, I'll fight him right back."

Her shoulders slumped. She opened her mouth to speak, but her thought was interrupted by Corinne and Emory's entrance.

"Oh my god, you're even more beautiful in person," Corinne declared. She slipped into the other side of the booth and reached for Sam's face, squishing her cheeks. "Look at you. How are you real? You're so pretty."

Sam flushed. "Th-thank you."

Emory slapped Nico on the back. "No Lee yet?"

"It's still quiet—what do you think?" Nico asked.

Emory chuckled and shook his head as he took a seat next to Corinne.

Corinne released her death grip on Sam, her face bright. "Wow, isn't this a fun surprise. We've heard so much about you, Sam."

Sam's face shifted a fraction in Nico's direction. "Oh yeah?"

"All horrible things," Nico said, leaning against the table. "That you're terrible at fake dating."

"*I'm* terrible at fake dating? Who's the one who insisted we go on a real date before the holiday party?"

"I think you're both terrible at fake dating," Corrine said, shaking her head. "I mean it's been, what? Two weeks since agreeing on your little contract and you decimated it as soon as you could?"

Nico smiled and covered his face with his hands. He divided two of his fingers and looked at Sam, noticing the way she was blushing as she took a silent sip of her beer.

"Suckers." Emory laughed.

Nico curled an arm around Sam's waist and pulled her close. "Something like that," he said, then dipped down to kiss her cheek.

"*AWWWW!*" screamed a voice at the other end of the bar.

Nico, Corrine, and Emory sighed. "Lee," they all said at the same time.

Leon ran up to the booth, a huge smile on his face. He

snatched his phone from the pocket of his bomber jacket. "Wait, do it again. I want photo evidence."

"Stop it," Nico said, pushing his phone away.

Leon laughed. "Hey, I hope you don't mind, since we're having a *Meet the Parents* moment, I invited my new girl too."

Corinne's eyes widened. "You did?"

Emory grinned. "Finally. More people to be around who know nothing about coding or computer science."

"Where is she?" Nico asked.

"She had to stop at the pharmacy." He turned toward the door. "Oh, I see her, hold on."

Leon ran away. Corinne shook her head, then leaned her elbows against the table, eyes on Sam. "So, does your brother know yet?"

Sam was visibly taken aback. "Excuse me?"

Corinne hummed. "Isn't that what caused the drama to begin with?" She pointed a thumb in Nico's direction. "I mean, this one pined for you for *years* after that night. We wouldn't want him to strain himself again from all that yearning, now would we?"

Sam opened her mouth, then clamped it shut.

Nico glared at Corinne. "Hey, stop. It's none of your business."

Corinne lifted her hands. "I just want to make sure you guys don't get hurt, especially if he's your best friend."

Nico sighed heavily, then placed a hand on Sam's thigh underneath the table.

She didn't return the gesture.

Leon reappeared, his arm slung around a pair of slim shoulders. "Guys, I would like you to meet—"

"Yumi?!"

Yumi froze, mouth falling open at the sight of Sam sitting in the booth.

Nico's eyes blew wide.

Leon's brow furrowed, looking confused, his head darting back and forth between them. "Wait, you know each other?"

Yumi pointed to Sam. "We're roommates. And best friends," she explained to Leon.

Corinne leaned back in the booth, picking up the beer in front of her. "Oh this just got *good*."

"Wait..." Sam pushed a finger into Nico's arm, motioning for him to move so she could get out of the booth. "This is the guy you've been seeing?"

"Well, yeah! I didn't tell you his name?"

"*No!* You referred to him as 'Hottie McHottie Pants.'"

"Right!" Yumi laughed. "Such a good nickname."

Leon turned, showing off his butt. "Nico, to confirm, do you think these pants are hot?"

Nico scratched his head. "Are you asking me to check out your butt?"

Leon laughed, then his mouth went wide, like something dawned him. "Babe, wait, this is the roommate you were telling me about? Who's finally with her unrequited love? Her love is *Nico*?!"

Yumi threw her hands up. "*Yes!!*"

Sam sunk deeper into the vinyl bench.

"I think it's time for another round," Emory declared.

After another round of beers and half a dozen exclamations of "of all the people in New York and all the dating apps,"

Yumi grabbed Sam's hand and forced her to the bathroom so they could "debrief."

When they entered the women's bathroom, Yumi screamed and threw arms around Sam's shoulders.

Sam shook her head in surprise, returning the hug. "What was that about?"

"You did it! You got the D!"

"*Yumi*, shhh! They probably heard that across the bar."

Yumi laughed out loud, then stepped back and tugged on Sam's shoulder as they made their way to the mirrors. "I want to hear everything. *Everything.*"

Sam shook her head, watching as Yumi checked her makeup and hair. Sam turned to face her own reflection, realizing what a ratty mess she made. She had rogue hairs sticking out near her ears, her hair tied up in the sloppiest bun of her twenty-three years of life, and her clothes had certainly seen better days after a day outside in the snow. "I look worse than a subway rat."

Yumi closed her eyes and shivered. *Fucking subway rats,* she grumbled. Then she checked Sam out and smirked. "Doesn't matter. Nico looks at you like you're the moon and the stars."

Sam rolled her eyes. "No he does not."

She leaned against the sink. "Oh, he certainly does. And he also can't keep his hands off of you. He is so smitten, sometimes it's hard to watch."

"Why would it be hard to watch?" she asked, her voice almost in a whisper.

"Because..." Yumi tapped her foot. "It's like the kind of love you see in the movies, or read about in books. That star-crossed-lovers, there's-no-one-but-you kind of love. He looks like you could utterly destroy him, if you so choose."

Sam released her hair from the elastic band and ruffled

it, the black strands spilling out into a wavy, frizzy mess. "I don't want to destroy him."

"I know, babe." Yumi hopped up on the sink and crossed her legs. "Okay, so...the sex. Good?"

"I mean, I have no concept of what good sex is, but..." She blushed. "I liked it."

Yumi chuckled. "Liked it or...?"

Sam rolled her eyes. "Okay, I looked like the mind-blown emoji after."

Yumi kicked her feet and squealed.

She pulled her hair back into a low ponytail, trying to make it look *somewhat* neat. "I honestly thought that it would be bad, ya know? You used to tell me how bad sex is when you start out, that it takes time." Her face pinched. "How was it so good for me the first time then?"

"Maybe because you're, oh, I don't know, madly in love with him?"

Sam slapped Yumi's leg. "I am not."

"Deny it all you want, babe, but it's clear from the way you look at each other. But hey, what do I know." She hopped down from the sink. "I will say this. Let me give you some advice, from someone who has had her fair share of romps in the sheets."

Sam closed her eyes and shook her head. "Do not say that again."

Yumi laughed, then took Sam's hand. "Listen. It's always better when you're with someone you trust. Your body just sort of"—Yumi moved her arms in a soothing motion—"relaxes, and enjoys it. No parts of you are on edge, you're not trying to perform or impress someone. You get really comfortable and enjoy making each other feel good."

Sam crossed her arms. "And is it that way with Leon?"

Yumi smirked. "You're changing the subject."

"I am! Yumi, he's *hot*."

They both laughed, then stifled their giggling as someone walked into the bathroom.

Yumi's face relaxed and she placed her hands on Sam's shoulders. "How'd the interview go yesterday?"

Sam smiled. "Yu, it went *really* well."

Yumi smiled, but her expression seemed sad.

Sam's face fell. "What? Are you feeling weird about it? I don't have to take the job if it's going to make things weird between us."

She shook her head. "No, that's not it." She sighed as she released her hands, jingling her bracelets with the motion. "Sam, there's something I need to confess to you."

"Okay?"

Yumi took a deep breath. "I put in my two weeks at Sigmond."

Her eyes went wide. "You did?"

"Yeah...I did, like, a week ago."

Sam's mouth fell open. "Wait, *what*? Why? Did you get another job?" Her lip quivered. "Are you...moving to Seoul?"

"And leave you when things are just starting to get good? Babe, *god*, absolutely not."

Sam's shoulders relaxed. "It would be really selfish of me to say I'm happy, right? I mean, you're so far from your family."

"You're also my family."

Sam's bottom lip quivered again, then the two were hugging it out. She could feel the slight buzz from the two beers, the tears coming easy to her. "Why didn't you tell me?"

Yumi sighed. "I was nervous. I didn't want to upset you, or make you think that I was giving up or abandoning you or…I don't know. I was feeling a lot of guilt that shouldn't have been there and I should have told you about what was going on."

She squeezed her arms around Yumi. "You can *always* talk to me, Yu. Don't listen to the guilt. You can count on me. I'll always be here, and we'll work it out no matter what."

Yumi choked out a sob. "So eloquent. I'm so happy we have each other."

"Me too." Sam sniffled. "What are you going to do now?"

She stepped back, wiping tears from her own eyes. Then Yumi placed her hands on her hips and made a super-hero pose. "You are now in the presence of the new staff writer at *Who What Wear*."

Her mouth fell open. "*NO!*"

"YES!"

"NO!"

They both screamed, then Sam threw her arms around Yumi in another big hug.

The other woman in the bathroom exited her stall at that moment. "Drunk girls," she grumbled while washing her hands.

Sam apologized softly as the woman exited. Yumi didn't bother with an apology and instead yelled a *yeah we're drunk, and we love each other!* very loudly as the door snapped shut.

Yumi pulled the elastic from Sam's hair and told her to turn, then started weaving it into a braid. She was going to miss Yumi at work, but was beyond thrilled for her best friend. The fashion writing job made more sense for someone like Yumi, who was always styling Sam and caring about every clothing decision she made with great detail, even down to how her hair should look with each outfit. Even now, Yumi cared about those details. Sam felt beyond lucky to have a friend like her.

"Yu, I've been meaning to ask. Do you want to come home with me for the holidays? It's...going to be a juicy one. Nico is going to be at our annual Christmas Eve dinner with his moms and we're almost positive Jeff is going to propose."

Yumi gaped at Sam in the mirror. "Are you serious? How do you know that?"

"It's a gut feeling. Both Nico and I agree." Sam shrugged. "Jeff has been pretty persistent that we both be there."

She swiftly tied off the end of Sam's braid. "God damnit, I so badly want to say yes. But now that I'm, um, free...I booked a ticket to Seoul to spend the holidays with my parents and Halmeoni."

Sam grinned. "That's amazing! I'm so happy for you."

Yumi tugged on the braid to make sure it was secure, then slid it over Sam's shoulder and tapped her back. "Thanks, but don't worry babe, I'll be home for New Year's."

"Let me guess, is it because you want to be with a certain Hottie McHottie Pants on New Year's Eve?"

Yumi's face turned red. "Am I that obvious?"

"Yumi, you're *blushing*!"

"*Stop*, oh my god."

The two exited the bathroom, arms linked. She looked over at their booth, and Nico's eyes instantly locked on hers. He smirked and cocked his head. *Get over here*, he mouthed.

Yumi shook Sam's arm. "See? The moon and the stars."

Her heart burst in her chest, and for what felt like the

first time, Sam was able to pinpoint what happiness truly felt like. A snowy day in New York, sitting in a cozy bar wearing damp clothes, drinking beers with friends; her best friend on one side, the man she never stopped dreaming about on the other.

After four years in New York, Sam felt like she'd finally made it. And she didn't need her career to make it happen.

As they approached the table, the group was laughing at Nico as he shook his head.

"No," Nico protested. "I won't. I'm sorry."

"Oh, come on man, it's one word, it doesn't really matter." Leon bit his lip hard, like he was waiting for Nico to join him.

"There is science behind it," Corinne said, holding up a finger. "There's like, a cathartic energy with swearing. It releases all this tension."

Nico shook his head.

"Nerd. Did you read that in a book?" Emory teased Corinne.

"And so what if I did?!"

Yumi smirked as she looked between Sam and Nico. "Wait, Nico, you don't swear?"

"Nope." He smiled back. "Swears are filler words. They don't really have a purpose in a sentence, they're unoriginal."

Sam's stomach swooped.

Yumi covered her mouth in disbelief as she turned to Sam.

Corinne threw her arms up. "But they *do* have a purpose, like I said! Stress relief! And with a strike going on, I have a feeling you have a lot of tension that needs to be released."

Leon shot Nico a devilish grin. "Oh, I think this man has other, *new* ways to release that tension."

"Enough," Nico demanded. He reached an arm to Sam, then twisted his hand and wiggled his fingers like, *Come here.*

She smiled and obliged, sliding into the booth. Being next to him didn't seem good enough, as he snatched her waist and lifted her onto his lap.

Yumi slid in too, and Leon threw an arm around her shoulder. "So, are we going to talk about it?"

Corinne looked confused. "Talk about what?"

Yumi slammed her hands against the table. "The fact that Sam *also* doesn't swear and Nico refuses to because of her?"

Corinne's mouth fell open.

Leon burst out laughing. "*What a sucker!*"

Yumi laughed along with him, the two of them clinking their glasses conspiratorially.

A large basket of fries was placed in the center of the table, distracting the group from the topic at hand.

Sam twisted around so her back was to the wall, her legs draped over Nico's. "Is that true? You don't swear because of me?"

He shrugged. "Someone once told me swears are dirty and gross," he mumbled.

Yumi snatched a couple fries, then handed one to Sam. "Moon and stars," she repeated.

Sam shook her head, ignoring Nico's confused face as the two of them tapped their fries and gobbled them down.

Chapter 22

Sam sat on Yumi's desk, eyeing the empty cubicle around them. What was once covered in colorful stickers and pins and pictures was now back to bare, grayscale walls, all her glittery possessions shoved into a single cardboard box.

"Ugh, I can't believe you're leaving us," Tally said. She sat in Yumi's desk chair, feet kicked up on the desk.

Yumi continued to stuff loose papers and sticky pads with outfit doodles into her box. "I know, right? Who will give you all the hot office gossip if I'm not here."

Tally groaned and leaned her head back. "Clearly not Sam. She's too goody-two-shoes to gossip."

Sam shrugged. "Hey, it's none of my business."

Tally rolled her eyes. Then her mouth opened in an O and she leaned forward. "Did you guys hear the rumor about why they had to fire Garrison?"

"No," Yumi and Sam rushed out in unison.

Tally smirked. "Apparently one of the articles he edited had a link that went directly to a porn site."

Sam covered her mouth. "*No.*"

Yumi's jaw dropped, then she laughed so loud, the people working around them stood up and told her to *shhhhh!*

"How did that slip through edits?" Sam asked.

"And how did they find *out?*" Yumi asked after. "Was it on the site for long?"

"Apparently it was up for twenty-four hours before someone commented on the article and said it linked to some, like, anime porn site. I mean, to each their own, you do you boo. But at *work?*"

"Why was he even copying the link in the first place? How did it end up in there?" Sam kept firing off questions, wondering how in the *world* an editor at a top publication could let that slide. "He should have double-checked all of the links."

"Sure, he should have, but we all know he was a lazy motherfucker," Yumi added, tossing the last of her gel pens into the box. She turned to face them and crossed her arms. "Sam is going to be so much better at that job."

Sam narrowed her eyes and shook her head. "I haven't heard anything. I doubt I got it."

"Sam, you're the only one truly in the running." Tally leaned forward again and lowered her voice. "Barbara interviewed four people for the position, and two of them have already been told they aren't getting it."

The pace of her heartbeat quickened. "Seriously?"

"That's it, we're going out and celebrating." Yumi shut down her computer for the last time. "Tequila sodas, on me. I have a fifteen-hour flight at midnight and I wouldn't mind boarding it with a little buzz."

Sam looked down at her phone, hoping *maybe* that would be the moment Nico would reach out. It was Friday, three days after their snow day, and she hadn't heard much from him. She knew he was slammed with OmniCorp's strike. It was probably selfish for her to want to see him with everything going on, but when in her life had she allowed herself to be a little selfish? Especially since they were heading to Willow on Sunday, and they had yet to really talk about Christmas and Jeff and how they were planning on handling all of it.

If Jeff was truly proposing, she was beyond excited for him. But a small part of her deep down felt kind of bitter that her and her brother never truly got to the *root* of the problem in their brief discussion at Thanksgiving.

Tally leaned in, noticing the background on Sam's phone. It was a selfie of her and Nico on the ice rink at Central Park. He had his hands around her waist, holding her up as she took the photo, light pink hat still on his head, that goofy Nico smile shining bright.

"How's the boyf?" Tally asked.

Sam sighed. "Busy with work. OmniCorp is a mess right now."

"Oh my god, he works at OmniCorp? Is he not on strike?"

"He should be, with the way they are treating him," Yumi grumbled. "That boy deserves better."

Sam tucked her phone in her blazer pocket. "I'm a little worried about him. He's only sent a couple good-night texts the past few days, and they're always at like, two or three in the morning. I'm worried he's not getting enough sleep, or eating properly."

"Let's be clear, it's more than a little *good-night text*," Yumi chided. She leaned toward Tally. "He's requested pictures three times."

"*Samantha!*" Tally squeaked, nudging her leg with her heeled boot.

"Samantha," echoed a stern voice behind them.

Sam popped up from Yumi's desk and turned to face Barbara. "Barbara, hello. Apologies that I wasn't at my desk."

Barbara sighed. "It's not a problem. I know it's Yumi's last day." She held out a hand to Yumi. "Good luck on your next venture. I've been a loyal subscriber to *Who What Wear* for years, and I look forward to reading your work."

"Th-Thank you, Barbara. That means the world," Yumi replied, looking a little starstruck.

Barbara nodded and dropped her hand. "Samantha, my office, if you have a moment."

She nodded, her stomach churning. "Yes, of course."

Sam followed Barbara round Yumi's cubicle, then turned to look at her friend.

Yumi held up two thumbs. *You got this!* she mouthed, then blew her a kiss.

She blew one back, then stepped into the office.

Barbara closed the door, but remained standing. "So, I think it's rather obvious at this point."

Sam's heart fell. "You chose someone else for the position."

Barbara looked surprised. "The opposite. I want you for the job."

Sam sucked in a breath. "Seriously?"

"Of course. Rather than boast about how great you would be at the position and toting on and on about your accolades—I hate when people do that—you were the only one who came to me with a strong argument and game plan on how we can make improvements. You proved to me in less than ten minutes that you have a business mindset that will help drive this publication forward. I like what you proposed, and I want to get started on things immediately."

"Immediately?" Sam breathed.

"Yes, well, as in, after the holiday." Barbara folded her hands in front of her. "I would love to have some big splashy piece up on the site on January first, something that makes it clear that we are entering a new era here at *Nourished*. I know it's a quick turnaround, but I think if we really put our heads together, we can make this happen."

Sam rubbed her chin, her mind racing with possibilities. "I don't hate the idea. My only concern is finding a freelance writer to put something together in enough time. Especially now that so many of them aren't taking pieces for the rest of the year."

"Then write it yourself."

Her eyes widened. "Seriously?"

"Of course." Barbara crossed her arms. "What better way to enter a new era than to have the one driving it to welcome us in? It doesn't have to be long, but something that will create enough buzz. I've already asked the art department to put together something for the site and for social."

She worried her bottom lip, her mind on Nico and OmniCorp and its employees. "Barbara, I don't want people to feel overworked. We are nearing Christmas, and we're supposed to have this week off."

"I had a meeting with them and promised two extra weeks of paid vacation in the new year, which they are allowed to take starting February first, after our busy season. They were not mad about that, I promise you." She nodded her head. "I take good care of my employees. And I will trust you to do the same. Advocate for them."

"I will," she replied confidently. "I'll make sure of it."

"Good. Can you have your piece to me by the twenty-ninth? I will also need you to evaluate résumés that have come in for Yumi's position. We will need a solid writer on our team when the new year hits."

"Absolutely, I can do that." She held out her hand. "Thank you for this opportunity. I won't let you down."

Barbara's smile turned into something soft, something Sam hadn't seen on her face before. "You will, Samantha. That's how it is in this kind of job. I expect your best work, but I don't expect perfection. Understand?"

Sam swallowed. "Yes, I understand."

Barbara nodded as Sam dropped her hand and went to exit the office. But before she did, her mind played over what Barbara told her. She'd gotten the job, not because she worked her way to the top, but because she proved that she was the smartest person for the job. It didn't take sucking up to the boss to get there. It took strategy and guts. It took standing up for herself and having faith that she could do it, just like Nico told her. And it worked.

She turned back to Barbara. "Barbara?"

Barbara smirked. "Yes?"

"I would also like two extra weeks of paid vacation to use in the new year, since I will be working over the holidays."

Barbara's face peeled into a genuine smile. "Of course, Sam. Request granted."

Sam nodded. "Thank you."

Then she exited the office. She closed her eyes, took a deep breath, then swiped open her phone.

Nico paced back and forth in his apartment. He still had his gym shorts on after getting a quick workout in the building's gym that morning before he glued himself back at the desk. Somehow the day got ahead of him and it was five o'clock at night, and he had yet to shower.

He was unsure how to handle what he'd discovered in Snipbit's files of code. *A secret broadcasting platform.* Despite what they'd previously believed, it seemed the former video-sharing app did have a new live broadcasting user experience they were working on. Nubo could attempt to convert it into their platform—and by New Year's, no less —but he wasn't sure if he could get it done by himself. He needed help.

He groaned, then opened up his email. He'd avoided contacting anyone from his team until that point. It wasn't like emailing them was against the rules, they just might not respond. They had a right to peacefully protest, and as long as Nico didn't threaten that right, he would be fine.

To: jkonicki@omnicorp.com

From: nguiliano@omnicorp.com

Subject: I found something.

Jer,

I was culling through all of the code Snipbit sent us, and I found the base work for a live broadcasting platform. They must have been working on it in secret. The interface is built up enough that we could seriously make this work. I have attached the file so you can take a look.

Wanted to keep you informed. Hope all is well.

Nico

He couldn't ask Jeremy to come back to work and help him, but he secretly hoped his email would be enticing enough. He hoped that the camaraderie he'd built with him over the past couple of months would have built up some kind of empathy.

He doubted it. OmniCorp had been awful to all of them.

His phone rang.

Hopeful that it was Jeremy, Nico immediately answered, not looking at the caller ID. "Hello?"

"Okay so it's the thirty-fourth floor, but what *number?*" Sam asked.

Nico's mouth fell open. "Are you in my building?"

"And on your floor."

He could hear her voice echoing in the hallway outside.

Nico ran to the door and pulled it open.

Sam spun around, halfway down the hall. She was still in her work clothes, her black tote around her shoulder, a plastic bag with takeout containers dangling from her fingertips. "Hi," she whispered.

"Samantha." He leaned against his doorframe. "What are you doing here?"

She lifted the bag. "Feeding you."

"How'd you know where I live?"

"You're the one who wanted to share our locations." Her eyes scanned his chest. "Where's your shirt?"

"Never put one on today."

She scrunched her nose. "Have you even *showered?*"

He grimaced. "No."

"It's so much worse than I thought," she grumbled. She walked toward him. "Move, let me in."

He did without a fuss, letting her stomp her way into the apartment and drop the takeout onto his counter.

Her eyes bulged out of her head as she scanned the inside of his apartment. The floor-to-ceiling windows with the view of East River and the Brooklyn Bridge. The eighty-five-inch flat screen and the mahogany shelf of carefully organized vintage video games. His corner office facing the window with four computer monitors. His gold bar cart with bottles and bottles of the small-producer whiskey and gin he liked to collect.

She walked to his bedroom, her mouth falling open at the king-sized bed. Then she made her way to the bathroom. "Oh my god, is that a *bathtub?* With jet streams? And a walk-in shower?"

He smiled. "It has a rainfall shower head."

"*NICOLAS!*" she screamed. "How much money do you have?!"

He chuckled to himself, drifting over to whatever delicious-smelling thing Sam brought in. Curry and sweet coconut wafted when he unsealed the bag. *Thai food.*

She appeared in his living room, coat slung over her arm. "Nico!"

He smiled and leaned against the counter, looking her in the eye. "I have a lot, okay? I've done well for myself."

"Yeah, you think?" She turned slowly, scanning his apartment again. "This is *crazy!*"

"Well, I may not have it for long." He rubbed his face and groaned. "Not unless I can figure out how to make this live video platform happen by New Year's."

"He's still demanding that?" Sam asked softly.

Nico's jaw ticked. "Yes. And if I don't, I'll probably lose my job."

Sam sighed and kicked off her heels, then made her way to him. She took his hands. "Come on. Time for a shower."

"Sam, I have so much to do—"

"Give me one hour. *Just one.* Shower, eat, let your brain rest. Then I'll leave you alone to get back to it." She chewed her lip. "Maybe we could also discuss Christmas?"

"Don't remind me," he grumbled. "Fine. I'll take the bait. But only because you're cute."

"Hence why I'm here," she teased. "Come on, let's go."

She pulled him to the bathroom, then turned on his shower. Nico watched as she scampered away, then returned with little bottles of essential oils that she must have unearthed from her tote bag. He removed his socks as she sprinkled a couple drops into the shower then lit the candle propped next to his sink.

"Okay." She paused. "Get in."

"Are you going to watch me strip?"

"Yes. I want to make sure you actually get in there."

He sighed, then removed his boxers and got in.

Sam didn't leave. Instead, she sat on his counter. "Want a shower beer or something?"

He laughed, slathering his hair with shampoo. "A shower beer? Did you bring some?"

"Yes. I picked a six-pack up from the bodega." She tapped her foot. "I had a feeling your fridge was empty."

"You're unfortunately correct," he mumbled. He scrubbed his scalp and rinsed, then opened the door slightly, steam escaping into the bathroom. "Although I'll take a shower Samantha, if it's available."

She frowned. "Be serious."

"I *am* serious," he said, lowering his voice to make his point. "Get in here with me."

She tapped her foot.

Before Nico had the chance to jump out of the shower and get her blazer and trousers wet, Sam stood up and undid her belt.

Chapter 23

By the time Sam stepped into the shower, Nico was already hard as a rock. Watching Sam strip out of her work clothes was certainly the worst kind of tease, given that she wore quite a few layers thanks to the cold. By the time she got to her bra and revealed it was the kind that unhooked from the front, it took everything in him not to start touching himself.

Sam closed the door and stepped into the stream, the water smoothing out her hair, her mascara dripping down her cheeks.

She smirked, then pointed at his dick. "That thing is dangerous."

He laughed and snatched her waist, then backed her up against the cool shower wall, pressing into her stomach. "It really doesn't take much when I'm around you, baby girl."

"*Mmm,*" she hummed, looping her arms around his neck. "Guess what?" she whispered.

He pressed his nose into her cheek, breathing in her familiar scent. "What?"

"I got the job."

He grinned and faced her. "Of course you did. I didn't have any doubts."

She smiled back at him. "Although I'm probably going to have to work a bit over the holidays."

"You and me both," he grumbled.

She pressed in closer, adding pressure to his groin. It drove him mad. "We could hunker down together, if you want," she teased.

The thought of being together around Christmas was too depressing at the moment. Nico knew he wouldn't get the chance to touch Sam like this. "I don't want to talk about Christmas," he whispered. "I don't want to talk at all, actually."

She smirked. "You don't want my words?"

"I said *I* don't want to talk." His eyes dropped to her lips. "You, on the other hand, can tell me all of the dirty things you want me to do to you."

She wiggled, the slippery feel of her skin in his hands driving him absolutely bananas. "Putting me in charge, huh?" she asked.

"Sammy girl, you're *always* in charge."

Her smile was devious. *Evil.* "Touch me again, Nico."

"Gladly," he growled. Then he twisted her around and pressed his dick against her back, squishing her between himself and the cool shower wall.

She whimpered as he tucked a knee between her legs. She moved slowly, grinding on his thigh, and he could feel every wet slip of her cunt.

He grinned and bit her ear, sliding one hand to her breast, the other on her hip. He squeezed her nipple. "You like that?"

"I thought you didn't want to talk," she rasped.

"You're right. Then talk to me." He slipped his tongue inside her ear.

She gasped.

He chuckled, then drifted toward the warm spot between her legs, releasing his knee so he could feel all of her on his fingertips.

"Move in circles," she demanded. "Like last time."

He did as he was told, moving in slow, excruciating beats, her body shaking against his as she whimpered. He squeezed her nipple again.

"Faster," she demanded.

He quickened his pace, but only slightly. Then he slipped two fingers inside of her and pumped in and out.

"Oh god," she breathed, throwing her head back to his shoulder. "That, right there."

He flicked her clit with his thumb, and she cried out.

"*Mmmmm*," he hummed.

Sam pressed her ass into his groin, his length finding a home between her cheeks.

He groaned.

"You like that, huh?"

"*Evil*," he whispered. Then he curled his fingers inside of her.

Sam gasped, slamming her hands against the wall. "Oh god. I'm gonna—"

"Give it to me, baby girl," he whispered. He squeezed her nipple again. "Show me you want me."

"I want you," she gasped. "I've always wanted you."

He pumped his fingers, faster and faster. "Tell me how you want me."

She leaned her head on his chest again, eyes closed. "I want you to make me orgasm as hard as last time. I want to scream. Then I want to taste you, Nico, until you can't stand it anymore. You'll sit on that bench over there and I'll climb on your lap so I can feel what it's like being on top."

"*Jesus*," he growled, pressing hard into her back, wanting desperately to sink his cock into that pretty little cunt. "Samantha Carter and her dirty mouth."

She smiled, and *my god*, she was stunning. Wet mascara and all.

He slipped a third finger into her, and it was enough to completely undo her. She clenched so hard and, true to her fantasy, it made her scream.

"That's my girl," he whispered, licking her neck. He kept circling her clit. "Keep going, show me how much you want it."

She crested into another orgasm, her body shaking underneath the weight of his.

She slipped out of his grasp, then to his surprise, quickly whipped around and grabbed his shoulders. Then, with a force he'd never seen, Sam turned him around and pinned him against the wall.

His dick was throbbing. She was staring at it.

"You're in control," he repeated. "What do you want to do with it?"

Sam smirked up at him, then got down on her knees.

His eyes widened. The water from the shower plastered her hair to her face. He brushed it away, then curled the strands around his fist. "Is this really what you want?"

Sam bit her lip, which made him laugh. Then she leaned forward and stuck out her tongue, licking from the base of his shaft all the way to the tip.

He gripped her hair hard. "*Sam*, I have to confess something."

She cupped his balls. His cock twitched. "Right now?"

"Remember how you said that swears are filler words?"

She squeezed again, and he whimpered.

"Well, in this moment, when you're being all hot and touching me, I really, *really* want to swear."

She hummed, running a hand up and down his cock. "You really, *really* want to, huh?"

He nodded, watching her. *How was this happening?* "Yes. I can't think of other words," he admitted.

"I think you can," she teased. She licked at his tip, and he wasn't sure if he would even make it to the part where she got to screw him on top. "But I'll make you a deal."

"Y-yeah?"

"I'll allow one swear. Use it wisely."

He grinned. Then in a moment, Sam flattened her tongue and swallowed his cock.

He gripped her hair harder, slamming a fist into the wall.

She moved in and out, her tongue at the soft spot underneath his shaft, and he was almost positive he was going to scream. "God, you're so hot. How are you this perfect?"

She hummed, and the sensation had him slamming his fist again.

She laughed, releasing his dick with a soft *plop*. "Nico, don't break the shower!"

"It would be absolutely worth it."

She laughed and sat back on her heels.

He shook his head, helping her up. "It's a good thing you stopped. I was not going to last long."

She grinned as they curled together under the water, falling into a mind-numbing kind of kiss, his heart beating faster and faster. *Sam, Sam, Sam*, it seemed to say. He was completely and utterly gone for this woman. And he wasn't scared in the slightest to admit that to himself. He'd do anything for her. *Anything.*

She moved a head back, detaching her lips from his. "Condom?"

He threw his head back and groaned. "It's in my nightstand." He squeezed her ass. "Want to move this to the bed?"

"Nope." She slipped out of his grasp, then opened the door. "Stay right here."

"*Sam!*"

But she was already gone, making a dash for his nightstand, leaving droplets of water across his oak floor. She was shivering when she returned, but he warmed her up quickly, roaming his hands across her body, licking her nipples as she peeled off the wrapper and covered his cock.

She pointed to the corner bench. "Sit."

"Gladly."

He took a seat as Sam climbed onto his lap. He rubbed her clit as she kissed him, then she sank slowly onto him until he was fully inside her.

She straightened, snapped her eyes shut. "Oh god."

He leaned forward, muscles tensing. "Does it hurt?"

She scrunched her nose. "Will you...do the thing you did last time?"

He slipped a hand between her legs and touched her wet cunt. "You're like velvet in my hands. I don't think I'll ever get over how you feel."

He felt Sam relax around him as she began to move up and down. Up and down. "This...this feels good," she moaned.

"I *live* to make you feel good," he replied, removing his hand and gripping her hip, digging his thumb below her hipbone.

Sam blinked her eyes open, looking surprised by what

he said. But she was easily distracted, moving at an even faster pace.

The pressure built up in his thighs. He sucked on one of her breasts, rolling her nipple against his tongue.

"*Nico*," she moaned, so soft it was barely a whisper.

He grinned and leaned back, watching his girl ride him, the water cascading down her breasts that bounced, so luscious and full. "Sam?"

Her eyes remained closed. "Y-yes?"

"I want you to fuck my cock so hard that you *scream* my name."

She gasped, raking her hands through his hair and pulling hard, bringing his face close to her.

"I want everyone in this building, everyone in *Manhattan*, to know who you belong to."

He slipped a hand between them, touching her in the way she liked, and she moaned again.

"Who do you belong to, Sam?"

"You," she whispered.

His hand moved faster. "Louder."

In and out. In and out. "*You*," she insisted. He could feel her tightening around him.

"Louder," he growled. He squeezed her clit with his pointer finger and thumb.

She screamed his name so loud he was almost positive the neighbors heard them. And he was mighty proud of it, especially after she clenched around his dick so hard that he came instantly, his roar even louder than hers.

He kissed her, guiding her slowly through her comedown.

"Now that..." she breathed, wet hair falling forward as she pressed her forehead to his. "Is a great use for a single swear word."

He smiled into her mouth.

Chapter 24

SAM SAT on Nico's couch, bare legs draped across his lap, bowl of green curry chicken and rice in her hands. She watched Nico as he politely scarfed down his meal, his hair still wet and slicked back. She smiled at the sight of him, of what they did in the shower, at the feel of her deliciously sore thighs.

I live to make you feel good. The words he'd spoken played over and over in her head. How similar they were to Yumi's advice mere days ago. Everything with Nico, even down to the ways he touched her and took care of her, felt like they were cosmically divined—written in the stars. The sex wasn't the only thing that felt good. When she was around him, everything felt good. She felt good. More than good—she was superbly happy.

Would her brother see that? Would he understand?

Nico placed his empty bowl on his coffee table, then began massaging Sam's calves. "Just so we're clear, since I was beyond distracted before...I'm really, really proud of you for getting the job."

She smiled. "You did make it clear earlier, but...thanks."

He leaned back on the couch, eyes on her. "How are you feeling about it?"

She pursed her lips. "Nervous, because I don't want to screw things up. I think I need to accept the fact that I probably will a few times, but I can still give this job my best."

Nico's mouth curled into a soft smile. "That's a lot more mature than how I handled my promotion."

"How'd you feel?"

His smile faded. "Like I was going to throw up every five seconds. That someone would walk into my office at some point and let me know they made a mistake, and they actually meant to give the job to someone else."

"But they never did," she pointed out.

He sighed. "I know. But I still feel that way sometimes. Especially with everything going on. Now it's less about them making a mistake and more about them realizing that hiring me was a bad call."

She placed a hand on his. "That won't happen."

He shook his head, like he wanted to avoid the conversation. "Let's get back to you. You said you have to work over the holidays?"

Sam launched into the project Barbara proposed, the cadence of her voice building and quickening with each sentence. She was surprised she was excited by the prospect of it. It made her want to sit down and start writing.

"But I did tell her that I would like two more weeks of paid vacation next year since she's asking this of me," she explained.

Nico's eyes widened with glee. "You said that to her?"

Sam nodded, setting her empty bowl next to his. "Yes, I did."

He chuckled then pulled on her legs so she was lying down, then curled his body next to hers, nose pressed to nose. "I shouldn't be surprised. You're going to take this world by storm, Sammy girl."

She beamed, running a finger down Nico's cheek, drawing a line to his neck. She tugged on his crew neck. "We'll see, baby dog."

"Okay, can we talk about the nickname? I think we can do better."

Sam pretended to look shocked. "But you were the cutest little baby dog."

Nico growled and clamped a hand around her wrists, pinning her to the couch cushions. She laughed out loud as he rolled on top of her and nipped at her neck. He stuck his tongue out and licked her skin.

She gasped, then wiggled underneath him. "Give me my arms back," she demanded.

"Hmmm." Nico lifted his head. "How about no."

"That's it, you're mean."

He barked out a laugh, then dipped low, kissing his way down her neck, tucking his hand underneath the New York Knicks T-shirt he'd let her borrow. "Oh, I can show you mean."

She grinned. "Oh yeah?"

"*Yeah.*"

Before Nico's hand could explore any further, two phones dinged in the kitchen. His, and hers.

They both froze.

Sam's brow furrowed. "Do you think that was a coincidence, or—?"

Their phones dinged in unison again.

They both sighed. "Jeff."

Nico jumped up and retrieved their phones, handing Sam hers when he returned. "He must have some kind of telepathy for when we're together."

She sat up, crossing her legs as she swiped her screen open. "I doubt it."

Nico sat down next to her. "He doesn't have your location, does he?"

"No, Nico. You are the only one."

He grinned. "Really?"

She glared at him. "Don't let it get to your head."

"It is *way* too late for that."

She shook her head as she glanced at the group text Jeff started.

JEFF

T-minus two days!!

Need me to pick you guys up at the station? Which trains are you taking?

Nico blinked up at her, left brow raised.
Sam stuck out her tongue and typed back.

SAM

That would be great! I'm planning on the 3:30pm out of Grand Central.

Nico chuckled.

NICO

Funny, I was too.

Sam dug her toe into Nico's ribcage. "You are such a liar."

"No I'm not. You don't know what my plans were."

She shook her head. "What were your plans?"

"To get on whatever train you were planning on."

She shoved her foot at him again and he laughed out loud.

> JEFF
>
> What a coinky dink! Daniel and I will pick
> you both up then.
>
> Sam, bring me the good bagels.

Sam rolled her eyes.

"The good bagels?" Nico questioned.

"It's that spot near my apartment you went to. He says they're better than the shop in Willow."

"Every bagel spot is better than the one in Willow."

She crossed her arms. "*Wow*, you've lived in the city for three months and are already a bagel snob?"

"Isn't that a rite of passage? And don't even get me *started* on the pizza."

"What about the cannoli?"

He smirked, tugging on Sam's arm until she climbed into his lap. "There's only one spot I'll go to, and with one person," he said, twirling a strand of her damp hair with a finger.

She sighed. "I'm nervous about being around him," she confessed.

"Then let's just tell him. Rip the Band-Aid off."

"Nico, no."

"Come on, baby girl. I can't stand the thought of having to fake it around you for a few days. It's going to drive me crazy."

"You've faked it with me before, remember?"

"That wasn't ever fake, Sam. It was all real to me. The whole time."

Sam pressed her lips together, afraid to speak what she felt deep in her soul. *It wasn't fake for me either.*

He squeezed her waist tighter. "What are you so afraid of?"

"I don't want to upset him," she whispered.

"Will he really be that mad about this? I don't understand why he wouldn't be happy to see us together."

"It's just...different, with him," she replied, careful with her choice of words. There was so much Nico didn't know. And even if it was the thing standing between the two of them ending up together, it still wasn't her story to tell. It had to come from Jeff.

Nico exhaled.

"I'm sorry I'm making you wait," she confessed.

"I'll do whatever makes you comfortable, baby. He's my friend, but more importantly, he's your brother. I don't want to ruin what the two of you worked so hard to build. But I —" His exhale sounded pained. "I'm frustrated that he hasn't really talked to me about why he was so mad all those years ago, for the way he shut me out."

She nodded, wiping at the water that pooled in her eyes. "I think the two of you should talk it out. But...after Christmas, okay?"

Nico sighed, then planted a soft kiss on her lips. "Will you stay the night?"

"You don't have to keep working? I don't want to be in your way, and I have to pack."

"*Please*, Sam. I need you. Stay."

She brushed her fingers through his hair. "Okay. I'll stay the night."

Sam swept through the turnstile at Grand Central, zigzagging through narrow spaces as tourists gathered throughout the station. It was her own fault for thinking the place would be quiet on Christmas Eve, that the stations and the streets would be free from the bustle of workday traffic and people traveling home. No, even after four years of living in Manhattan, Sam had a lot of lessons to learn.

And now she was late for meeting Nico.

Meet me by the golden clock, he'd texted.

Their train was set to depart in nine minutes. She jogged through the station, trying her best not to slip on her heeled boots as she snaked her way through bodies and into the main terminal. The place was crowded with people taking photos of the iconic turquoise ceiling dotted with constellations.

She grumbled, standing up on her tiptoes, trying to see where Nico was.

It wasn't hard to find him and his tall physique. He leaned against the marble at the side of the information desk, the golden clock above him, his head towering over everyone. He wore his caramel wool coat over a sweater and slacks, a leather duffel slung across his shoulders.

Her shoulders relaxed as she made her way over to him. "Thank god you're so tall or I would have never—"

Nico stopped her midsentence with a mind-numbing kiss. He squeezed her waist and lifted her up, his hand moving to her hair as he cradled the back of her head. His kiss was devouring and full of devotion.

A small applause broke out from tourists around them.

Nico let her down gently, then dipped her low, peppering more kisses on her lips and her cheeks.

"*Nico*, we're going to miss our train."

Kiss. Kiss. Kiss. "We have a few more minutes." He moved his mouth to her neck.

"We're. In. Public," she mumbled between kisses.

He steadied her, then took the handle of her suitcase. "I needed to get my fill."

She shook her head and took his free hand.

He lifted their joined hands up, twirling her in a full circle, then dropped his arm on her shoulder, tucking her close.

They made it with three minutes to spare, but that didn't give them much of a choice on where to sit. The train was already packed with other New Yorkers heading home for the holidays. They found two seats across from one another next to the window, squeezed next to two strangers near the aisle.

Nico slid their bags overhead, then frowned as he took his seat. He leaned forward. "I was really hoping I could make out with you this entire ride."

The middle-aged woman sitting next to Nico turned to him with a look of disgust.

Nico held up a hand and gestured toward Sam as he faced the woman. "What? Can you blame me? Look at her."

She frowned and shook her head, then opened the book on her lap.

Sam covered her mouth and tried not to laugh as the train rolled forward and pulled out of the station. She reached into her tote bag and pulled out her laptop. "It's okay. I need to work anyway, and I don't need a distraction."

"But I love distractions."

"*Nico.*"

"Ugh, *fine.*"

Nico also pulled out his laptop, the two of them working in silence as the train zipped north, across Harlem and the Bronx and up the east side of the Hudson River.

Sam crossed her leg, computer balanced on her lap as she typed sentence after sentence. She knew what she had was already far too long for what Barbara probably expected, but she didn't care; she'd edit it down later. Right now, it was a matter of getting all of her best ideas on the page. And she had a lot of them.

Every few minutes, between the moments he furiously typed, Nico placed a hand on Sam's leg and massaged her thigh, a crinkle between his brow as he stared at whatever was on his screen.

"Next stop, Willow, in ten minutes. Please make sure to take all of your bags and belongings as you exit the train."

Nico sighed and eyed Sam, no trace of the earlier tension on his face. After a number of stops through the Hudson Valley, they finally had their rows to themselves. He leaned in and cupped her cheek. "One for the road?"

Sam smiled and kissed him on the lips. She could sense Nico's desire to linger there, but she pulled back and leaned on the vinyl seat. "So what's our plan?" she asked.

Nico sighed as he closed his laptop, then leaned against his elbows. "You're the one in charge, Sammy girl."

She tapped her foot.

He moved a hand to her calf. She eyed the way his hand practically covered the circumference. "Okay, for starters, you probably shouldn't touch me like this."

"But what if no one is looking?"

She tilted her head and narrowed her eyes. *Be serious.*

He groaned.

"No kissing, no touching."

"It would probably be weird if I didn't, like, hug you?"

She pursued her lips. "Fine. Hugging is fine."

"Brilliant."

She rolled her eyes. "But you have to act like we're just friends."

"While I die slowly on the inside."

She slapped his leg and he laughed. "Be serious, Nico."

"I *am*." He placed a hand on his heart. "But I promise to be on my best behavior when I'm around everyone."

The train began to slow, the Willow station coming into view. "Thank you," she replied.

He sighed as he looked out the window. Then he dropped his grip on her calf and leaned back.

Sam followed his gaze to the gray Honda Accord and the couple huddled together, waiting for them. Daniel wore his tweed jacket and jeans, one arm looped around a shivering Jeff, who was in only a sweatshirt. But her brother was smiling, his eyes scanning the windows like he was trying to spot them.

She stood up and shuffled out of the row as the train rolled to a stop. She raised an arm to snatch her suitcase, but Nico stopped her.

"Nico, come on, we can't look like—"

"Samantha, I think if I walked off this train and *wasn't* carrying your bag, your brother would kill me." He shooed her away. "Now move."

She grumbled to herself as she stepped off the train, Nico with their bags close at her heels.

When Jeff saw them, he threw his arms in the air. "They're *here!*" he yelled.

Sam's stomach churned as she descended the station steps.

Jeff didn't hesitate to pull her into a hug and squeeze her tight. "I missed you."

She smiled and melted into his embrace. "I missed you too."

Daniel popped the trunk and helped Nico load their bags.

Jeff stepped back, hands on Sam's shoulders. "I haven't heard from you, you're so busy these days."

She swallowed. "Yeah, I am."

Nico stepped toward them, a devious twinkle in his eye. "Probably because she got a big promotion."

Jeff's mouth fell open, eyes darting between them. "*What?* A promotion?" He dropped his hands and looked at his best friend. "Wait, how did you know before me?"

She sucked in a breath.

He pointed at the train with his thumb as it slowly crawled away from the station. "We caught up on the train."

"Oh, right, duh."

"I only found out a couple days ago," she answered, her words coming out fast. "My boss wanted me to start right away, so I've been super busy."

"What's the job?"

"Nutrition editor."

"*Seriously?!* But like, you only just started at the company!"

"I know."

"We all know that doesn't mean she's not qualified," Nico butted in. He winked at her.

Her chest squeezed. *God, he's handsome.*

Daniel placed an arm around Sam's shoulders. "Congratulations, my girl."

She relaxed, remembering how much she liked Daniel. "Thank you."

"Shall we go?" he asked. "Nico, we'll drop you at home on the way?"

"Yes, thank you."

"You suckers are in the back," Jeff said, playfully pushing Nico's shoulder. Nico pretended to punch him, then the two broke out in one of their usual fake fights.

"Have they always been like this?" Daniel asked, the two of them watching in fascination as Jeff threw a punch and Nico ducked it, his wool coat flaring up behind him from the wind.

Sam sighed. "Yes. Get used to it."

Daniel chuckled. "Not much changes, huh?"

Nico gripped Jeff's head into a headlock, then gave him a noogie. Jeff screamed about Nico ruining his hair, but Nico didn't budge. Instead, he looked up at Sam with a devilish grin on his face.

Her heart pounded in her chest. *Some things do change though.*

They eventually all piled into the car, Jeff's face flushed red while Nico still looked easy-breezy, completely unfazed. They settled in beside one another in the back, the console conveniently dividing the space between them.

Nico went to lift it up, but Sam slammed it back down with her forearm, eyes slitted. *Don't you dare.*

He suppressed a smile and placed his hands in his lap as Daniel backed out of their spot.

"So you guys caught up on the train, huh?" Jeff swiveled around in his seat. "Did Nico complain about his job the whole time?"

"I don't complain about my job," he deadpanned.

"I wouldn't blame you if you wanted to," Daniel said, stopping at a red light and flicking on the right turn signal. "That strike is not looking good."

"How bad is it?" Jeff asked.

Nico tilted his head forward. "Bad. The numbers jumped to eighty-five percent of the company on strike."

"*What?!*"

Nico's face fell. "How do you not know this? Don't you live on Nubo?"

"I deleted it for my mental health! I've been overwhelmed by all the—" His eyes flicked to Daniel, then back to Nico. "Inspiration."

Nico nodded, like he understood.

Jeff whirled around and faced forward, snatching up his phone. "Although I am redownloading it right now because I need to see this."

They rode in silence for a few minutes, slowly making their way through the winding hills of Willow. The trees were covered in snow, and the backstreets were barely plowed enough to grant them access.

Sam crossed her legs and leaned her head back, doing her best to avoid the awkwardness that hopefully only *she* felt between all of them.

Nico's phone screen lit up in his lap. Sam quicked a look, noticing his wallpaper was a picture of *her*. The selfie she sent him from the office weeks ago.

She panicked, looking at her own screen and the generic holiday background she'd replaced with a picture of them. She picked it up and typed.

SAM

Change your background now.

Nico raised a brow at the text, then smirked as he replied.

NICO

I like living on the edge.

SAM

NICOLAS.

Nico didn't reply as he gazed out the window, placing his phone in his lap and settling his forearm on the console, brushing it against hers. Then a warm hand gripped her suspended ankle. His expression was completely blank as he blinked and tilted his head toward her.

"This strike is nuts, Nico," Jeff said. "I'm so sorry this is happening."

Nico didn't respond, eyes still on Sam.

She attempted to pull her leg free, but he only tightened his grip.

"Wait, Sam, did you get me the bagels," Jeff said, whirling around.

Nico dropped her ankle before Jeff could notice.

Sam exhaled, face feeling hot. "Yes, they're in my tote."

"And you got the *good* ones?"

She tilted her head. "Yes, there are five jalapeño cheddar bagels in there."

Jeff turned back around. "Fantastic. You're the best."

She exhaled as she looked over at Nico. His lips were pressed together, like he was trying not to laugh.

Jerk, she mouthed.

He chuckled to himself as Daniel pulled up to the Giuliano house, his black Bronco parked out front, the snow already scraped off the top.

She watched his shoulders loosen at the sight of his car and his childhood home.

"I forgot how big that car is," Sam said, eyeing the giant wheels that seemed like they were perfect for this weather.

Nico turned to her with a grin so devious, she knew she was in for it. "So *big*, huh?"

Jeff laughed so hard he dropped his phone.

Sam kicked Nico as he got out of the car, laughing hysterically as well. "You are so inappropriate!" she screamed as he slammed the door shut.

She watched as Nico removed his duffel from the trunk,

then closed it. He leaned forward so they were eye to eye through the back window, then gave her a subtle wink.

She shook her head, watching as he made his way up the walkway to his front door, then escaped into the house.

When she turned to face the front, she noticed Daniel watching her through the rearview mirror.

Chapter 25

SAM
Best behavior, huh?

NICO
I don't know what you're talking about.

SAM
You broke the no touching rule in less than five minutes!

FIVE.

NICO
Whoops

SAM
NICO

NICO
* sends devil horns emoji *

Nico chuckled to himself as he read through their texts again, sitting in the driver's seat of his Bronco.

Mom helped Mama into the back, then climbed into the front seat. "What are you smiling at?"

"I haven't seen that smile in *years*," Mama commented, pointing at him through the rearview mirror.

He turned the ignition, the car lights dimming off, the night sky shielding the expression he tried to work into submission.

Mom poked his arm. "Is it a girl?"

Nico placed a hand on the passenger seat and glanced behind him as he backed out of the driveway.

Mama inhaled, a hand flying to her mouth. "A girl?!"

"Stop," Nico said as he switched the gears, making his way down the road for the two-minute drive. Normally he would walk to the Carter house, but with all of the snow and the three of them dressed in their holiday best—along with the roasted carrots, fluffy dinner rolls, and peppermint brownies Mama made—driving made more sense.

"What do you mean *stop*? Is that a yes?" Mama screeched.

Mom squinted her eyes. "You're keeping something from us."

"No, I'm not," he answered coolly, eyes on the road.

"Nicolas Giuliano, do not lie to me." Mama pulled on her long muumuu dress. "Let me remind you I gave you this body."

"Yes, respect your mothers, Nicolas," Mom deadpanned.

He pulled into the driveway behind Jeff's Honda Accord and cut the ignition. "All right, fine. There is a girl."

They cheered. He tried shushing them by pressing a finger to his mouth.

"Please don't say anything tonight," he pleaded. "It's still really new and I don't have much to say."

"Does Jeff know? He has to know." Mama beamed. "Our inseparable boys."

Nico clenched his jaw. Both of his mothers continued to believe that Jeff and Nico remained best friends, even if they didn't see one another for years. He used the excuse of not seeing each other on finishing school and working new jobs and not having enough money to travel. It was easier than explaining the truth to them—that his best friend refused to talk to him until *he* deemed it okay to do so. "Jeff actually doesn't know. I haven't had the chance to tell him yet."

"Well, let's go tell him!" Mama moved to open her door.

Nico panicked. He grabbed her knee. "Don't. *Please*. I think he plans on proposing tonight. Let's not make tonight about me, okay?"

"Proposing?!" Mama squealed.

"How do you know that?" Mom asked.

"Just a hunch," he replied. "Sam feels the same way."

"You talked to Sam about it?"

Nico nodded. "We rode the train together this afternoon, remember?"

Mom lifted a brow in Nico's direction as Mama squealed again and hopped out of the car.

Nico helped carry the trays of food, following close behind his mothers as they were greeted by Jeff and Sam's parents at the door. Mama and Mrs. Carter hugged, talking a mile a minute as they exclaimed how they didn't hang out enough despite living so close.

"Nico, my word, I forgot how tall you are." Mrs. Carter had her hand around Mama's waist. She reached up and pinched his cheek. "And so handsome, look at you!"

He grinned as he placed the trays of food down, then dipped low and enveloped Mrs. Carter in a hug. "Thank you for having us."

She patted his back, then squeezed him tight. *You're growing up too fast*, she always said. Her hair was down, curls wild, and she still smelled like cinnamon and clove. He wondered if it was her everyday scent, or whether she'd recently baked her pumpkin pie. Regardless, he associated it with her. It brought him back to the many Christmas Eve dinners of the past, and he hoped, deep in his heart, there'd be many more of them to come.

Mrs. Carter released him with a tear in her eye, then swept up the trays of food with Mama. "Let's get these in the kitchen."

Daniel came into view, patting Nico on his back. "Jeff will be down in a minute," he relayed to Nico. Then he reached for a tray in Mrs. Carter's hands and helped carry it to the kitchen.

Nico removed his shoes as everyone in the foyer dispersed—except for one smaller figure in the corner.

Sam leaned against the wall, adorned in a velvet evergreen babydoll dress that cropped short at her upper thighs. Black lacy stockings covered her legs, and her feet were tucked into fuzzy Santa slippers.

He bit his lip and turned his gaze down, concentrating on his shoes. "Samantha."

"Nicolas," she drawled.

He rubbed his face, then peeked to the entrance leading to the kitchen and up the stairs. No one was coming, no one was watching.

He stalked over to her and placed a hand on her waist. "*Evil*," he whispered.

She grinned. "You like it?"

"What do you think?"

She chuckled, watching for approaching family herself before returning her gaze to his. She traced a finger down his navy cashmere sweater. "Navy, huh?"

"You like it?"

She rolled her eyes, and then they both were silently laughing.

Nico snatched her hand and kissed the top of it. "You're stunning, baby girl," he whispered.

He heard pounding footsteps from upstairs and stepped back, shoving his hands in his pockets as Jeff appeared.

"Ah, my two favorite humans," he said, throwing his arms around their shoulders and squeezing them tight. Nico had to lean over to get at the right height, his face close to Sam as Jeff pressed them all together. Her face flushed at their proximity.

"Are you saying that a certain hottie in the kitchen *isn't* your favorite human?" Sam teased.

Jeff scoffed. "He's barely human. Daniel is a god."

"No I'm not! Stop saying that to people!" Daniel yelled from the kitchen.

Jeff threw his head back and laughed, then released his grip on them and shoved Nico's chest. "*Smash Brothers* later?"

"Would it be Christmas Eve without an attempt at breaking your streak?" Nico joked.

"You will never break it," Jeff replied. Then he pointed to Sam. "Are you at least going to *try* to play this year?"

Sam frowned. "I'm so bad at that game."

Nico nudged her. "I could teach you."

"She isn't wrong," Jeff butted in. "She's a lost cause."

"*Hey.*" Sam placed her hands on her hips. "Couldn't we play a different game? *Mario Kart*, perhaps?"

"No," Jeff and Nico responded at the same time. Then they high-fived immediately. The entire interaction felt like no time had passed at all. Like they were back to being middle schoolers and driving Samantha Carter absolutely insane.

She glared at them. "I hate you both."

"Dinner!" Mrs. Carter yelled from the kitchen.

Jeff cheered and charged for the kitchen. Nico and Sam stood there and watched as Daniel snatched Jeff's face and kissed him on the lips.

Nico turned to Sam, noticing the way she was glowing watching her brother. He so desperately wished Jeff would do the same for her, to see the way she relaxed and smiled and laughed when they were together.

She blinked up at him, her eyes sparkling.

Nico grinned, then held out a hand. "After you."

She lifted a brow and stepped past him. As she walked down the hall, she swiveled her hips *just* so. Before entering the kitchen, she looked back at him with a smirk.

He bit his fist and turned away, hearing her chuckle as she disappeared through the doorframe and headed for the dining room. Nico followed, forcing himself to think of the cold snow and cold showers and anything *but* those hips.

The dining room table was draped with a cream lace cloth, and boasted the usual fanfare: roast beef and crispy Brussels sprouts and thick cranberry sauce, and the burgundy-colored cotton napkins, tied together with twine and mistletoe, were delicately placed over the Carters' special china.

Everyone was already coupled up; his moms, the Carters, Jeff and Daniel. Two chairs were left next to each other as they entered. He watched Sam freeze at the sight of it, no doubt realizing that—yet again they'd be forced to squeeze in right next to each other. Nico wanted desperately to touch her. Actually, if he was honest, he'd wanted to touch her on Thanksgiving too. Both clearly a bad idea.

He pulled out the chair for Sam. "After you, Samantha."

"Aw, Nico, you are always such a gentleman," Mrs. Carter said, swaying a little as she raised a glass of Champagne. "To raising gentlemen."

Sam sat down and Nico helped her push the seat in, then settled in beside her.

His parents picked up their glasses. "To friends that feel like family, after many, many years," his mom added.

Jeff beamed, then turned and kissed Daniel on the cheek. Then he lifted his glass higher, in Sam's direction. "To family that feel like friends."

Sam's throat bobbed as she swallowed, then gave Jeff a watery smile.

Nico cleared his throat. "To creating families of our own," he said, tipping his glass in Jeff's direction.

Jeff's shoulders tightened as he leaned over, eyes darting between Nico and Sam. Daniel didn't seem to notice his reaction as he threw an arm around Jeff and kissed his temple.

They all clinked glasses at the center of the table.

"Getting engaged?" Sam whispered to Nico, soft enough so no one could hear them.

Nico lifted his glass to his mouth with a single nod, keeping his eyes on the table and *not* the dip of her cleavage so clearly in his view. "Definitely."

Plates were passed around the table as everyone helped themselves.

Sam leaned forward for the roasted carrots, her thigh pressing into his, her dress dipping even lower.

Nico tipped his glass back and downed it, then grabbed the bottle beside him.

"Isn't this nice, being all together again?" Mama asked, spooning sprouts onto her plate. She pointed a spoon in his direction, then at Jeff. "The two of you were working too hard for too long."

Nico pressed his lips together.

Jeff smiled. "We had a lot of growing up to do."

Mrs. Carter turned to Nico. "Yes, but never coming home for the holidays? Or during the summer? Were you really *that* busy?"

He swallowed. Clearly Jeff hadn't told his parents about their fight either. "Yes. Those first four years at Nubo were all consuming. They barely give us time to breathe."

"Clearly," Mr. Carter grumbled. "That strike is certainly something."

Nico felt a pinky finger trace delicately up his thigh from under the table.

He shifted in his seat. "If it's alright with you, I don't feel like talking about work tonight."

Mr. Carter nodded.

"So, Daniel, what does your family do for the holidays?" Mama barrelled on. "I'm sure they're going to miss you this year."

Jeff's lips tightened at the question, but Daniel seemed relaxed as he reached for his glass. "They won't miss me," Daniel explained. "I haven't spoken to them in seven years."

Mrs. Carter dropped her fork.

Mr. Carter wiped at the corners of his mouth, then carefully folded his napkin. "Daniel, you do not have to talk about it if you don't want to. You're only just getting to know us."

He nodded. "I know. But Jeff has made it clear that I

can adopt this family as my own, and if it's okay with you, I would like to do that."

Sam threw an arm across the table, hand reaching for Daniel. "We would like that too."

Daniel grinned at her as he grabbed her hand and kissed it. "I'd want nothing more than to call you my sister."

Nico locked eyes with his best friend across the table. He lifted a brow, hoping that Jeff understood what was unspoken between them.

Jeff pressed his lips together, then nodded slightly.

Nico grinned and leaned back as he lifted his glass.

Sam wiped at her eyes as she leaned back. He pressed his thigh into hers, and this time, she didn't shy away. They remained pressed together, hidden underneath the tablecloth.

Jeff placed his hand on the table, palm up, inviting Daniel to take it.

He did, threading their fingers together, eyes on their joined hands. "Seven years ago, I told my parents about my sexuality, and, well, they weren't as supportive and loving as this family." Daniel blinked up at Jeff, who smiled back at him. That look of such vulnerability and love had Nico's heart squeezing in his chest. How special it was to love so deeply, and to feel that wholly in return. For a moment, Nico imagined what that could feel like. Then, in a flash, realized maybe he already did.

He downed his glass again.

"Oh, honey." Mrs. Carter stood up and rounded the table, throwing her arms around Daniel's shoulders from behind. "We are so happy to have you here."

Daniel rubbed a hand on her arm. "Thank you. And thank you for raising an incredible son."

Mrs. Carter hugged Jeff next, squeezing hard. "My boys. How rich we are to experience your love."

To experience your love. Nico wanted more than anything for everyone at that table to also experience his... love? Was that how he felt for Samantha Carter? Was he in love with her?

Feeling buzzed from the wine, Nico slipped a hand underneath the table and placed a hand on Sam's knee.

She sucked in a breath, so quiet that he was the only one to notice. Everyone at the table was too preoccupied with Daniel and Jeff as he slid his fingers to the inside of her thigh and moved his hand up, up, up, until it was underneath the fabric of her dress. He could feel how warm she was, even with the thin layer of nylon between them. His hand was so close to her hip he wanted to scream.

Sam bit her lip and pinched his hand, then removed it from her thigh. She then pressed both of her palms to the table and stood up. "I'm going to start on the dishes." She stood up and turned to him with the best poker face of all time before gathering dishes in her hands.

He grinned.

"Oh, honey, it's okay! We'll do it."

Nico stood as well. "No, all of you cooked. Please, stay." He snatched his plate, then collected the others.

"See, such a gentleman!" Mrs. Carter exclaimed.

"And a gentlewoman," Mom added. She eyed Nico with a look that he didn't care to try and decipher. He had more important things on his mind.

He turned and made his way to the kitchen where Sam escaped to. He found her at the sink, spigot on, already rinsing off dishes and placing them in the dishwasher. He glanced behind him to make sure no one else was coming, then stepped up behind her, sliding the dishes into the sink.

He bracketed his hands around her, chest pressed to her back, and leaned his head down, face close to hers.

"Someone could come any minute," she whispered as she continued to work.

Nico responded by running a knuckle down her jaw, turning her face toward his. Then he tipped her chin up with his forefinger and thumb.

Laughter burst out from the group in the dining room, but neither of them moved.

She blinked her eyes closed. "*Nico*," she whispered.

Nico felt his heart pounding in his chest, his throat closing tight. *I love her.* He wanted *this*, forever. Christmas at the Carters. A shared apartment in the city. Kids who grew up with Jeff's. He wanted the family he'd grown up with to become part of his *real* family. He wanted to run his hands in velvet black hair and sleep in sheets that smelled like coconut and vanilla.

The sounds of screeching chairs jolted him back into reality. He stepped away from Sam and scratched the back of his neck.

"Nico," she whispered, sounding urgent.

He whirled around, taking in Sam's flushed face. She looked embarrassed.

It was on the tip of his tongue. *I love you.* He felt ready to say it. Man, how much he wanted to tell her how he felt.

But the moment was over as Mrs. Carter and Mama burst into the kitchen, followed by Jeff who demanded his presence in the basement.

Chapter 26

IT WAS EARLY on Christmas morning, but Sam was already awake. She had on her silky pajamas—a ruby-colored set with long sleeves and shorts—tucked under her pink childhood quilt, her phone perched up on her knee.

Yumi was on FaceTime, wearing the matching set but in green, which she demanded they both wear on Christmas despite the fact that it was already seven o'clock at night in Seoul and she was about to have dinner with her family.

"I appreciate the dedication to the bit," Sam said. "Thank you for my pajamas."

"Well, I had to after you found Mister McStuffin's *twin*." Yumi beamed as she placed a smaller stuffed bunny into the screen, almost identical to the one her best friend had become rather obsessed with over the past year. "Missus McStuffin misses her man."

Sam smiled and leaned her head against the stuffed animal next to her, then yawned.

"Ugh, I'm sorry. It's so early." Yumi pressed her face closer to the screen. "How was your night? Did we get any ring action?"

Sam rolled her eyes. "No. I honestly think he chickened out."

She'd waited the rest of the night to see what Jeff was planning on doing. After all, he had *insisted* that she and Nico be there on Christmas Eve. But after an hour of watching Nico get utterly destroyed in *Smash Brothers*—and making sure to sit on the *opposite* end of the couch, far away from his hands and his legs and pretty much everything about him that set her entire body on fire—Jeff didn't make a move. Daniel fell asleep on the couch, cuddled up next to him, and eventually her brother called it quits. Nico asked her if she wanted to play, a twinkle in his eye. But she shook her head, knowing that if she stayed in that dark basement with him for more than five minutes, there was no way she'd remain clothed.

"Do you think he's still planning on doing it?" Yumi budged.

Sam nodded, shaking out of the thoughts of Nico in the dark stripping off her dress. "Yeah, there's definitely something up. Nico is convinced as well."

Yumi smirked. "And how'd *that* go last night?"

Sam turned down the volume of her phone. "He looked yummier than my mom's pumpkin pie."

"Now that's saying something, because your mom's pie is *bomb*."

"There was this moment though, in the kitchen..." She hesitated, thinking of the way Nico had pulled her close, like he was going to kiss her. There was a look in his eye, a new kind of expression she couldn't read painted across his face. Then he'd backed away from her, looking like he was full of regret. Had Nico looked at Jeff last night and begun to change his mind about them? Was what they were doing taking its toll?

She'd made sure to keep her distance after that.

"I'm wondering if he's second-guessing things," she finished, chewing on her lip.

"*Pffft.* Nico? Second-guessing how obsessed he is with you? I highly doubt it." There was a noise in the distance on Yumi's end. She looked up, then smiled. "Halmeoni! Come say hi to Sam."

Sam grinned as Yumi's grandmother came into view, her soft wrinkly cheeks and short gray hair looking like she just woke up from a nap.

"Who's Sam?" Halmeoni asked.

"You remember Sam," Yumi explained. "My roommate? We work together? She's kind of a slut."

"*Yumi!!*" screamed her mother from the other room.

"What?" Yumi yelled back.

Halmeoni smiled at the screen. "She's very pretty. Is she your girlfriend?"

"Yes. Forever."

Sam smiled. "Not if you keep calling me a *slut.*"

A small thud came from her window. She sat up, noticing the outline of a snowball.

"What was that?" Yumi asked.

"I think that's...Oh my god," she whispered.

A very tall figure appeared at her window. Nico crouched on the roof and knocked on the glass, wearing a Berkeley hoodie and a pair of sweats.

"Oh my god," she repeated, "Nico."

"*See?* You slut. Get some. I'm hanging up." Yumi was off the phone before Sam could comprehend what was happening.

She ripped her quilt from her and shuffled over, then unlocked the latch and ripped it open. "What are you doing here?" she whisper-screamed.

He grinned. "Lock the door," he demanded.

Sam silently moved across her room and locked the door as Nico climbed through the window, snow tracking in from his sneakers. She leaned against the door as he closed the window, then turned to face her.

He silently lifted a hand and motioned for her to move closer. *Get over here*, he mouthed.

She did, moving soundlessly to his direction. When she was within reach, Nico grabbed her neck and yanked her toward him, claiming her mouth like it was his alone for the taking. Sam was okay with his possessiveness though. Ever since that fateful night—not twenty feet from where they now stood—her lips had only ever belonged to him.

He moved her to the back wall, pressing her up against her collage of posters and photos from high school she hadn't bothered taking down. His kiss was hungry and consuming as he slipped a thigh between her legs, pinning her to the wall. He kept kissing her and kissing her as he fumbled with something in his sweatshirt pocket. She felt his hands at her neck as he placed a cool chain on her skin.

She released her lips as Nico linked the chain at her nape, then pressed his forehead to hers.

She picked up the necklace. White gold with a pink diamond dangling at the center, in the shape of a heart. She pressed a hand to her mouth, shocked. *This must have cost him a fortune.*

"Merry Christmas, Sammy girl," he whispered.

She blinked up at him. "But I didn't get you anything."

He shook his head, his expression serious. "You've already given me more than you know."

"Nico," she breathed as his hands returned to her sides. He pushed the silk fabric of her shorts up until he hit the bare skin at her hips.

He sealed their foreheads together. "*God*, Sam," he grumbled low.

"I wasn't expecting company," she whispered.

"You feel so good in my hands." He drew circles into her skin with his thumbs. "Can I take these off?"

She answered by pinching the bottom of his sweatshirt and peeling it off him. He threw it to the ground, revealing a bare chest underneath.

"Couldn't even bother putting on a shirt?" she teased, tracing her finger down his clavicle.

He shook his head. "I dreamt about that dress all night long."

She grinned, pressing her palms to his abs. "Had to see me?"

"Desperately." He tucked his hands underneath her shirt and moved them up her stomach. "I climbed that tree outside your window."

She shook her head. "You're insane."

"When it comes to you? Absolutely."

Then he was back to consuming her, his kisses wet and sloppy, his groin hard and pressing into the soft spot between her legs.

A knock sounded at the door.

Their mouths broke apart, and they froze.

Another knock, this one persistent. "Sam, why the fuck is this door locked?" Jeff grumbled on the other side. "Let me *in*, we have to talk!"

Sam's eyes widened. She went to say something, but Nico covered her mouth and shook his head.

"Oh my god, *fine*. I'll unlock it myself, if I must." She heard tinkering at her doorknob.

"Remember that time you guys looked up how to pick locks?" she whispered to Nico.

His eyes widened.

Sam jumped away from him and opened the window.

"Seriously?" he whispered back. "It's going to be—"

The door knob clicked.

Nico shoved his feet into his shoes and jumped through the window, stepping out of view.

Sam slammed the window shut, then jumped on her bed right before Jeff swung the door open.

"Since when do you lock the door, Sam? Are we twelve again?"

"Habit," she snipped. "Since when do we *pick* locks, Jeff? *Are we twelve again?*"

Jeff ignored her and looked into the hallway, like he was making sure no one saw him. Next to his foot was Nico's hoodie, the Berkeley logo *very* clearly facing up.

Sam jumped up and snatched it, then shoved it under her bed. She then grabbed the pink diamond and swiveled it around so it was tucked under the back of her pajama shirt.

Jeff, completely unaware of Sam's awkward maneuvers, closed the door and made himself right at home on her bed.

"What?" she snipped, aware that Nico was waiting on the roof, without a shirt on, probably freezing. "What is it?"

Jeff's face softened, then he reached into his pocket and pulled out a box.

Her shoulders melted as she took a seat next to him.

He popped the box open, revealing a titanium engagement band. A stripe of gold swirled through the center, connected by two tiny diamonds embedded into the metal.

"Oh Jeff," she said, picking up the box, her other hand at her mouth.

"I was going to do it last night," he whispered. "But...I got nervous. And he was sharing his story and— I don't know, it didn't feel right yet."

"Then when are you going to do it?"

"Is it...cheesy to give it to him as a present?"

Sam blinked up at him. "Why would it be cheesy?"

Jeff rolled his eyes. "All that talk last night about being each other's families and all that. I don't know, maybe it's laying it on too thick."

"Or, it's laying on *just* the right amount."

Jeff relaxed, looking relieved. "Yeah?"

"He's perfect, Jeff. And he seems right at home with us." She handed the box back to him, eye on the ring. "What better time to make him a true part of our family than on Christmas Day?"

Jeff smiled, then pulled Sam in for a hug. "I can't wait to see this happen to you some day."

She swallowed, eyes on a strip of blue sleeve that was still visible underneath them. "Y-yeah. Me, too."

He squeezed her, then jumped up, wiping at his eyes. "I wanted to have Nico here for it. I think he knows I'm going to do it."

Sam smiled. "He's going to be so happy for you." She paused, rubbing at her neck. "And we both sort of saw this coming."

He grinned. "It was so great having the gang back together last night."

She bit her lip and nodded, thinking of Nico's hand on her leg underneath the table, his chest pressed into her as she did the dishes. All in secret. All in hiding. "Yeah," she murmured. "Back together."

Jeff shoved the ring box back in the pocket of his pajamas. "Okay, see you downstairs."

She watched as Jeff exited, then waited a beat before making her way back to the window. She quietly opened it and stuck her head outside

Nico was curled up in a ball, shivering.

"Oh god, get in here," she whispered.

He did as she asked, closing the window behind him as she grabbed his sweatshirt. She went to hand it to him, but he shook his head as he cupped her face. "One more," he whispered. "Warm me up, baby girl."

Then he was kissing her again, and Sam lost all ability to think. Which was unfortunate, because if she *had* been thinking, she would have remembered that she forgot to lock the door again.

Jeff opened her bedroom door. "Wait, Sam, I forgot to tell you—"

Nico's grip on her face tightened as they broke apart and looked to the doorframe.

Jeff let the door go, the metal knob slamming into the wall. His face was red, and it was all like a cruel version of déjà vu.

But this time, his face wasn't red with anger. And he wasn't yelling at them. Instead, there was a new expression on his face. Hurt. Betrayal, maybe.

"You promised," he said to her.

Nico released his hands, looking between the two of them. "Promised?"

Jeff turned on his heel and walked away, his footsteps padding down the stairs.

"Jeff, wait," Nico yelled. He snatched his sweatshirt from Sam and ran after his best friend, leaving her alone in her bedroom without a backward glance. She stood there, still frozen as she listened to the swish of the back door sliding open...then the sound of distant yelling.

Chapter 27

Nico followed Jeff out the back door of the Carter house, his strides long as he made his way down the path that led to the river.

"Jeff, stop. *Jeff.*" Nico caught up to him and grabbed his arm. "Please, will you listen to me?"

Jeff shrugged off Nico's hold. "How long has this been going on?"

Nico inhaled, then exhaled. *Deep breaths.* "Since I saw her at Thanksgiving."

Jeff let out a single laugh. "Jesus, one look at her and you can't keep it in your pants?"

"For your information, I kept it in my pants for a while. I waited until she was ready."

"*Ew*, god, so gross." Jeff shimmied his arms, like he was shaking off a bad feeling.

Nico held up his arms. "Is it really that gross?"

"*Yes!* It's weird!"

"*Why?*! Tell me why you're not okay with it?"

Jeff rolled his jaw and said nothing.

Nico shook his head, letting his arms fall to his side, heart in his throat. "Do you not trust me, or something?"

Jeff's eyes widened, his jaw going slack. "Of course I trust you."

He took a deep breath. *It's now or never.* "It sure doesn't seem like it, man."

Jeff crossed his arms. "Oh yeah? How so?"

"Let's see." Nico held up a finger, knowing he'd likely regret this later, but he was angry, and it was finally time to admit how he felt. "You catch me kissing your sister and you stop talking to me after sixteen years of friendship." He held up another finger. "After countless times I tried to reach out to you, you ignored me. The only time you bothered to reach out was through an email years later."

Jeff's face deepened to a darker shade of red.

Nico held up a third finger. "When I finally hear from you, nothing felt right. I call you my best friend but you avoid any kind of real conversation and avoid the Sam topic with me." He ran a hand through his hair, taking a deep breath before he said something out of anger he wouldn't be able to come back from. "You're the only person I've ever been able to really talk to about my life, but after everything, I felt like all of it vanished. And you made it seem like it was all my fault, even though you were the one who got angry and avoided any kind of confrontation for years."

"You shouldn't have lied to me."

"Do you blame me, though? I'm afraid to come to you about anything, because what if it all blows up in my face again?"

Jeff worked his chin, his cheeks still red, eyes glassy. "It sounds like you're the one who doesn't trust me."

Nico exhaled, his words cutting deep. "Yeah. Maybe you're right."

Silence befell them.

"Look." Nico dropped his hand and clenched his fist, then released it. "I'm in love with her, Jeff."

Jeff twisted to face Nico, his expression blank. "I had a feeling that was coming," he replied.

Nico gestured an arm to the house behind them. "I don't know what kind of promise you made her keep all those years ago, but *please*, let it go. Let her be happy. Let *us* be happy." He stepped closer. "Jeff, I'd be so good to her. I promise."

Jeff closed his eyes, sucked in a breath, then took a step back, squaring his shoulders in Nico's direction. "When I was five years old, I met a boy in the sandbox."

Nico's brow furrowed. *Why is he telling our story?*

"He was playing with a truck bigger than mine, and I wanted it, because it was so much cooler."

"Of course it was. I've always had better taste."

Jeff held up a hand. "Please, Nico. Don't joke about this."

Nico hesitated, then nodded. "Okay. I'm sorry."

Jeff nodded back. "We started a fist fight and our moms forced us to apologize, and then worse, made us have a play date. Our hatred didn't last long because, well, we're actually great friends. You're the only boy I got along with, and you were certainly far more fun than my dumpy little sister."

Nico sucked in his lips. "Dumpy?"

Jeff ignored him. "As time went on, I realized that..." Jeff rubbed his neck, splotches of red climbing up his neck. "I realized that maybe the reason why I only got along with this one boy and didn't like anyone else was something more, and my feelings got confusing. You started talking to me about girls you liked at school and I couldn't help but think 'why would I want to hang out with girls when I like hanging out with you the most?'"

Nico's stomach dropped.

"By the time high school came around, I was positive where I stood with my sexuality. The problem was, I had these really big feelings for my best friend, the one guy I counted on for everything. But I couldn't tell him, because I *knew* he didn't feel the same way in return. And what would be the point of admitting all of this if there was the possibility of losing my friendship altogether?

"When I went to college, I finally let myself explore more of who I am, and got more comfortable with it. I found that I was really happy allowing that part of myself to finally be free. But anyone I met still didn't come close to these feelings I had for you, so I figured I was screwed for life." Jeff exhaled, long and slow. "Then that summer, I caught you kissing Sam."

Nico examined the way Jeff's face twisted into something sad and vulnerable. He wasn't sure what to do, so he turned to face the water, hands in his pockets, giving Jeff the privacy to voice what he had to.

"That night, when she got back in the house, I admitted the truth to her, and I made her promise that she would never be with you."

He slammed his eyes shut.

"I love my sister, I really do. Even through all the years that she annoyed the shit out of me, I loved her and I've always wanted what is best for her. But...I couldn't see her with you. Not after all these years of pining for you and having nowhere to put those feelings except deeper into this dark place in my heart where I kept stuffing more and more of my secrets."

"Jeff..."

Jeff shook his head, not wanting to hear what Nico had to say.

So he clamped his mouth shut.

"You know the rest, I think. She and I got close, but we never talked about you. I selfishly tried to encourage her to get out there and meet new people, hoping that we could put this behind us, hoping that I could work through my complicated feelings and finally get my best friend back. It... took me time, yes. And I'm sorry for that. But I needed the time.

"Then I met Daniel and, well, everything changed." Jeff walked over to Nico, making sure he was in his line of vision. "I fell in love with him so fast that I realized my feelings for you were complicated, yes, but absolutely nothing in comparison. That what I felt for you is a mix of a crush but also deep, *deep* platonic love. And I fucked it all up."

Nico scratched the back of his neck, unsure what to say next. What was there to say, when your best friend told you he'd had feelings for you all along?

"Is it going to be weird between us, now that I've told you the truth?"

Nico exhaled. "I don't know? I don't think so."

"Are you mad?"

He shook his head. "I admit, I was, for a while. But now...I'm glad you told me. The distance you created makes a lot more sense now. I just wish I knew the context sooner."

"I hadn't talked to you about any of this yet because, well, I didn't really know how to. I avoided the conversation. But unfortunately, that meant my best friend and sister couldn't trust me with telling the truth. That...that makes me livid. And really, really sad"

He exhaled. "I'm guessing this is why Sam kept her distance all this time?"

"Yeah," Jeff whispered. "I-I'm sorry."

Nico pressed the heels of his palms to his eyes. "She kept saying how she didn't want to ruin her friendship with you, and now...it makes so much more sense. It was more than friendship. To her, it probably felt like betrayal." He dropped his hands. "And I had no idea. I felt angry with you and I just...kept pushing her."

"So you decided to lie."

"We wanted to tell you, after Christmas."

"I wish you *told me immediately*."

"And look how well that went the last time."

"*Fucking A*," Jeff choked out. "What a mess."

Nico's phone went off in his pocket. He didn't bother reaching for it because there certainly wasn't anything more important than *this*. The moment that he had been simultaneously hoping for—and dreading—since that night four years ago. The moment he could finally be honest with his best friend and admit how he felt.

But his phone kept going off.

Jeff eyed him. "Are you going to get that?"

"No, I'll silence it." When he reached for it though, he blinked at the name on his screen.

JEREMY

Fuck, I should not be contacting you on Christmas.

But you're right, this code works

Don't tell anyone, but if you need help...

Nico closed his eyes and pinched the bridge of his nose.

"All good?" Jeff asked.

"N-no." Nico sighed heavily, sliding his phone back in his pocket. "Work. I think I need to work today."

"*Today?*"

He held up his hands. "If I don't make this integration happen, I could be out of a job."

"Would that be so bad? They treat you like shit."

Nico laughed, but it was more of a wheeze. He was so tired. "If I get fired for not pulling this off, then any other tech company will see me as a failed engineer. It could ruin my career."

"While eighty-five percent of your company is on strike? I'm sorry but I do not fucking believe that." Jeff crossed his arms and shivered. "Go. Get the work done."

Nico gestured toward Jeff then the house, where Sam was probably waiting for him. "We have to figure this out."

He shook his head. "Not right now. I'm going to go in there and propose, and I really would like to not deal with this today, if that's all right with you."

Nico blinked. "You're going to do it?"

Jeff reached into his pocket and pulled out a box. "Yes. And you're kind of ruining the moment."

"I seem to ruin everything, don't I?"

"No, Nico. I clearly did." He shoved the box back in his pocket. "I'll tell Sam you left."

"C-can you just…" He hesitated. "Can you tell her I will call? That everything will be okay?"

His friend shifted back and forth.

"*Will* everything be okay?" Nico asked, heart pounding.

"I…I don't know." He backed away. "Let me talk to Sam first."

"Are you telling me not to call her?"

"I'm telling you to give me a moment to fucking *breathe* so I can propose to the love of my life." Jeff took a deep breath and closed his eyes. "Can you at least let me have that?"

"Yes," Nico answered quietly. "I'm sorry, Jeff."

He opened his eyes. "Me too."

Then he watched him leave, and for the second time in his life, Nicolas Giuliano stood in the alcove next to the river, behind the Carter house, wondering if this was the end of it all.

Chapter 28

Sam watched from the sliding glass door as Jeff made his way up the hill back to the house. Nico stood there watching his best friend go, then ran a hand through his hair and turned, walking in the direction of his home. He didn't look back to the house. He didn't seek her out.

Her heart sank deep into her belly.

Jeff slid the door open, then softly closed it shut. He leaned against it, his eyes on the ground. Everyone in the house was still asleep. Or at least she hoped so after their raised voices outside. The winter breeze was burly enough that it drowned out whatever they were saying. Sam couldn't catch a word.

"I'm sorry," she whispered.

Jeff ticked his jaw and blinked up at Sam. He had tears in his eyes. "I wanted today to be perfect."

"It *will* be." She took a step forward.

He stretched away from her, looking like she'd slapped him in the face. "Sam, please."

She stopped, then took three steps back.

Jeff stood up straight and rubbed his arms. "I want this

to be a Christmas to remember," he said. "I want this to be something we look back on as a family and remember for the rest of our lives. Tell our kids the story of our love. Take pictures and keep them in frames until they turn yellow from age because they've been sitting out for so long."

Tears filled her eyes. "And we will," she whispered.

"Can you let me have this, Sam? Let me have this day?"

"Yes. Of course."

Jeff nodded. "I promise, we'll talk soon. I just...need this. I know I'm being selfish right now."

"You're not. I'm the selfish one."

His face softened. "Sam. I don't think you even have the ability to be selfish."

Sam watched as her brother exited the kitchen. She heard the twinkling of ornaments on the tree as Jeff switched on the lights, getting the room ready. Making everything sparkle for the perfect proposal.

She swallowed and wiped her eyes, vowing that she would give him his moment. Today, and the days following.

It was ten o'clock in the morning and Nico already felt like he needed a drink.

His laptop was hooked up to his old desktop with a USB-C port and an HDMI cord he found in the back of his closet. The screen certainly wasn't big enough for him to evaluate all this code, but it would have to do. Especially if he was going to try to figure out how he could convert it to the Nubo algorithm in enough time for New Year's Eve.

"I mean, you're right, the framework is all here," Jeremy said.

Nico had him on FaceTime on his phone, propped up

by the basketball trophy he won at States his junior year of high school. "We would need to beta test it though. We can't just add it to the code and expect the best. The feed could collapse again."

"Obviously," Jeremy grumbled. "Does OmniCorp plan on pushing videos still on New Year's?"

Nico sighed. "Frank never gave me an answer. He simply expects live streaming to happen and hasn't told me if they want videos without it, or if we should wait to push all of it at once this spring."

"What do you think?"

Nico rubbed his face. *God, this day.* "I really think we should wait. It gives us enough time to figure out how the algorithm can work alongside our current photo sharing so those posts don't get lost in the mix. If we push video now, they will."

"But what happens if you wait?"

"I could lose my job."

Jeremy barked out a single laugh. "Please don't tell me he threatened that."

Nico let out a laugh as well. "He did."

Then they were both laughing. Two grown men on Christmas, huddled over their computer screens and not downstairs with their families, trying to push an agenda for men who could care *less* if either of them had a normal holiday at home.

Nico wiped the tears in his eyes from laughing and opened up Nubo on his computer. He scrolled, looking at the photos of friends sharing about their days, pictures of families and pets wearing reindeer noses and delicious cinnamon buns and lit menorahs.

Then he came across a photo of Jeff. He was smiling bright, still in his pajamas from this morning, arm thrown around Daniel. Daniel was covering his mouth, and a new ring was on his left hand.

Forever and always, Jeff had captioned.

Nico swiped through the carousel of images. There was one with Jeff down on one knee, one of them kissing, one of them holding glasses of Champagne. Then a selfie with the entire family.

Sam's face was covered in happy tears. Her hair was blocking her neck, so he couldn't see if she was still wearing the necklace he'd bought her. He wondered what she was thinking. He wondered if his asinine decision to go over there this morning decimated any and all chances of having her for good. All because he couldn't keep it together for two whole days.

"What's the plan?" Jeremy asked. "Do you want to keep trying?"

Nico bit his lip, then shook his head. "No." He reached for his mouse and powered down his computer. "No, I'm done."

"Done?"

"This is not okay anymore." He shut his laptop and began unplugging cords. "Nubo is meant to be a place to share moments." He thought of Jeff and Daniel and those beautiful pictures, how they would have all gotten lost in the mix. "I wanted to be a part of this company because I care about human connection. I care about the experience of being online. I want people to have a positive one, even if the world says social media is all garbage. I may sometimes be a cog in the machine, but at my core, that's what I want."

"Okay, valiant and all. But what does that mean for you?"

Nico tapped his fingers on his desk. "Will you send me those files that everyone posted about going on strike?"

Jeremy perked up. "Are you joining us?"

He exhaled. "Yeah. I think I am."

Sam sat on her bed playing with the chain dangling at her neck, the metal and the diamond warm from her skin after not taking it off for four days.

They all got swept up after Jeff's engagement. Sam gave her brother and his fiancé her full attention, making the moment as special as possible. It was magical watching the way Daniel bloomed in her brother's presence, how he seamlessly folded into their family. It killed her knowing that somewhere out there, a family had a Daniel-sized hole in it that they didn't care to fill. How could they not want this special man in their family? How could they not want to witness such pure, beautiful, passionate love?

She didn't mention Nico, and neither did Jeff. They dedicated themselves to ignoring the situation. That night, after a Christmas Day feast of takeout Chinese, Sam curled into her bed and checked phone. She didn't have a single text message from him. Not a call. Not anything.

Maybe this is for the best, she thought to herself. *Being with Nico has never not been a mess.*

The days following, she dedicated herself to writing her article, to preparing for the next huge chapter in her life. Once she told her parents about the promotion, she holed up in her room and worked, readying the project she was looking forward to launching.

She was giving her piece one last read before sending it over to Barbara when someone knocked on her door.

"Come in," she said, saving her work.

"Promise it's clear in there?" Jeff asked.

She rolled her eyes. "Funny."

He stepped into her room, then closed the door gently. "Too busy being a girl boss to talk?"

She looked down at her article. At this point, it was as good as it could possibly be. *A New Era at Nourished: Less Noise, More Truth.* It was dramatic, but it did the job. It painted a picture of the changing tides, of a focus more on journalism that mattered to the public, versus trying to chase the latest fad or search keyword. She knew it would turn heads and cause a stir online, but she didn't care. She was ready to get out there and make a difference. And she was thankful that Barbara was the one readying the ship for sail.

"Yes, once sec." She attached the document and emailed it to Barbara, then pushed her laptop aside.

Jeff took a seat beside her, propping his knee up so he could face her fully.

She smiled. "How are you feeling?"

He grinned, twirling an arm in the air. "Blissful. Happy. Like my heart could burst out of my chest and make you all sick with my undying love and devotion and obsession."

She laughed. "Who knew you were such a poet."

His grin softened as he settled in. He took Sam's hands.

"I'm sorry," she whispered. "That I broke your trust, and your promise. You asked one thing of me, and I didn't listen."

"You're right." Jeff tilted his head. "You bitch."

Her eyes widened at that.

Jeff's mouth curled into a smirk.

She slapped his arm. "That was mean."

He laughed, then snatched her hands again. "Okay, okay, no more jokes." He squared his shoulders and huffed. "I am mad at you, yes. Not about you breaking your promise, but the fact that you felt like you couldn't come to me."

"How could I?" She twisted her lips. "Jeff, I'm still hurt that you never told me about the emails. About becoming his friend again. It made me feel like you couldn't trust me after everything we've been through. I didn't know *how* to come to you after all of that."

He squeezed her hands. "I know I was the one who created that divide, and I'm sorry. I was the one who made you feel like you couldn't talk to me. I let all of my complicated feelings get in the way that I didn't give you or Nico the space to really talk to me about what was going on. To tell me how you felt."

She sniffled and turned her head, her nose pinching. She didn't want to cry in front of him. She hadn't cried yet, and she was afraid if she did, she wouldn't stop.

"I know. If I had swallowed my pride and finally had those conversations, I would have been able to witness my best friend and sister falling in love."

She twitched, eyes widening. "Falling...in love?"

"Y-yeah." Jeff opened his mouth, then closed it. "Shit."

Sam jumped up and paced across the floor. "Did he say that?"

"Well, he didn't really have to. Have you seen the way he looks at you?" Jeff shivered. "Even at the dinner table on Christmas Eve. I tried to pretend like it wasn't there, but come on, Sam. I'm not that blind."

"That isn't love, that's...I don't know. Lust?"

"Then how come he told me on Christmas that he loves you?"

She stopped pacing, her hair falling in front of her face. She blew it away. "So he did say that to you."

"Yes. Among other things."

She felt like she was spinning. She pressed her fingers to her temple. "Why does this always feel so complicated between the three of us?" She dropped her hands. "Maybe I need to find someone with absolutely no ties to this family or our history. Someone unproblematic. Someone—"

"Who you can't admit you're in love with because you'll always harbor feelings for someone else?"

Sam bit her lip as a *whoosh* sound came from her laptop.

Jeff peeked at the screen. "Someone named Barbara wants to know if you can come into the city."

She lunged for her computer and scanned the email. "She wants me in for a photoshoot first thing tomorrow morning, to go with my article."

"Okay *fancy*." He shoved Sam's arm. "Are you going to go?"

She looked up at Jeff, then back down at her screen. *Yes.* She needed to get away from all of this. She needed time to think. "I was planning on being in the city for New Year's, so there's probably no reason for me to come back to Willow."

He jumped up. "Then let's go! Sam's day in the spotlight. We can drive you to the train."

She scanned her room, in a daze. "But, Jeff...I—"

"Sam." He pressed his hands to her shoulders. "This is your moment. Don't waste it."

Her chest swelled. She stood up and nodded continuously. "You're right. What do I wear?"

Jeff snatched his phone and opened FaceTime. "Calling reinforcements," he said as he tapped on Yumi's name.

Thirty minutes later, Sam was climbing out of Jeff's car, reading through the list of instructions Yumi had texted. The outfit was a combination of items from both of their closets back in the city, and Yumi gave her exact instructions on where to find them and how they should be styled.

YUMI

Do not disappoint me, slut.

SAM

You are so good to me. I'll see if they will give you styling credit. ;)

YUM

You better.

Love you. The camera is going to break from your hotness.

Jeff collected her things in the trunk as Daniel gave her a hug. "I'm so proud of you," he said.

She squeezed him back. "And I'm so happy you'll be part of us," she admitted. "Will you guys still come to the city for New Year's?"

"Is that even a question?" Jeff teased, pulling out her suitcase.

"We'll be there, sweetie." Daniel held her arms as he looked her in the eye. "Have you heard from him?"

"F-from who?"

Daniel rolled his eyes. "Sam, be serious. I picked up on it that night at the pub."

"Nico?" she whispered, afraid Jeff would hear.

He tilted his head. "Do you really think Jeff hasn't told me the story? That I wouldn't know every detail about the man I'm spending the rest of my life with?"

She moved her head back, her nose cold from the December chill. "No, I haven't heard from him. But I haven't reached out either. I think...I think maybe it's for the best. Things between us have always been messy, from the start."

"But do you love him?"

It hit her then like a ton of bricks. Maybe she had always felt that way. But she was too scared to admit it. Too scared to dive in deep, afraid that everything would collapse into ruin.

"What if he doesn't want it anymore? What if he also feels this way, that it's all *too much*."

Jeff rolled her suitcase over to her. "Sam, come on. Stop being stupid. You know that's not the case." He paused. "Do you love him?"

She gritted her teeth and took the handle of her bag, tightening her grip.

"Do you?" Jeff egged on.

"*Yes*." The word rushed out fast. "I'm head over heels and I'm really, *really* scared."

Daniel grinned and squeezed her arm. "Love is scary, sweetheart. Love means taking a chance, sacrificing for another, putting it all on the line. It means betting it all on a person. But if you love them, if they are the kind of partner you know them to be, then the bet is *always* worth the risk."

Jeff smiled and hugged his fiancé from behind. "Show him," he said to Sam. "Show him how much you love him. Don't hold yourself back from being happy. Don't wait."

The train was set to arrive in three minutes. She had to get back to the city, and she wouldn't get the chance to tell Nico to his face. She didn't want to say what she needed to on the phone. She needed him in person.

Sam looked down at the list of styling tips Yumi sent her. She pursed her lips, then she made one adjustment to the outfit plan.

Chapter 29

Nico sprawled out on his childhood bed, staring up at the blue ceiling in his room, bored beyond belief. He'd tried everything he could to stay busy, to ignore the fact that he might have blown up his career and blown up his chance to be with the love of his life. He hadn't heard anything from her or Jeff the past six days, and he was starting to think he might have lost them all over again. So he filled his time doing busy work for his moms to get his mind off it, like shoveling the driveway and updating the software on all of their electronic devices.

His door swung open. "Nicolas, are you still planning on fixing the leaky sink in the bathroom?" Mom asked.

He perched up on his elbows. "Yes. At some point."

"Okay, well, I wasn't sure because Jeff is waiting for you downstairs."

He sat up. "Here? At the house?"

"No, in the North Pole. *Yes*, this house."

He scrambled up, then looked at the mirror and attempted to tame down his hair. "Only him?"

"Only him. No Samantha."

Nico stopped fussing and looked at his mom.

"Nico, I'm your mother." She leaned against the wall. "I think I have enough intuition to see when my boy is in love."

"How?"

"Oh, I don't know, maybe the fact that I practically saw you swallow her whole on Christmas Eve near the kitchen sink?"

He covered his face. "You saw that?" he mumbled.

"I went in there to help, but saw the two of you were having a moment, so I backed away and distracted every-one." She frowned at him. "*Please* tell me Jeff knows."

"Yes, he knows." He sighed. "Although he didn't know that night."

"Then you better go down and fix it."

"Unless I screwed up everything so bad that it's unfixable."

"Nicolas Giuliano, I did not raise you to be a quitter."

He chuckled to himself. "Actually, you did. May I remind you that I joined this union strike?"

"That doesn't make you a quitter. That makes you humane."

He pinched his lips as his mom pressed a hand to his cheek.

"That family has been so good to you," she said. "They've been so good to *us*. They made this town's first bona fide lesbian couple feel welcome and loved. I will always be grateful to them, to the ways they helped us raise you. And I know how much they all mean to you in return. Be the man we raised you to be, the one I know you *are*."

He stretched for her and wrapped her in his arms. "Thank you," he said, pressing his chin to the top of her head.

She squeezed him again, then reached up and gave his cheek a little love tap. "Get down there."

He did as his mom asked. Jeff waited for him by the door. He was dressed up in nice slacks and a sweater vest.

One look at Nico and his best friend frowned. "You look like hell."

"Good to see you too," Nico replied.

They stood there awkwardly for a moment.

Jeff sighed then held out an arm, gesturing for a hug. Nico took it, patting him on the back with a fist.

Nico rubbed his mouth and pointed at Jeff's attire. "Where are you off to?"

"Um, the city? It's New Year's Eve."

His throat tightened. Nico knew Sam was in the city. In a moment of weakness, he checked Find My Friends two days ago. He watched as her avatar moved slowly down the Hudson, along the train line heading back to New York. She left Willow and didn't even say goodbye. Didn't say *anything*. He figured he deserved it.

"Are you going to invite me to sit, or are you going to keep being an asshole and make me stand by the door?"

"Sorry, yes." Nico gestured toward the living room. "Please, come in and sit."

Jeff smirked. "Sorry, I actually need to run soon, so I'm going to make this quick."

"You are such a—" He shook his head.

Jeff's smirk widened into an evil smirk. "Say it. Call me a dick. You know you want to."

Nico continued shaking his head.

"When did you stop being so fun? Why do you not swear anymore?"

"Come on, Jeff. You know why."

Jeff's face fell. "Oh. Wow. I didn't put that together until now."

Nico shifted back and forth. "If you didn't come to stay, then what did you come for?"

"To apologize. I'm sorry, Nico. For everything. For keeping secrets and not trusting you. For making you feel like you couldn't trust *me*."

Nico swallowed. "Thank you for saying that."

Jef nodded. "I also came to patch up the mess I made."

He clenched his jaw. "You told me not to reach out. So I haven't, and she hasn't either. I haven't heard anything from Sam, and now I'm wondering if it's on purpose."

Jeff tilted his head back and let out a deep, exaggerated sigh. "The two of you are impossible." He tipped his head to Nico's phone on the coffee table. "Have you seen the photos?"

"The...photos?"

"On Nubo? They are all over, dude."

"I'm not on Nubo right now." He shoved his hands in his pockets. "I joined the strike."

"Ah," Jeff's smirk returned as he twisted his body back and forth. Nico knew that move well; it was what Jeff did when he had a secret. Something he knew that Nico didn't.

"What photos, Jeff?"

"Oh, you know..." Jeff grinned and placed his hands together. "Photos of a very gorgeous someone who has taken the internet by storm thanks to an insanely smart and provocative article she wrote."

His jaw fell open. "Sam?"

"Yes, you idiot. Check your phone."

Nico slid to the table, almost tripping over his socks as he snatched his phone and opened the app.

Jeff wasn't wrong—there were photos of Sam all over

the internet. People were reposting the photos and the link to her story. There were a number of opinions and hot takes about what she'd written, but he didn't pay attention to them. His eyes landed on a close-up shot of his girl.

The backdrop was a simple green, the same color as the *Nourished* logo, and it made those honey-green eyes he loved so much pop. She was a vision. She wasn't smiling, but he could tell there was a hint of a smirk at the corner of her lips. A mastermind in the flesh, and all of this was part of her master plan. She wore a pink tank top, tight around the chest, hair tucked back to show off the big floral green earrings she wore. And at the center of her chest, dangling on a white gold chain, was his pink diamond.

He could feel his heart racing, blood pounding in his ears. He traced his thumb across the screen, across those lips. It was a sign, right? She was sending him a message?

"Oh my *god*," Jeff moaned. He snatched the phone out of Nico's hand. "How the two of you survived without me for this long is *beyond* me."

Nico grinned, attempting to grab his phone back. Jeff backed away, holding it out of reach.

"Give it back, man." Nico laughed, unable to contain the bubble of excitement in his chest. "Please."

"Not until you tell me you're going to do something about it."

Nico froze. "Of course I'm going to do something about it."

"You still love her?"

He held his arms out. "Clearly!"

Jeff tilted his chin up, sizing Nico up. "How much?"

He dropped his arms. "How much? Like she is the sun and I am the moon. I'm a mere reflection of her and all of her joy and her light and her goodness. How I was able to live without her for so long and not know that she is my entire *world* still kills me to this day. That I could meander through this life and not realize how insanely, radically, neurotically in love with her I am."

Jeff chuckled and shook his head. "Damn, dude. Yumi's right. You *are* a sucker."

Nico reached over and shoved Jeff's arm so hard his best friend almost fell back. Jeff went to fake punch him, but Nico caught his fist. "I need to make a plan."

Jeff snatched his hand back and pointed a thumb to the door. "Want to come with us to the city?"

He looked at his phone in Jeff's hand, thinking of Sam and what felt like a big, grand gesture.

It was time to make a grand gesture of his own. "No," he replied. "I have a better idea."

Sam entered Spritz & Fizz at ten o'clock, feeling exhausted. The past couple of days had been a complete whirlwind at work. The photoshoot, the social media firestorm, the number of emails she'd received from freelance reporters with feature stories they wanted to pitch her. She finally felt like she could come up for air an hour ago, and was able to slip on the black dress and heels she'd brought to the office and make her way to the cocktail bar downtown.

Sam squeezed past crowded groups dressed up in sparkly outfits with plastic hats and glasses, party blowers going off every couple of seconds. Streamers covered the surface of the ceiling, and a disco ball hung at the center.

"The queen is here!" Yumi yelled from a table across the bar.

Cheers broke out as Sam joined her friends. Yumi jumped

out of Leon's arms and pounced on her. "I missed you! I can't believe you weren't at the apartment when I got home."

"Needed. To work." Sam coughed. "Can't. Breathe. Yu."

Yumi landed a loud kiss with a *smack* on Sam's cheek. "You looked amazing in those photos. Although I didn't approve the necklace choice."

Sam smiled, throwing her coat across a barstool, feeling a little sad. "I needed a little something from me."

Corinne handed Emory her drink and slid her arms around Sam. "You look gorgeous, my dear."

"Have you heard from him?" she whispered.

Corinne leaned back, face close to Sam's so no one would hear them. "Except for the fact that he went on strike with the union? No. Nothing."

"*What?* How do you know that?"

"He posted it on his Nubo."

Sam's mouth fell open. "Oh."

"Did you not see it?" Corinne asked.

"I'm never on that app, but especially the past two days. People seem to have *strong* opinions about my article."

Her forehead pinched. "Is he not talking to you?"

"Things are...complicated right now."

She sighed. "Do I need to kill him?"

"*No.*" She eyed the group, clearly not paying attention to their side conversation. "Can we keep this between us, please?"

"Of course, honey."

Yumi cheered again, this time for Jeff and Daniel's entrance. Their faces were flushed, like they'd rushed to get there. Or maybe from making out in the cab. Sam assumed it was probably the latter.

She stood on her tiptoes, eyeing the door, hoping that *maybe* he'd come with them. When she didn't notice any sign of him, her heart sank.

Jeff stepped up to her, bouncing on his toes, swiveling back and forth. "He's not here."

Sam glared at him. "Thanks for rubbing it in."

"Who's not here?" Leon looked through the group. "Oh, wait, shit. Where's my boy?"

"*My* boy?" Jeff squealed. "Who are you?"

"Nico's best friend. Who are you?"

"Nico's *actual* best friend."

"All right, now," Daniel said, patting Jeff's back. "Let's not get rowdy."

Corinne's mouth fell open. "*You're* the brother?"

Jeff did a little bow. "That's me!"

"Why do I always feel like I'm in a reality television show with this group," Emory teased.

Jeff turned his attention back to Sam. "Samantha, I think you should grab your coat."

She felt everything inside her squeeze tight. Like the hug Yumi gave her, Sam felt like she couldn't breathe. "Wh-why?" she choked out.

Jeff grinned, then reached into his pocket and handed her an envelope.

They all went silent as Sam examined the scrawl on the top.

Sammy girl

She blinked up, looking at Yumi.

"Moon and stars," Yumi said.

Sam grinned, then ripped it open.

Meet me where it all began. Midnight.

Her heart was pounding in her ears. *Thud. Thud. Thud.* She didn't need to check his location to know where he was. She knew exactly what he meant.

She checked the clock above the bar, noticing it was already ten fifteen. There was no way she was going to make it.

"I-I have to go," she said, snatching her coat.

Raucous applause and screaming broke out among their friends. Heads turned as their group made a spectacle of Sam putting on her coat and grabbing her bag. They chased her out of the bar.

"I don't think I'm going to make it," she exclaimed to Jeff as her brother opened the door for her. "Should I text him?"

"You don't think he's thought of that?" Jeff replied, knocking his head to the street.

Waiting for her outside was a black limo, a driver leaning against the passenger seat, holding a sign that said *Baby Girl.*

She covered her mouth.

"Oh my god, Samantha. Get in the car *now.*" Jeff opened the door and shoved her in.

A box of cannoli waited for her in the back. She rolled down the window as the limo driver made his way to the driver seat.

Jeff leaned against it. "Sam?"

She grinned. "Yeah?"

"I like seeing you in love."

Tears sprung up at the corners of her eyes. "I like seeing you in love too."

Chapter 30

Nico stood outside in the freezing cold. He checked his watch to make sure he was seeing things correctly. Twelve ten. It was ten minutes past midnight, and she still hadn't arrived.

Maybe she didn't even get in the car. He left his phone back at home, so he wasn't able to track where she was. He didn't have a desire to be on his phone in general, knowing that the Nubo video launch was a complete flop. Ryan Seacrest wouldn't be going live on their app, and he had no idea what Frank or Theo's reaction was, given that he was avoiding all work communications. Now that he was on strike, Nico realized how desperately he needed support, for him *and* his employees. He needed people to advocate for him, and with the strong negotiations taking place between the forming union and OmniCorp, he had a feeling that things were going to look a little brighter moving forward.

If only everything in his life felt that way.

He shivered and crossed his arms, looking out at the stark blackness behind him, toward the frozen river. It'd started to snow, and it felt like the weather was taunting him. Reminding him of the last snow storm and who he was with, and now he was not.

He scratched his head, looking down at his suit, feeling incredibly stupid for wearing it. Not caring if he got his nicest suit wet, he took a seat on the snow that piled on the grass and took a deep breath, closing his eyes. He lifted his face to the clouded sky, snowflakes melting on his cheeks and lashes.

"Get up, you can't be that drunk."

He grinned, eyes still closed. He no longer felt cold. Every part of him felt warm. "I haven't had anything to drink."

"Me neither, my night of boozing got interrupted by a *limo*."

He laughed as he stood up and opened his eyes. She looked stunning. She still had on her New Year's dress, her long black coat around her shoulders, a pair of fuzzy boots on her feet.

She shook her head and crossed her arms. "Nicolas, I would like to point out that driving *anywhere* on New Year's Eve is a bad idea."

"Oh god, really?" He stepped closer to her. "Was the driver bad? I can report him—"

"No, he was lovely." She shook her head. "It's the fact that there was so much *traffic* and it took me forever to get here, so I stress ate all of those cannoli and I was crawling out of my skin the whole time because I thought that maybe if I was late you would...That you would think..."

He grinned. "That I would think what?"

She huffed. She didn't respond, but she didn't need to. That little pout was on her face, and it was still the cutest thing in the whole world.

Sam glanced around her, at the alcove behind her

house, next to the river. "I also was wearing heels, so I had to run inside and get appropriate shoes—"

Nico was only half paying attention as he took another step, looking at the necklace sitting at her collar. He touched it with the tips of his fingers, and Sam's words faded midsentence. His fingers played with the diamond, then brushed against her bare skin.

"Sammy girl?"

She blinked, eyes on his lips.

"I have a proposition for you."

She looked amused. "Another one?"

He nodded and smiled, drawing his fingers around her neck and to her nape.

"What is it this time?" she breathed.

"I think we should kiss."

She chuckled and shook her head. "For science?"

"Obviously."

"And what kind of outcome are you hoping for with this...experiment?"

He tilted her head up, eyes locked. "To confirm what is already true."

He listened to her sharp inhale of breath.

"And what is true?" she asked.

"That I am hopelessly—" He pressed their foreheads together. "Irrevocably—" He brushed their noses together. "In love with you."

She grinned and grasped the lapels of his jacket, nuzzling herself closer to him. "I love you too, Nico."

He closed his eyes, taking in the moment, because he knew *this* was what he was going to want to remember forever. The moment that everything changed. The lightly falling snow. The feel of her soft neck in his hands. The smell of her, coconut and vanilla and the rest of her unique scent that made up *her*. The quiet of Willow at the start of the new year, at the start of *everything*. Finally, everything in his life felt right. Even when he wasn't sure what was next for his career, the path he chose still felt like things were finally clicking into place. Because with Sam, it felt like everything made sense. He was exactly where he was meant to be.

He moved his other hand to her waist and pulled her close. "Happy new year, Sam," he whispered.

She exhaled with a small hum. "Nico?"

"Yes?"

"Do you think if we kiss it's going to ruin our friendship?"

His lips brushed hers as he smiled. "Oh, I'm counting on it."

Then he kissed her. Soft, tender, and gentle. Because this time, Nico didn't rush having Sam in his arms. There wasn't someone to hide from or a timeline they were racing to beat. With Sam, now he had all the time in the world.

So he kissed her, again, and again, and again, and ruined their friendship for good.

Ten Months Later

Epilogue

SAM HOOKED a finger around the curtain for the canopy tent and whisked herself inside. It was an unusually warm day for October in Ithaca, the sky a crystal-clear blue, the grape leaves right on the brink of turning, with yellow tips that gave the landscape of New York wine country a golden hue. They were surrounded by row after row of vines, the perfect backdrop for the perfect day.

She paused at the figure in the tent. Clean cut black tux with sharp angles that perfectly fit the body she had come to know so well.

Nico turned to face her. His eyes blew wide at the sight of her, and to her delight, his expression was almost identical to the one in the grocery store almost a year ago. He seemed shocked. Taken aback. Speechless.

She frowned. "I know I already said this, but I'm going to say it again. I think it's *really* weird that I'm wearing white on my brother's wedding day."

He shoved his hands in his pockets and tightened his jaw, working it back and forth as he eyed her dress.

Sam frowned. "*Nicolas.*"

Nico jumped, like he was remembering where he was and that she was clearly trying to *talk to him*. Then he took three strides, his long legs bringing him right in her orbit. He kept his hands in his pockets as he leaned down and murmured in her ear. "Sammy girl."

She huffed. "Yes?"

"Remember how I said I like you in red?"

"I'm pretty sure at this point you've told me I look good in every color." She paused for effect. "And you told me I look good in *no colors*."

He hummed. "I take it all back. I have a new favorite."

She felt her face flush. "You do?"

He grinned, dipping down to nibble on her ear lobe before he whispered. "I really like you in white."

She arched her head back to get a look at him. Nico's eyes were twinkling bright. She could feel the heat of his body, so close, surrounding her, engulfing her. It didn't take much for her to slip a hand to his cheek and kiss him, fusing herself to him. He hummed in response, smoothing a palm around her cinched waist, his hand gripping the chiffon fabric at her hip as he pulled her closer.

Her heart beat fast at his touch. *Closer, closer, closer.* She slid her hand to the nape and raked her fingernails down his neck. *Mine, mine, mine.*

"Oh my god, *we get it.* You're into each other."

Sam felt her face go hot as she broke away from Nico, turning to face Jeff who stood at the entrance of the tent, arms crossed.

He had a gleeful smile on his lips. "How come every time I come looking for you two, I always find your faces superglued together?" he joked.

Nico chuckled, then dipped low to kiss Sam's neck.

Jeff whipped out his phone in his pocket and took a picture.

"Jeff, come on, you have to stop with the pictures," Sam quipped.

Her brother grinned and slipped it back in his pocket. "Not until it gets old. And, unfortunately for you, it never does."

"You're right about that," Nico replied, squeezing his hand at Sam's hip.

Jeff beamed, then flicked his wrist. "Okay, now that you've gotten that over with, it's time to pay attention to me. Today's all about me."

"When is it *not* about you?" Sam teased.

Nico and Jeff both barked out a laugh. Then Jeff galloped forward and threw his arms around them both, squeezing their bodies together, like they were kids again. "I'm getting married today."

Sam relaxed in her brother's embrace. "You're getting married today."

Nico patted Jeff's back.

Jeff tapped Sam's nose. "Thanks for standing by Daniel."

She felt tears forming at the corners of her eyes. "Of course. I'm so honored to."

Jeff beamed, then his face fell as he unlatched his arms. "I can't believe none of his family showed up."

"It's sickening," Nico added.

"I don't get it." Jeff shook his head. "Imagine living this whole other life and *not* being able to fully share yourself with the people you love."

The three of them froze. Sam could feel the pull of tension between all of them, the way the words lingered like a haunted memory.

"Well, it's a good thing we've never had that problem," Jeff quipped.

Nico barked out a laugh as the two of them fist bumped.

Sam crossed her arms. "You two are insufferable."

"Aw, Sam, you love us." Jeff threw his arms around her and landed a loud kiss on her cheek. "Although you probably love one of us more than the other."

"Yeah, who do you love more, Samantha?" Nico joked.

"We are *not* playing this game."

Jeff jumped back and held out his arms. "Oh, *come on*! It's my wedding day. You have to do what I say."

Sam bit her lip, then turned to look at Nico. He grinned then cupped her face and planted a delicate, featherlight kiss to her mouth.

"Yeah okay, I know who you love more." Jeff playfully punched Nico's arm. "I can't believe the vice president of engineering at OmniCorp had enough time to grace me with his *presence* today."

Nico smirked at Jeff as he pressed a hand to his chest. "Who, me?"

Sam rolled her eyes. "Cocky."

He laughed, wrapping his arms around Sam's waist from behind and kissing her bare shoulder.

She grinned and shook her head, proud of the way her man stepped up for the company during the strike, for speaking out about OmniCorp's impossible standards they were all held to. When the union finally made an agreement with OmniCorp at the end of January and everyone went back to work, Nico also communicated the other more private things to human resources, like the comments Frank made about Nico's personal life or the inappropriate things he said to Sam. Apparently he wasn't the only one who voiced concerns about Frank, and a couple weeks later, Frank was out and Nico was assigned to that office.

Even if he pretended to be his usual cocky self, on the inside, Sam knew Nico was struggling with his imposter syndrome. He didn't think he deserved being promoted *again* into a role he felt he was not old enough for. Yet Sam saw the way he handled the work, how good he was with their employees and the ways he advocated for their well-being. Because of the culture Nico created, the engineering team was healthy enough to find a solution for live streaming and they launched videos on Nubo in June.

Nico stepped aside and reached to open up a small cooler on the table. He sighed, then unpacked two chilled beer glasses, two miniature mysterious green bottles, and two silver and blue cans.

Her inhale was sharp. "*Nico*, no."

Jeff noticed what was happening, then screamed with laughter as Nico poured the energy drinks into the cold glasses. "You are outdoing yourself with your best man duties," Jeff said.

Nico handed him a glass. "I thought it would be appropriate to send you off and out of your crazy single years with one last Jägerbomb."

Sam pinched her nose. "I can't believe you guys are going to drink those when we are literally in the middle of *wine country*."

"Oh, we'll drink the fancy stuff later." Jeff shrugged her off. "Right now is the time for debauchery."

"Yeah, Sammy girl, don't ruin our fun."

She shook her head. "I wouldn't ever dream about getting in the way of the two of you."

Jeff and Nico fist bumped again, this time without having to even look at one another. The two were back to being inseparable, texting memes nonstop, streaming video games late every Tuesday night. They spent those evenings talking about everything and nothing as they killed zombies or aliens or whatever other game they decided to play that wasn't *Smash Brothers*, which was now off limits because it always ended up with the two of them screaming at one another. Sam made sure to not bother going to Nico's those nights, and instead spent a night with Yumi cooking a lavish recipe with a bottle of wine in their new apartment in Crown Heights. Brooklyn was certainly a change of pace compared to Manhattan, but finding a two-bedroom they could afford was enough to draw them to another side of the city. Plus, when Sam looked up her commute to Nico's and realized it would take her half the amount of time to get to him, she wasn't complaining. Neither was Yumi when she revealed that Leon was only a ten-minute walk away.

Yumi thrived in her job at *Who What Wear*, writing in-depth think pieces on celebrity fashion and what it means in the greater landscape of culture and art. Sam was always amazed when one of Yumi's pieces came out, and every day was thankful that her best friend decided to leave *Nourished*.

But replacing her hadn't been easy, and neither was being someone's boss. Sam oversaw the two full-time writers who filled their former positions. She challenged them as an editor, nit-picking every bit of their piece to make sure they were ready to publish. While she knew how tough it was giving extensive edits to her writers, she saw the ways their work improved with each article. Barbara said this type of work is needed to sharpen the best writers for major national publications like theirs. She had become a close mentor to Sam over the ten months since taking on the role, especially now that her project was bringing in five times the amount of traffic they were making compared to the year before.

It was a lot of work, which meant her Tuesday nights with Yumi were sacred, mostly because every other night of the week they didn't see much of each other. Yumi spent most nights at Leon's, and Sam and Nico would split their time between their two places. Nico hadn't asked her to move in yet, but after buying her a dresser and slowly filling it with clothes—that he bought for her, of course—Sam knew it was only a matter of time. She had a feeling when their lease was up on the two-bedroom next May they would both be going their separate ways. Yumi a ten-minute walk. Sam five subway stops up north.

Nico unscrewed the green bottles and handed Jeff one, then lifted his glass. "To making many more memories."

"And more mistakes," Jeff added with a grin.

He grinned back. "And always coming back together, no matter what."

Jeff's eyes went teary. "Sam, count us down."

She sighed, then held up her hand. "Three, two—"

They tipped the green bottles into the liquid, then slammed their drinks.

"*Jeffery Carter!* If you don't get your ass out here right now so I can fasten this custom Gucci bowtie on you I'm going to shove it up your—"

"YUMI!" Jeff screamed back, handing Nico his empty glass. "I regret the day I asked you to help me with wedding attire."

"Is Samantha in there?" Yumi yelled from outside the tent. "She wore the dress, right?"

"I still can't believe you made me wear white!"

"It was your stupid brother's idea!"

"But I look ridiculous!"

"You look hot!"

"It's true," Nico added, threading their hands together. "You do look hot."

Yumi huffed. "*Jeff!*"

He sighed heavily and exited the tent. "Oh my god, *fine!* Way to ruin a cute moment!"

The two of them stood there in silence, listening to the sound of their bickering as it faded into the distance.

Nico brushed a finger under her chin, tilting her head up toward him. "Baby girl?"

She grinned. "Yes, baby dog?"

His eyes danced with delight. Then he blinked, his chestnut-colored irises dropping to her lips. "I like you in white."

Also by K. Sinko

Sunday Supper

Call Of The Loon

THE SCOOPS SERIES

Safe Harbor

Always Choosing You

The Offer

NOVELETTES

Please Be Mine

Notes &
Acknowledgments

Oh, how I loved writing this book. A challenge in so many ways, but also such a joy. Writing my first holiday romance was something special, and setting in my favorite city in the world was such a treat.

Speaking of my city, I have to make a few notes. As you know, *Ruin The Friendship* is a work of fiction. While there are some spots in New York City that are real places, some of them are also fictitious. This book is a collage of both, all based on what the story needed. Plus, I couldn't help but throw one of my favorite Italian meatball spots in there. *Wink, wink.*

While I always take the time to do thorough research for my stories, sometimes I take creative liberties when it comes to certain parts of the story. I certainly did for Nico's job. The world of social media and tech is a complicated one, and while I touched on some very real issues in regards to the types of projects and work-life balance, in reality launching a live streaming platform for a social media app requires a *multitude* of engineers. But for the sake of a good story, I put it all on his shoulders.

Of course, I wouldn't be where I am without all of the wonderful people who championed my work, supported me, and got me to the finish line. This one was truly a team effort, and I am blessed to have the absolute best team in the world.

To my beta reading team, thank you for always being

honest with your feedback *and* hyping me up at the same time. You each individually make me a better writer and I'm so thankful for it: Abby Hancock, Taiko Endo, Alexis Wierenga, and Meagan Williamson.

My confidence as an artists is always boosted after a thorough talk (and belly laughs) with my writing group, Creatives Who Cry. You guys make this job so much fun. I am thankful we have each other, even if it's virtually from across the globe.

To my other teammates who helped me get this book ready: Britt Tayler for her editing genius that always make my books stronger, and Hannah Hill for her beautiful cover art that had me swooning from the start.

Lastly, and as always, I have to thank my number one supporter, artistic sounding board, and partner for life. My husband is the true MMC of my dreams, with a support and a love that I didn't even think existed in real life. I am truly the luckiest woman in the world to have him by my side. Love you babe.

About the Author

K.Sinko is an indie published author with a deep love for love stories. She is the author of *Sunday Supper, Call Of The Loon, Please Be Mine,* and the Scoops Series—a trilogy of stand-alone romances centered around a fictional ice cream shop. Her debut novel *Safe Harbor* became an Amazon best seller for young adult contemporary romance and is the winner of two Indieverse Awards. *Ruin the Friendship* is her seventh book. Follow her on Instagram and sign up for her newsletter to get the latest book updates.

tinyurl.com/ksinkonewsletter

www.ingramcontent.com/pod-product-compliance
Lightning Source LLC
Chambersburg PA
CBHW020231010826
48973CB00006B/1463